# HELSINKI HOMICIDE: COLD TRAIL

## JARKKO SIPILA

Translated by
Kristian London

IceCold Crime

Originally published in Finnish as *Kylmä Jälki* by Gummerus, Helsinki, Finland. 2007.

Translated by Kristian London

Published by
Ice Cold Crime LLC
5780 Providence Curve
Independence, MN 55359

Printed in the United States of America

Cover by Ella Tontti

Library of Congress Control Number: 2013905662

ISBN-13: 978-0-9824449-8-6
ISBN-10: 0-9824449-8-2

# Also by Jarkko Sipila

**In English:**

*Helsinki Homicide: Against the Wall* (Ice Cold Crime, 2009)
*Helsinki Homicide: Vengeance* (Ice Cold Crime, 2010)
*Helsinki Homicide: Nothing but the Truth* (Ice Cold Crime, 2011)

**In Finnish:**

*Koukku* (Book Studio, 1996)
*Kulmapubin koktaili* (Book Studio, 1998)
*Kosketuslaukaus* (Book Studio, 2001)
*Tappokäsky* (Book Studio, 2002)
*Karu keikka* (Book Studio, 2003)
*Todennäköisin syin* (Gummerus, 2004)
*Likainen kaupunki* (Gummerus, 2005)
*Mitään salaamatta* (Gummerus, 2006)
*Kylmä jälki* (Gummerus, 2007)
*Seinää vasten* (Gummerus, 2008)
*Prikaatin kosto* (Gummerus, 2009)
*Katumurha* (Gummerus, 2010)
*Paha paha tyttö,* with Harri Nykänen (Crime Time, 2010)
*Muru* (Crime Time, 2011)
*Suljetuin Ovin* (Crime Time, 2012)
*Valepoliisi* (Crime Time, 2013)

**In German:**

*Die weiße Nacht des Todes* (Rohowolt Verlag, 2007)
*Im Dämmer des Zweifels* (Rohowolt Verlag, 2007)

**In Italian:**

*Morte a Helsinki* (Aliberti Editore, 2011)

# HELSINKI HOMICIDE:
# COLD TRAIL

# CAST OF CHARACTERS

Kari Takamäki...................Detective Lieutenant, Helsinki PD Violent Crimes Unit

Suhonen.......................Undercover Detective, VCU

Anna Joutsamo....................VCU Sergeant

Mikko Kulta........................VCU Detective

Kirsi Kohonen .....................VCU Detective

Jaakko Nykänen...........Head of Intelligence, National Bureau of Investigation

Turunen............................Head of the SWAT team

Helmikoski ...............On-duty Lieutenant, Helsinki PD

Timo Repo ...........................Convicted murderer

Erik Repo...............................Timo's father

Otto Karppi...........................Erik Repo's neighbor

Lauri Solberg..........................Espoo PD investigator

Aarno Fredberg...............Supreme Court Chief Justice

Eero Salmela.............Suhonen's old friend and ex-con

Tomi Manner...............Owner of a hit-and-run vehicle

Jorma Raitio.............................Career Criminal

Juha Saarnikangas.........................Junkie

Sanna Römpötti...........................TV crime reporter

Mary J. Juvonen...........................Tabloid reporter

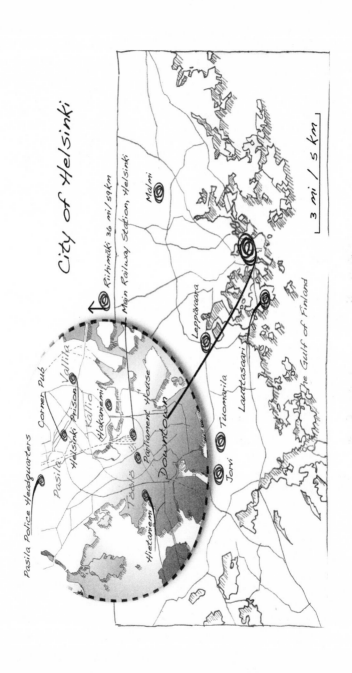

City of Helsinki

Pasila Police Headquarters

Corner Pub

Vallila

Helsinki Prison

Kallia

Hakaniemi

Riihimäki 36 mi / 59km

Main Railway Station, Helsinki

Malmi

Leppävaara

Parliament House

Downtown

Töölö

Hietaniemi

Torvi

Tuomarila

Lauttasaari

The Gulf of Finland

3 mi / 5 km

# MONDAY,
# OCTOBER 8, 2007

# CHAPTER 1
## MONDAY, 2:45 P.M.
## HIETANIEMI CREMATORIUM, HELSINKI

The coffin was the cheapest model available. Behind it, the pastor once again shifted uneasily from foot to foot and tentatively recited, "The Lord is my shepherd; I shall not want."

Aside from the clergyman and his customer, three men in dark suits were the only other people in the large, lofty chapel. The pastor read the Twenty-third Psalm from his book:

"Yea, though I walk through the valley of the shadow of death, I will fear no evil: for thou art with me; thy rod and thy staff they comfort me."

The final phrase prompted Timo Repo, who was sitting in the tenth row, to raise his head. Thy rod, exactly, he thought. His father, who was lying in the coffin, hadn't been one to spare it. It felt like an eternity has passed since those days—or at least decades. Timo Repo was now fifty-two years old, and Erik Repo had lived more or less the average age for a Finnish male, seventy-six years.

Timo hadn't seen his father in six years and hadn't even learned about the cancer that brought his death until after the fact, from his medical records at the hospital.

"Surely goodness and mercy shall follow me all the days of my life, and I will dwell in the house of the Lord forever."

Repo wondered if this was the young pastor's first funeral. Repo wasn't a big man, clearly under six feet.

His face was angular and his dark hair slightly disheveled, as if it had been combed with nothing but his fingers.

The pastor urged those present to pray. "Our Father who art in Heaven, hallowed be thy name..."

The younger man with a shaved head sitting next to Repo crossed his hands. Repo knew the prison guard by last name only: Eskola.

Repo kept his heavily veined hands apart. The funeral's third attendee sat a couple of rows in front of them, his gray head lowered. Repo knew it was his father's neighbor.

In a way, Timo Repo was pleased that there weren't more mourners. More than anything, he felt uncomfortable. Grief was beyond his reach.

Luckily, Mom had died back in the early '90s and hadn't had to suffer through later events. Timo did wonder why his older brother, Martti, wasn't there. Maybe he was off in Thailand again. Rumors of these jaunts had reached Timo. But his big brother hadn't even visited him in the joint. Not once.

The prayer droned on, but Timo wasn't listening. He had lost his faith in God eight years ago, after he had been sentenced to life in prison for murdering his wife. Timo's God wasn't merciful; he was an avenger.

The interment continued for another twenty minutes. Afterwards, the coffin slid slowly out of the chapel toward the oven, to a recording of "The Lord is My Shepherd."

The guard was the first to stand. Eskola was about six inches taller than Repo.

"Well, that was that."

"Yeah," Repo answered. They stepped into the aisle.

"Ready to head back?"

"I need to hit the...," Repo began.

2

The gray-haired man, who moved with difficulty, interrupted. Extending both hands, he squeezed first Repo's hand and then Eskola's.

"Thank you for coming. Erik deserved a bigger send-off, but what can you do." The old man focused his gaze on Timo. "You're the younger son."

Timo nodded.

"My deepest condolences."

"Thank you," Timo replied politely. The old man looked like he was on his last legs. He might well be the crematorium's next customer. "And thanks for taking care of the arrangements... I heard you..."

"I carried out Erik's wishes. He knew death was approaching."

And still didn't bother to get in touch, Timo thought. That ate at him, but it was typical of his father. Timo wished he could have asked him a few questions.

"Nice service."

"Yes, I apologize for not introducing myself. I'm Otto Karppi, your father's neighbor. You'll come to the reception, won't you?" asked the old man. "The pastor can't make it."

Repo glanced at his escort, who nodded. Prison rules stated that prisoners attending an interment under escort were also allowed to attend memorial services.

"We can take the prison car," said the guard. "Did you drive?"

Karppi grunted. "Doc took my license away three years ago."

"Well, the state will give you a ride. The weather's so bad there's no point walking," Eskola said, turning to Repo. "Didn't you need to use the bathroom?"

"I can wait till we get to the restaurant," Repo answered.

3

* * *

The three men in dark suits were sitting at a six-person corner table at Restaurant Perho. There were only a handful of other customers in the beautiful, wood-paneled establishment. A young woman in a traditional black-and-white wait-staff uniform poured them coffee from a gleaming pot.

Karppi had placed a photograph of Erik Repo on the table and lit a candle in front of it. The elder Repo had a hook nose and vaguely pronounced cheekbones; his hair was gray and short. Timo felt like his father was staring at him and him alone with his grim, almost angry eyes.

No one seemed to have much to say. Eskola's and Repo's dark suits were both from the prison's limited selection of loaners, from which both prisoners and guards could borrow for such occasions. Eskola's suit was a little too small and Repo's a little too big.

Eskola broke the silence. "So how does cremation actually work?"

Repo glared at the guard. "They burn the body."

"As a matter of fact, it's not quite that simple," Karppi interjected. "They heat the oven with natural gas until it's hot, and then they push in the coffin. It self-ignites and burns for a solid hour, as long as they keep on blowing air. It's more cremation than burning."

"So what's left over?" Eskola asked.

"All organic material burns away. The only thing left behind are the inorganic elements from the bones."

"So pretty hygienic then," Eskola reflected.

"That was the original idea behind cremation. The custom began to spread through Europe during the nineteenth century because of the poor conditions at cemeteries."

Repo sipped his coffee.

"Well, there are still a few practical issues to deal with regarding Erik," Karppi said. "The urn will be ready in about a week, and I can take it to the vault in accordance with Erik's wishes. If that's all right."

Timo nodded.

"Then there's the matter of the estate. There's an inheritance of sorts to be divided up. The assets consist primarily of your father's house. And, as far as I'm aware, the heirs are yourself and your brother."

"Don't our kids get anything?"

"Do you have children?" Karppi asked.

"I have one, and I'm assuming my brother does too, although I don't know how many."

"According to the estate law, grandchildren don't get anything if the children are alive."

Repo noticed the pretty waitress approaching with a plate of sandwiches.

"Uh, listen, I need to hit the john now. My stomach's acting up."

The woman placed the sandwiches on the table.

"You guys go ahead and start. I'll be right back," Repo said, standing.

"No funny business?" Eskola asked.

"'Course not. I'm just going to the bathroom."

"Okay," Eskola said, giving Repo a stern look. He checked his watch: 4:05 p.m.

The bathroom was near the front door. Repo walked there with rapid steps. He knew Eskola's eyes were on him. There was a line of sight from the table to the front door, but not to the bathroom area, which was tucked into a small niche near the coat racks.

Repo made it around the corner and paused for a moment at the coat rack. The parties at the other tables seemed to be in the middle of their meals or just getting started. No one was paying attention to him. Repo pulled a gray trench coat that looked about the right size from a hanger. No one started shouting, at least not immediately.

The restroom, with two urinals and two stalls, was empty. There was no window. That would have been too easy, Repo thought. He'd have to go with plan B.

He bent over the sink and examined his thatch of hair. He drew an old plastic tortoise-shell comb from his breast pocket and tidied his mane. The front door was his only alternative. Eskola had a direct view of it from his seat and would definitely be keeping an eye on it. Repo needed a head start of a few minutes; prison life hadn't exactly improved his endurance. He wouldn't stand a chance against the young guard in a flat-out race.

Repo decided to wait a minute or two, until Eskola would be distracted by his sandwich.

The situation made Repo nervous enough to take a leak, wash his hands, and comb his hair again. He put on the gray coat and tried to get a rear-view glance of himself in the mirror. It just might work, he thought. Eskola wouldn't get more than a few-seconds-long look at him. And if he changed his gait into more of a shuffle, that might help, too.

The prisoner tightened his shoelaces. His black ankle-boots were a size too large, but he couldn't let that get in his way now.

Repo gave himself a final once-over and stepped out of the restroom.

There was no one at the coat rack. That's all he would have needed, the coat's owner standing there, wondering where his missing trench coat was. Repo tried to take small, tight steps. He had an impulse to look over in Eskola and Karppi's direction, but that would have been a huge mistake. Repo could feel the back of his shirt dampening with sweat.

He walked over to the door, expecting the whole time to hear a loud "Stop!". But it never came. Maybe Karppi was lecturing Eskola on the history of cremation while the latter munched on his sandwich. How did Karppi know so much about it anyway? Repo thought, pushing open the door to the vestibule. Two more steps and he'd be outside. The urge to look backwards was overwhelming, and Repo almost bumped into a middle-aged couple entering the restaurant.

"Excuse me," he said, rudely shoving his way out between them. Now was not the time for politeness.

A tram was clattering down Mechelin Street, and a bleak wind was blowing. The rain on his face felt cold but good. Repo turned right so he wouldn't have to walk past the restaurant's windows. After a couple of shuffling steps, he broke into a run, headed north. Now he needed to put some distance between himself and Eskola.

\* \* \*

Eskola had finished his sandwich and was starting to get antsy. Maybe he shouldn't have let the prisoner go to the bathroom by himself after all. But as they had been driving out of Helsinki Prison, Repo had promised to be on his best behavior. Nothing in the inmate database indicated that Repo was a flight risk. He had already done eight years of his life sentence without chalking up any incidents. He would be allowed to start taking unescorted leaves in a year's time. Besides, Eskola had been hungry, and the sandwich had looked tasty.

He had kept an eye on the door, and hadn't noticed anything out of the ordinary. There had been a little activity, but no one who looked or moved like Repo. Still, he was uneasy. Eskola glanced at his watch: 4:14

7

p.m. There was still a minute to go of the allowed ten-minute bathroom break. Eskola decided to go check on things anyway.

"I'm gonna go to the bathroom, too."

"What's wrong with you young men?" Karppi said.

Eskola marched into the bathroom, checked the stalls, and swore a blue streak. He rushed back out into the entryway and scanned the restaurant. Then he flew out the front door, but Repo was nowhere to be seen.

* * *

Repo had slowed to a brisk walk. He had two reasons for doing so: he was out of breath, and a man running in a dark suit and trench coat always attracted attention. He tried to remember when he had last walked down Arkadia Street toward the railway station in the rain. He couldn't even remember doing it on a sunny day.

The past eight years had gone by in various prisons. Before that he had lived in Riihimäki, forty miles due north from Helsinki. He had rarely visited the city—except maybe his father's place in the northern part of town. But even there pretty infrequently, and that had all been before his life sentence. Some kid in a hoodie rode past on a dirt bike, and Repo was reminded of his own bicycle from the '60s, with its banana seat, chopper-style handlebars, and frame decorated with old bottle caps.

Repo quickly shook off the vision and concentrated on his surroundings. By this time, Eskola would have noticed his disappearance and reported him to the police. Should he ditch the gray overcoat? Would it be mentioned in the description? Or would they say he was wearing a black suit? Repo wasn't sure and decided to hang on to the coat, partly because of the rain. He might arouse more suspicion in the chilly weather in just a suit.

When Repo reached the Museum of Natural History, he picked up the pace again. He wondered what new building had risen where old Little Parliament restaurant used to be.

Little Parliament had had a pleasant patio, even if its prices had been a little steep for Repo's budget. He remembered having been there once, on a warm summer evening. The bar's windows and doors had been pulled open, letting in a refreshing sea breeze. If he wasn't totally off the mark, he had even succeeded in picking up some female company that night.

What the hell? Repo thought. A tall brick-and-stone building now stood where the old restaurant had been. When he got closer, he noticed that the name was still the same: this granite monstrosity was the new annex to the Parliament building across the street. What a waste. Apparently the big boys had money to burn on such vanities.

* * *

"So your prisoner got away, huh?" the sergeant on duty said sarcastically. "Now how'd that happen?"

"What difference does it make?" Eskola shouted into his cell phone. He was walking northward up Mechelin Street. Arkadia High School was on his right. Its stucco facade had suffered badly from graffiti tag removal. "We have to find him!"

The sergeant, who had put in his time in the field, grunted. "Take it easy. Why don't we start with who needs to be found and where?"

Eskola took a deep breath. "Timo Repo. Fled from Restaurant Perho. From a funeral."

"A funeral at a restaurant? Sounds pretty strange to me. So when did this happen?"

"Less than ten minutes ago."

"He can't be far, then. Which direction did he go? And on what?"

Eskola turned onto Arkadia Street. He thought that Repo must have come this way. The only thing on the other side of the cemetery was the Hietaniemi cul-de-sac, where the road dead-ended into the Gulf of Finland. "I don't know which direction he went, and I'm pretty sure he's on foot."

"And who is this...Repo? Shoplifter or something? The name doesn't say anything."

"Timo Repo. He's hard-core, at least going by his sentence. Life."

The sergeant's voice grew sharper. "Life? Holy shit."

Eskola could hear the police officer tapping away at his computer. He assumed Repo's name was being queried from the database. Soon the police would have a photograph.

"What was he wearing?"

"We were at a funeral. One of those black prison loaner suits," Eskola reported, pleased that the sergeant was taking him more seriously now.

"Right. The computer describes him as age 52, height 5'8", average build, crew cut, and I'll add wearing a dark suit. That about right?"

"Everything except his hair is dark and medium length. Not a crew cut anymore."

"Thanks. I'll put your phone number here. If you see something, call right away."

Eskola tried to imagine where Repo might be headed, and why he'd break for it after serving eight years with good behavior.

\* \* \*

The sergeant gestured for Helmikoski, the lieutenant on duty, to come over. A dozen or so officers were milling around the new command center at Helsinki police headquarters in Pasila. The desk officers' workspaces were filled by computer monitors, and images from downtown surveillance cameras were projected onto one of the walls of the large room.

"Yeah?" asked the burly lieutenant.

"Prisoner Timo Repo, serving life, skipped out on his escort about ten minutes ago on Mechelin Street," said the desk sergeant, showing the photo of Repo he had pulled up on his screen. The image was almost ten years old; in it, the fortyish Repo still had a crew cut.

"Who is he?"

"Not in my bowling league, and none of those guys have heard of him either, even though they're all cops."

"Serving life, though?"

The sergeant nodded. "Missing somewhere downtown. No report of accomplices. Got the description of clothing and hair from the guard. Unlike most fifty-year-olds, his hair's longer now. Dark, medium length."

Helmikoski found his colleague's rambling style irritating.

He glanced at the map of downtown Helsinki projected onto the wall. All active police vehicles were marked on it by ID number, with their location status updated in real time via GPS. About ten units were patrolling downtown Helsinki.

"Let's try to pin this guy down pronto. Put out an APB," Helmikoski ordered the sergeant. "Give the description to all units and send the photo to those with the new computer system. Drop everything else; it'll be easiest to find him now, before the trail goes cold."

The sergeant started tapping away at his computer. He wasn't so sure about it being easiest now, because the streets were full of people and cars due to the afternoon rush hour. But of course it was worth trying. He took another glance at the surveillance cameras, which showed a central Helsinki that was exceptionally gloomy and gray. Raindrops had almost completely blurred out some of the images.

Lieutenant Helmikoski considered his options. The most effective alternative would be to seal off the entire downtown peninsula. Set up roadblocks and restrict all vehicular traffic. But that would cause such chaos that he'd be demoted to sergeant before his shift was over. He had to think of other alternatives. The Gulf of Finland offered an effective boundary to the west, beyond the Hietaniemi Cemetery. He wouldn't need any units there. He'd have to cut off the escape route north from the Helsinki peninsula. It had already been a good ten minutes; the fugitive would have made it past the city's narrowest point, the isthmus marked by Hesperia Street. Or would he? Beyond it, the neighborhood of Outer Töölö was such a maze that it would be tough finding anyone there.

"Send two units up to Hesperia Street. Let's set up a roadblock there."

The sergeant looked at the electronic map and immediately radioed the order to the two closest patrols.

"One unit over to Ruoholahti to sweep the southwest and two to Mannerheim Street. Tell them to patrol between Stockmann in the south and Hesperia Street in the north."

Helmikoski paused to consider the situation from Repo's point of view. The fugitive had to know that the authorities would be after him by now. He'd have two options: try to get out of the center as quickly as possible or find a hideout somewhere. From the police's perspective, it would obviously be best if Repo kept moving. What options did he have for getting out of downtown? Bus, metro, tram, or train. Of course foot and taxi were possible too, as was having an accomplice with a car somewhere. In the last scenario, they would have already lost the race.

"Send one more patrol south to Tehdas Street and the other four to traverse the area. Inform security at the bus terminals and the train stations and give them the description."

"Taxis?"

"Not yet. Let's not go public with this yet. With our luck there'll be some journalist in a cab somewhere and the news will be out before we know it," Helmikoski said, looking at the map. "You okay handling this alone?"

The sergeant nodded. Helmikoski briefed the other desk officers, too, and told them to keep an eye on the downtown surveillance cameras.

\* \* \*

Young, blond officer Esa Nieminen was sitting at the wheel of his patrol car, a Ford Mondeo. The number 122 was painted on the trunk. Sitting at his side was his partner, veteran officer Tero Partio. The police car was waiting at the lights at the intersection of the Boulevard and Mannerheim Street, nose pointed toward the Southern Esplanade. A few cars were idling in front of them. Raindrops splattered against the windshield. Nieminen thought the wipers were making a funny clunk. Which was no surprise, because police vehicle maintenance had always been pretty slapdash.

"Did he say Code 3?" Nieminen asked.

"No sirens," Partio replied. "The convict would hide as soon as he heard them."

"Yeah, you're right," Nieminen said. "But that would be cool, ten units tearing up and down the streets, sirens blaring."

"Yeah, really cool," Partio grunted.

The traffic lights at the Boulevard turned green, and the Mondeo turned left onto Mannerheim Street. Their progress came to a halt half a block later, at the crosswalk near the Swedish Theatre. Now three cars stood between them and the traffic light. A heavy stream of pedestrians was crossing the street in front of the Stockmann department store.

Nieminen was suddenly alert. "You see that? At least three fifty-year-old guys in black suits just crossed the street!"

Partio didn't answer. He was almost forty and had ten-plus years of experience in Helsinki PD work under his belt. "Yeah, I saw 'em."

"Should we pick 'em up?" Nieminen asked eagerly.

"Nah, they're going the wrong way. Our guy is probably headed down the west side of the street. Those suits came from the east."

The lights turned green, and the police car was the last vehicle to make through the light in front of Stockmann. The traffic coming from the North Esplanade had filled the lanes.

It took four minutes to drive the hundred yards to the statue of the Three Smiths. By then, Nieminen and Partio had seen about 30 fifty-year-old men in dark suits.

\* \* \*

Helmikoski was looking at the map where the police vehicles appeared as white dots. He turned toward the

14

desk sergeant. "How come they're not moving?"

He had envisioned the units sawing back and forth at the edges of the sector, effectively cutting off the area. And had it been nighttime, the plan would have worked, too.

"Four o'clock rush hour. Nothing's moving out there," the sergeant noted in a tired voice, gesturing at the images from the surveillance cameras. Mannerheim Street was jammed with cars from end to end. The streets were teeming with so many pedestrians that you couldn't make out their faces, and the umbrellas didn't make things any easier. Sure, you could zoom in with the cameras to get a really close shot, but in reality that required a target that was standing still. And it was pretty unlikely Repo would stop, if he even were headed downtown in the first place.

One of the junior officers walked up to Helmikoski. "You might find this interesting," he said. Helmikoski wondered what a guy who looked so fit was doing in the Emergency Operations Center instead of the field. His badge read Lehtonen. "A call just came in from the Perho restaurant. A gray trench coat was stolen from the coat racks. The caller's name is..."

"Doesn't matter," Helmikoski said, glancing at the sergeant sitting at the computer monitors. He was already informing the patrols that Repo was probably wearing a long, gray coat. That information should aid the search, at least a little.

"Lieutenant," yelled a dark-haired female officer sitting further off. "Helsinki Transport ticket inspectors are having trouble with a freeloader who's threatening them at the Kaisaniemi stop. Can we spare a unit?"

"Is it a male with short hair and a trench coat?"

"No, they said it was that old drunk Fuck-Jore. His hands are trembling worse than ever, but evidently his mouth moves just fine. He started going on about some knife in his pocket."

Helmikoski considered before responding. "Send one unit. Have the rest keep searching."

The officer checked the map, turned to her microphone, and sent over the closest patrol, unit 122.

* * *

A smile spread across Nieminen's face when the orders arrived. The car was still on Mannerheim Street, but had now advanced down to the Sokos department store. "Yippe kay-ay," he said, flipping on the lights and sirens. Traffic wasn't moving, but Nieminen bumped the car up onto the sidewalk. The pedestrians started at the noise and moved out of the way.

"Hey, take it easy!" Partio snapped. He would have much preferred to be at the wheel himself. He instinctively checked his pistol and mace. He always did when it was a Code 3. The third critical thing was his seat belt. That was on, too.

Partio remembered Fuck-Jore well; he was a regular customer. The fifty-year-old had gotten his nickname from the fact that every third word out of his mouth was "fuck," or some derivation of it. Not a total skid row bum yet, but well on his way. The gaunt drunk's eyebrows were as bushy as Brezhnev's, and he always wore the same flannel shirt. Fuck-Jore used to be a mid-level burglar, but booze had started to taste a little too good. Partio thought it was a minor miracle the guy was still alive.

At the old main post office, Nieminen whipped the Mondeo onto Posti Street, heading toward the main railway station. He did it a little too quickly for Partio's taste, missing a pedestrian by less than a yard. The streets were crowded, and everyone was staring at the police car with its lights and sirens blaring.

Although there wasn't anything remarkable about him, a man in a gray coat who was staring at one of the Sokos display windows caught Partio's attention. Partio tried to remember: it was a trench coat, wasn't it? Why didn't the guy look at them? Maybe he was deaf, but still.

Partio had learned to register everything out of the ordinary, but the man in the gray coat vanished from his thoughts when Nieminen hit the gas and swerved into the oncoming lane. A number 66 bus was headed toward them, and the Mondeo made it back into its own lane just in the nick of time.

"Goddammit! Take it easy, will you?" Partio yelled. Luckily, Nieminen would be able to jump up onto the tram lane at Kaivo Street. Driving along them instead of in traffic was safer for all concerned. The man in the gray coat still nagged at him, and Partio grabbed the microphone from the dash.

* * *

Timo Repo was sure he'd just gotten caught. He had heard the wailing of the police car before it turned the corner, but it had zoomed past. He had instinctively turned his face toward the display window and hoped for the best. He was envisioning a scene with the officer aiming a gun at him and ordering him to put his hands up.

And that's how it had gone down eight years ago. He couldn't imagine a worse way to wake up. The police officer slapping his face and shouting. Opening his eyes to find himself looking down the barrel of a pistol. And then the third thing he noticed was how sticky his hands were, and the sweet, sickening smell in the air. Repo remembered it all like it was yesterday. Coca-Cola? No, something red. Blood. He decided not to pursue those thoughts any further.

He needed to get out of downtown, and fast. The police car bothered him. Why had it passed him by? Why didn't it stop? Why didn't some gorilla in blue coveralls jump out, waving a gun?

Repo jogged a couple of steps and accidentally bumped a skinny punk in a hoodie.

"Fucking faggot. You wanna get your ass kicked?"

"Sorry. Late for my train," Repo apologized without stopping. In his younger days he might have mashed the guy's face into a pizza, but not now.

At the corner, Repo crossed over to the post office side of the street and set course for the central train station.

Just then a police car pulled up to the railway station taxi stand and two officers stepped out. Both scanned the crowd.

Repo turned in the direction of the all-glass offices of the *Helsingin Sanomat* newspaper, which stood behind the restaurant Vltava. Further ahead, toward Finlandia Hall, he saw another police car. He rapidly ticked off his alternatives: the old post office? No, he'd be trapped if he went in there. A small doorway nearby had a sign indicating it would lead him to the underground parking lot below Eliel Square.

Eliel Square was a busy transportation hub, with buses pulling into and backing out of loading zones.

At that instant a woman in a red coat ran past, and Repo noticed a bus on the verge of pulling out. He sprang after her. The bus was his best chance. It was already sliding back out of its parking spot, but the woman smacked its side. The driver stopped and opened the door. She stepped in, and Repo followed.

"Sorry," she said to the grouchy driver, flashing a card in front of some sort of reader that Repo didn't recognize. "Have to pick up my kid from daycare."

The driver didn't respond, just looked at Repo, who was clueless. "You wanna pay so we can get out of here?"

Pay! He didn't have any money. His hand reached into the pocket of the trench coat, where at least there was a comb. He fished deeper and felt coins. Repo pulled them out, but they looked strange. He had heard of euros, of course, but he had never held one before. The prison store worked on credit.

"Sorry," he said, trying to act the yokel. It didn't take much effort. "How much is it?"

"Where are you headed?" the driver asked.

Repo didn't even know what bus he was on. "Umm... End of the line."

"Three sixty," the driver snapped.

Someone yelled from the back, "Hey, asshole! Why don't you pay so we can get out of here!"

Repo fumbled with the coins, trying to see how much they were worth, but they all looked the same to him. He slapped them down on the driver's little tray. "You mind? Eyesight's bad," he said.

"So get some glasses," the driver retorted, picking through the coins for the fare. Repo took his ticket, swept up the remaining coins, and moved farther back into the bus. He kept his eyes on the floor and found a seat up front, on the left. The woman in the red coat was sitting next to him, but she didn't so much as glance in his direction.

The bus backed up and Repo stole a glimpse outside. The police car that had approached from the *Helsingin Sanomat* headquarters had stopped fifty yards away.

Repo examined the coins in his hand. One was bigger than the rest and had a big 2 on it. The second-biggest one was yellow and it was worth 50. Repo counted his funds and came to the conclusion that he had 4 euros and 70 cents. He noticed the woman in the red coat eyeing him, and he slipped the change into his coat pocket.

The bus drove past the police car. It passed the newspaper's offices on the left and some new hotel on the right as it continued down the street, following the railroad. Up at the front of the bus, red lights formed what appeared to be the numbers 194. Repo didn't have the faintest idea where he was headed.

## CHAPTER 2
## MONDAY, 4:50 P.M.
## HELSINKI POLICE HEADQUARTERS, PASILA

Detective Lieutenant Kari Takamäki was in his office browsing through his copy of Finland's statutes, which was marked with colored Post-it notes cut into narrow strips. Written on the Post-its in tidy, tiny stick letters were words such as MURDER, ARSON, TELESURVEILLANCE, POLICE LAW.

The detective lieutenant had a problem. A thirty-two-year-old redhead, Jana Puttonen, was being held in a cell at police headquarters.

The detainee, who originally hailed from central Finland, was a teacher at a North Helsinki elementary school. A few hours ago she had been arrested on suspicion of blackmail.

Detective Sergeant Anna Joutsamo had interrogated the suspect and then briefed her sharp-featured, close-cropped lieutenant. Three separate police reports had spurred the investigation. In each instance, Puttonen had sent dubious photographs to the homes of three separate individuals. The North Helsinki precinct had connected the dots between the incidents, and the case had been transferred to the Violent Crimes Unit, which handled blackmail cases.

In and of themselves, the photos were relatively innocuous. One was of a kiss; in another, a woman had her arms around a man's neck; and in the third, a woman's hand was placed provocatively on the man's thigh. There was a different man in each photo, but the woman was the same. In the pictures, Puttonen was wearing heavy makeup and a black wig.

During the investigation, the police had quickly figured out that all the men were fathers of students in Puttonen's class. The photos had unexpectedly arrived at the men's homes in the mail, the envelopes addressed to their wives. The fingerprints had matched Puttonen's, and she didn't deny having sent the letters. The problem in terms of a criminal investigation was that Puttonen wasn't demanding anything from the men or their wives. She had simply sent the photographs.

The teacher had revealed her motive during Joutsamo's interrogation. The children of the families had harassed her at school, and Puttonen wanted to get back at them. She had tried changing schools, but new bullies always surfaced. Puttonen had claimed she had no problem dealing with the thumbtacks left on her chair, but the sexist slurs and the vandalism, like the gum in her car lock, were too much. She had even arranged special parent-teacher nights on the theme, but the parents of the problem children never showed.

So she had wanted to get back at the parents. She had figured out who the fathers of the bullies were, and, at an opportune moment, had flirted her way into their company. Finding someone to take a photo with a cell phone was never a problem. Puttonen had told Joutsamo that she didn't have any demands as far as the men were concerned. Getting back at them was enough.

Takamäki had initially opened the green-covered book at the Post-it marked "EXTORTION." In order to meet the description of the crime, the perpetrator had to be guilty of coercing the other party to relinquish assets under a force of threat. The photographs could be interpreted as a threat, but no assets were at stake.

The photographs could also be interpreted as causing suffering or slander, but the disseminating of information infringing on one's privacy required that the photos be made accessible to a number of people. That had not occurred.

Libel was not an option, because no false statements were involved, nor did the images degrade the men. Their expressions indicated that they had been perfectly happy to appear in them.

Disturbing the domestic peace? Puttonen hadn't entered anyone's home or caused any sort of public disturbance, and she had only sent one photograph to each family.

Vandalism? Nothing had been broken. Fraud? No financial loss was involved. Violating a restraining order? No restraining orders had been filed in the case. They wouldn't be able to wring any kind of sex crime out of it—the prosecutors would laugh in their faces.

Takamäki couldn't come up with a crime, which didn't actually disappoint him. To tell the truth, his sympathies were with the teacher. If families didn't keep their brats in line, why should teachers have to? Especially when they had been stripped of all means of doing so. Not that Takamäki missed those days. He remembered his own detentions all too well, which during the 1970s had meant standing on the school's tile floor: your feet had to stay within one twelve-by-twelve-inch square.

This was one of the more bizarre cases to come to the Violent Crimes Unit. Still known colloquially as Homicide, the unit got all sorts of incidents to investigate, from improperly installed electric stoves to beached boats to missing persons.

Takamäki's cell phone interrupted his reverie, but it didn't matter anymore. He had already decided that they'd release Puttonen for the simple fact that no crime had been committed. One-time harassment was not a punishable offense.

"Hello," Takamäki answered. He never offered his name unless he recognized the caller's number.

"Takamäki?" asked a male voice.

"Who's this?"

"Helmikoski, EOC."

Takamäki remembered the broad-shouldered lieutenant from the Emergency Operations Center. If Takamäki's memory served him correctly, he had transferred there from the department in the neighboring city of Vantaa.

"Yeah, it's me. What is it?"

"Have a case for you."

Takamäki glanced at the clock on his computer screen. A few minutes past five. Theoretically the day shift had already ended, but the Puttonen case had demanded some extra time. No other VCU lieutenants were around, or at least available.

"What kind?"

"Escaped convict."

Wow, Takamäki thought. At least it wasn't a violent standoff between motorcycle gangs or a headless corpse.

"Who?"

"Timo Repo."

"Who is he?" Takamäki asked, writing down the name.

"Fifty. Doing life for murdering his wife."

"Doesn't ring any bells," Takamäki replied. The crime had probably taken place somewhere outside greater Helsinki, because Takamäki remembered all the local murders.

"Was at his old man's funeral at Hietaniemi. The prison guard let him go to the bathroom at Restaurant

Perho and the guy never came back."

"Of course not," Takamäki said, already planning how they should organize the search. "Any sightings since the restaurant?"

"Possible but not definite sighting near the railway station twenty minutes ago. I've got several units looking for him, and the security companies have been alerted, but there are a lot of directions you can head from the central train station."

"You guys are still keeping an eye on it, though, right?"

"Of course."

"Give me a little more on Repo. Gang member, or what's his background? I'm mostly looking for an assessment of how dangerous he is."

Helmikoski thought for a moment. "We don't know much about him. A photo and some details of what he's wearing, but that's it. The guard who called in the escape was alone and not totally coherent."

"Ri-ight," Takamäki said. Like all prison escapes, the incident was already starting to frustrate him. The police had done their part: investigated the crime and gotten the perpetrator behind bars to sit out his sentence. But as soon as some other department screwed up, the case was tossed back in their laps.

"Anyway, the guard let him go to the bathroom by himself. So in all likelihood he's not some hard-core gangster."

"Just a murderer, tops," Takamäki replied.

\* \* \*

A couple of minutes later, Takamäki rose from his desk. He had printed out a few pages' worth of background info on Repo. One was his photo.

Takamäki stepped into the room shared by Joutsamo, Kohonen, Suhonen, and a couple of other detectives. It was clearly larger than Takamäki's cubbyhole, but had less space per occupant. Dividers decorated with photographs and papers separated the workspaces. From the window you could see the old courthouse. It was going to be renovated into Police HQ II, but Homicide wouldn't be moving there.

Anna Joutsamo was at her computer, typing with her headphones on. The thirty-four-year-old brunette was wearing jeans and a sweater. There was no one else in the room. She hadn't heard Takamäki enter and didn't realize her supervisor was there until he was standing right next to her.

"What is it?" she asked, pulling off her headphones.

"The Puttonen interrogation, huh?"

"Yeah."

Takamäki tossed the papers onto Joutsamo's desk. "Forget Puttonen. Got a new one for you."

Joutsamo swore. "What the hell? What do you mean, forget it? Little Red Riding Hood is right over in that cell. I can't just drop it."

"Yes, you can," Takamäki said. "I've been thinking about the case. There's no crime there. Doesn't meet the description."

Joutsamo was silent.

"Believe me. There's no way to get a case out of it. If you ask me, society would be better off if it concentrated its resources on the twerps who were harassing her."

"So which one of us is going handle that? You or me? There's no one else here," Joutsamo said laconically.

Takamäki chuckled. "Let's release her. She's probably got a school day tomorrow. Transcribe the interrogation later when you have some time, and I'll write up a report closing the investigation, citing no crime."

Joutsamo turned to the papers Takamäki had tossed onto her desk. The photo was on top. "And who's this winner?"

"Prisoner Timo Repo, serving life. Killed his wife a few years back, but what most interests me now is his current whereabouts."

"Escaped convict?"

It didn't take Takamäki more than a minute to pass on the info he had received from Helmikoski.

"Goddammit, cases like this piss the fuc... I mean really annoy me. We do our job and then..."

The lieutenant cut off his subordinate's rant. "You're preaching to the choir."

"That's not what I meant."

"I know," Takamäki said. "This guy disappeared an hour ago. Find out where he might be or want to get."

"Timo Repo." Joutsamo savored the name. "I might have read something about him at some point."

"Well, that's a good start. So you guys are practically friends. Where's Suhonen?"

"Hmm, I wonder where he could be at five o'clock on a Monday?" Joutsamo said.

Takamäki chuckled. Joutsamo grabbed the previous day's newspaper from the top of one of her piles. "I was going to ask you about this earlier. Did you read this interview this morning?"

Takamäki glanced at the page Joutsamo was showing him from the Sunday section of the *Helsingin Sanomat*.

"Yeah, I read it," he said.

The newspaper had sacrificed two pages to an interview with Aarno Fredberg, the new chief justice of the Supreme Court. In the article, Fredberg described his liberal views on criminal justice policy. From the perspective of the policeman, and the policewoman too, the headline was harsh: "Prison Doesn't Do Any Good." According to Chief Justice Fredberg, society would be better off if it focused its resources on things other than police and prosecutors, because incarceration simply escalated the cycle of marginalization.

Joutsamo was still holding the paper. "Can I call Mr. Chief Justice and have him come down here to talk to a few victims of serial rapists? That might open his eyes."

"No."

"Seriously, how can the highest justice in the land say stuff like this publicly? It's going to have a direct impact—judges will be handing down more lenient sentences. The bad guys are going to be getting out faster and committing more crimes."

"Yes, of course, because prison doesn't do any good," Takamäki said sarcastically.

Joutsamo didn't notice the joke. She huffed, "What?"

"Listen, if the minister of the interior said police productivity has to increase even more, would you start working overtime for free?"

"No," Joutsamo replied tartly.

"Well, those judges don't believe everything they read in the paper, either. They're people, just like you and me."

"Still, the guy could think for a second before opening his mouth," Joutsamo snapped, flinging the paper back on the stack.

"Would you believe me if I said it would be better if Repo was back sleeping in his own cell sometime soon?"

Joutsamo laughed, and Takamäki continued. "Let Puttonen go. Apologize and say that the police have to investigate all reports of crime, even the ambiguous ones. Be apologetic enough, genuinely apologetic, I mean, so she doesn't lodge a complaint with the Ministry of Justice. Because if she does, you get to write the response. I can't stand doing them anymore."

"No?"

"No, actually I can't. They're such a joke. I'll go get Suhonen and see if we can't send Superman here back to his cell."

"Be sure and pack the Kryptonite," Joutsamo said.

* * *

Takamäki parked his unmarked police vehicle, a Volkswagen Golf, in the parking lot of the Helsinki Hockey Arena, a mile up Mannerheim Street from downtown. Luckily, Monday wasn't a game night, so there was plenty of space. On the way, Takamäki had called his wife, Kaarina, and told her he'd be at least a few hours late.

The rain kept coming down, and Takamäki hustled to the practice rink door on the east side of the building.

As soon as he entered the lobby, he could smell the familiar, vaguely pungent aroma of hockey arenas. He stepped into the elevator and went down a couple of floors, where the elevator doors opened to the clanking of a game. The soundscape was different from that of league games. There were only a handful of spectators and the sounds of play predominated—you could hear the swear words more clearly.

It looked like there was an actual game underway on the ice, as it was unlikely that any team would have brought a ref in zebra stripes just for a practice. Takamäki looked around for Suhonen but couldn't spot him. The players all looked alike in their gear. The police team was wearing electric blue jerseys that read "PUCK POLICE" in big letters. The other team was playing in red. He'd probably find Suhonen on the bench, Takamäki decided, and walked on.

Takamäki was well aware—there's no way he could have avoided hearing about it at the station—that a year ago Suhonen had started playing hockey with the Financial Crimes Division. The undercover detective had trained them in the use of unconventional investigative methods; in other words, how to use informants. At some point, Suhonen had mentioned having played hockey all the way up to the Under 16 team in his hometown of Lahti, which had inspired the guys in Financial Crimes to recruit him.

Takamäki jumped when the plexiglass boomed right next to him. One of the blue players had tackled one of the reds into the boards. The ref blew his whistle and skated over.

"Number 27, two minutes! You know there's no tackling in the veteran league!"

Number 27 tapped the plexiglass in front of Takamäki with his stick, and the lieutenant recognized that the smirking face belonged to his undercover officer. Suhonen started skating toward the penalty box.

Takamäki walked up to the bench and whistled loudly at the ref, who skated over. "What now? It was clearly an illegal tackle," the sweating official bellowed.

Takamäki flashed his badge. "I have a warrant for Number 27 there. Eject him from the game. I'm going to take him back to the station."

"Fine with me," the ref laughed.

He skated over to the penalty box, put his hands on his hips and announced that Suhonen was being kicked out of the game.

"What?!" Suhonen protested. "What'd I do?"

"Talking back to the ref! You're done! Out of here!"

Suhonen glared ominously at Takamäki, who was smiling on the other side of the plexiglass, skated submissively toward the team bench, and stepped off the ice.

"Nice tackle," Takamäki said. Suhonen snatched the key to his locker from behind the bench and headed into the locker room without a word. Takamäki followed him down the linoleum corridor.

The locker room reeked of years of ingrained sweat. The stench took Takamäki back to his patrol-cop years; their locker room had smelled the same. It was a good stink in a way, because it carried a whiff of action. Suhonen sat down on the bench and pulled off his helmet.

"What now?" he asked, irritated. The forty-year-old detective's black hair was long and sweaty. He was sporting a beard like the pros during the Stanley Cup Playoffs. Although Takamäki suspected that Suhonen wasn't as superstitious as the NHL players were about shaving and losing.

"You guys were ahead 6–2, so forget about the game," Takamäki said.

When Suhonen took off his blue shirt, Takamäki noticed the extra gear under his shoulder pads and began to laugh.

"Bullet-proof vest? Why?"

Suhonen looked a little sheepish. "Let's you take the corners a little harder. Almost all our guys wear them."

"Boy, you are Puck Police, all right," Takamäki said, sitting down on a bench. There were about twenty guys' bags and gear in the locker room. How many department-issued weapons were here? Well, these guys were financial crimes investigators, so probably not many.

Suhonen tossed his neck guard and shoulder pads into his bag and began unlacing his skates.

"What's up?" he asked, without raising his gaze from his skates.

"Work. A lifer escaped."

Suhonen stopped unlacing and gave Takamäki an intense look. "Who?"

"Apparently no one that bad."

"Who?"

"Timo Repo."

Suhonen went back to his laces. "Repo? Killed his wife somewhere in Riihimäki or Hyvinkää before the turn of the millennium?"

"Bingo."

"From prison?"

"Nah, his old man's funeral in Töölö. Ran for it."

"And you had to get me tossed from the game for that?" Suhonen said, drying and packing up his skates.

"You're on the clock," Takamäki chuckled.

Suhonen took off his bullet-proof vest and sniffed it. "Pretty fragrant. Hopefully I get to hunt Repo down with you and Joutsamo in the teeniest compact vehicle ever."

"Go take a shower."

# CHAPTER 3
## MONDAY, 7:00 P.M.
## THE CORNER PUB, KALLIO

Suhonen was sitting alone at a table in a stuffy bar in Helsinki's working-class neighborhood of Kallio. His hair was pulled back in a ponytail and he was wearing a leather jacket. A half-full pint stood in front of him. Salmela hadn't shown up yet. Half a dozen guys were standing at the bar, even though there was plenty of room at the tables. An elderly customer was watching some old soccer match from the muted TV bolted to the ceiling. Over the loudspeakers, a classic rock band was offering advice about socking cash away, but for the clientele of the Corner Pub, the advice had gone in one ear and out the other.

At the next table over, Suhonen heard a heavy-set guy recounting his weekend escapades to a couple of buddies. "Check it out, we were there at the strip bar and this chick came over to give me a lap dance and just kept going, 'Tip me, tip me.' So I dug a fistful of change out of my pocket and dropped it into her panties."

"Dude, hell no," laughed one of the other guys.

"And that's not even the best part," Fatso continued. "I figured she'd go right over to get the bouncer so I took out one more two-euro coin. I heated it with my lighter and when the goon showed up, I said, 'My bad,' and put the red-hot coin in his hand. Fuck, that dude screamed loud! I hauled ass out of there as fast as I could."

As the group burst out laughing, Salmela entered and walked straight to the bar. The forty-year-old regular had short hair and a brown bomber jacket; its faded lambskin collar was wet. He got his pint in no time and came over to sit next to Suhonen.

"What's up? Any good gigs lately?" Salmela asked.

Suhonen glanced over at the guys sitting at the next table. "Nothing worth talking about here."

Salmela tapped the heavy-set guy on the shoulder.

"Hey, why don't you guys move over to that corner table. Watch some TV for a sec."

Fatso was about to say something, but his buddy stepped in. "Sure, okay. No problem," he said, picking up his beer. The others followed in silence.

"Your reputation's growing," Suhonen joked.

"Sometimes it even comes in handy," Salmela answered. Suhonen looked him in the eyes. Suhonen thought they looked even harder than before. Suhonen and Salmela had been friends since childhood. They had both grown up in Lahti, a town of about 100,000 an hour's drive north of Helsinki. When they were teenagers, they had belonged to a small gang that burglarized attics. When the gang was finally busted, Salmela got caught, but Suhonen was at home with a raging fever. The best friends had ended up on opposite sides of the law, but their friendship hadn't ended. It had actually blossomed—Suhonen picked up street intel from Salmela and, in return, had helped his friend out of a few legal jams. Salmela had continued to earn his living fronting stolen goods, but now there were rumors that he had ratcheted up into more serious crimes.

"What about your gigs?

"Bah," Salmela said. "It's been quiet. Quiet."

Suhonen wasn't completely sure he believed him.

"You had something you wanted to talk about?"

"The name Timo Repo say anything to you?"

"Repo?" Salmela thought. "Unusual name. Nah, the only Repo I know is the guy who's doing life for icing his wife."

"That's the one," Suhonen said. He took a sip of his pint and waited for Salmela's reaction.

"A softy. I didn't know him personally. He pretty much kept to himself, like most wife-killers. They're not tough guys, usually they just snap. Sometimes for a reason, sometimes not. What'd he do?" Salmela asked, sipping his beer.

"Skipped out."

"From Helsinki Prison?" Salmela was intrigued. "That's interesting. How?"

Suhonen shook his head. "From his old man's funeral. Ditched the guard."

"Hmmm. Okay, not so interesting anymore. What's he to you guys?"

"C'mon, a lifer escaped. We need to get him back behind bars before the media gets its panties in a twist."

"But the guy's a total nobody," Salmela wondered.

"Still a murderer. Lieutenant figured we need to find him fast."

"Well, I can ask around, but I gotta say I'm a little confused by your, or I guess Takamäki's, enthusiasm. Old man's death can be a tough spot for a soft con like that. My money's on him downing a bottle of vodka and walking up to the prison gates to turn himself in once the hangover clears."

Suhonen shrugged.

\* \* \*

In the Homicide break room, Joutsamo poured hot water into her mug and dipped in a bag of tea. It was some green variety she didn't particularly care for, but it was all that was left. She'd have to remember to pick up some more Tiger's Daydream.

She walked back down the harshly lit corridor to her room, set her mug down on the sole corner of her desk not covered by stacks of paper, and sat down.

A few postcards were pinned to her cubicle divider, the most recent one from Panama. It had been sent by Joutsamo's good friend, TV reporter Sanna Römpötti. Joutsamo wondered where Römpötti got the money for her overseas trips, since Joutsamo could barely make the rent on her one-bedroom in Töölö. Maybe reporters made that much more than cops.

Takamäki had given her the background info on Repo, and Joutsamo had now fleshed it out. The Social Security database revealed that Repo was born on June 16, 1955 in Hämeenlinna, so he would be fifty-two now. His current address wasn't much use: Helsinki Prison.

Repo's mother had died in the '90s, and his father was deceased now as well, although that information hadn't been updated yet. Joutsamo had jotted down the father's address, which was somewhere in northern Helsinki, probably Malmi. Repo had a son born in 1995, Joel. The records indicated Child Protective Services had taken Joel into custody immediately following the crime. Timo Repo's mother tongue was Finnish, and he was a member of the Lutheran Church. He also had a brother, Martti, who was a couple of years older. Joutsamo tapped the brother's address into her computer, too.

The police database provided basic facts on the crime Repo had committed on November 3, 1999 in the city of Riihimäki. He had been charged with murder right from the start, rather than a lesser homicide charge. It also revealed that Repo had been sentenced to life in prison in 2000. Joutsamo had written down the number of the police report. It would lead her to the investigation documents, which might prove useful in tracking down Repo's acquaintances.

Repo didn't own a car. There was no mention of him in the "usual suspects" database, aka the register of repeat offenders.

She also had access to the *Helsingin Sanomat* newspaper's premium archives. There, Joutsamo had discovered a blurb titled "Riihimäki Wife-Killer Gets Life." The text itself was short and to the point, "The Riihimäki District Court sentenced Timo Repo, convicted of killing his wife in November, to life in prison. The court found the act unusually cruel and brutal: forty-four-year-old Repo slit his wife's throat with a knife. Alcohol was involved. Repo admitted to the crime in court."

Takamäki entered the room, carrying a cup of coffee.

"Do we have anything?"

"Not much more than a couple of addresses: father's and brother's homes," Joutsamo replied. "I thought I'd go by and check them out once Suhonen gets back from his field trip. Tomorrow I'm going to head up to Riihimäki to take a look at his preliminary investigation papers and see if I can find any mention of Repo's acquaintances in them. After that, make the rounds and ask anyone if they've seen him."

"Okay."

"You see this? The old *Helsingin Sanomat* piece about Repo's crime?" Joutsamo said, holding up a print of the article.

Takamäki read it. "Cold-blooded way to kill. We'd better round him up before he decides to cork another bottle. Of course, it may already be too late."

His cell phone prevented the lieutenant from further reflection. Caller ID said it was Kaarina, his wife.

"Hey hon," Takamäki said.

"Jonas got hit by a car. The Espoo Police called," Kaarina said urgently.

"How bad?" Takamäki asked. Sixteen-year-old Jonas was the older of Takamäki's boys. Kalle was fourteen.

"They don't know yet. The ambulance took him to Jorvi Hospital."

Joutsamo could tell something had happened and perked up her ears.

"When did it happen...and where?"

"I don't know exactly. Apparently not long ago, according to the policeman. Jonas had been riding his bike near the Sello shopping mall."

Takamäki thought for a second. "I'm heading straight to the hospital. How's Kalle?"

"He's at home. I'll come, too."

"Good," Takamäki said, ending the call.

Joutsamo gave her superior an inquisitive look.

"Jonas got hit by a car and was taken to Jorvi. I have to go out there."

"How bad?"

"Don't know yet."

"Anything I can do?"

Takamäki shrugged. "I don't think so."

"You want me to call a cruiser to take you?"

"No need. I'll drive myself."

Joutsamo stood up and gave Takamäki a quick hug.

# CHAPTER 4
## MONDAY, 7:20 P.M.
## MALMI, NORTHERN HELSINKI

Timo Repo sniffed the stale air and opened the window. He drew back the curtains giving onto the street. Not all the way, but far enough for the cold blue light of the streetlamps of Vallesman Road to filter into the living room. He was still wearing the black suit. The stolen gray trench was flung across the arm of the couch.

His dad had lived for years in an old wooden house in the north Helsinki district of Malmi. The elder Repo hadn't diverged from ingrained habit: the key had been under the mat, just like decades before.

Timo recognized some of the belongings. He had bought the Aalto vase as a gift for his mother in the 1980s. The china was the same old set.

The living room contained a threadbare sofa, an armchair, and an old TV. The room opened onto the kitchen at the far end. Near the dining table, a door led to the bedroom.

Repo's gaze fell on an old photograph on top of the TV. It had been taken some time in the late '60s, when the family had taken a weekend cruise to Stockholm. Mom and Dad smiled in the middle, with the boys on either side. His buzz-cut brother, Martti, grinned broadly in the photo. Timo remembered that he had had the same kind of haircut. You couldn't see it, though, because his face had been scrawled out with black marker.

Repo was exhausted. He didn't have time to sleep, but he could rest for a while on the couch. First, though, he went into the closet in his father's bedroom. He found a 9mm Luger in a brown leather holster in the hatbox on the upper shelf. It also held three small cardboard boxes, each containing twenty-five bullets.

He knew the gun. Dad had taught him to shoot it back in the day. The gun was still in good shape; it had been oiled well enough. He pulled back the pistol's slide, checked that the chamber was empty, and pulled the trigger. The gun clicked. He ripped open one of the boxes, loaded six bullets into the magazine, and pushed it back into the old gun. Repo drew the slide again. The bullet slid in impeccably. Good, no chambering problems. Repo clicked on the safety and shoved the gun back into its holster.

He stretched out on the couch and decided to close his eyes for a minute.

* * *

Suhonen was driving a green Peugeot 206 he had signed out of the police HQ garage. Joutsamo was sitting in the passenger seat. An old song by Metallica was playing on the radio. Joutsamo, a fan of heavy music, thought it was bubblegum rock. Suhonen disagreed heartily.

The car turned onto Vallesman Road. The houses were old and relatively small, and both sides of the street were lined with parked cars.

"I know this area. Picked up a member of the Skulls three, four blocks from here a few years back," Suhonen said. The Skulls—or, as it read on the gang members' leather vests, MC Skulls—wasn't a genuine motorcycle club; it was a criminal organization. "Found two Swedish submachine guns."

"Let's drive past it first and see if there are any lights on," Joutsamo suggested. "If there are, then we can stake the place out or call in the SWAT team."

"You got it," Suhonen said.

Joutsamo checked the numbers on the houses. "Two more, then it's the next one. At that streetlamp."

Suhonen slowed down and the car slid past the house, going under 20 mph. The place was dark.

"I didn't see any movement," Joutsamo said.

"And you're saying you would have been able to tell if there had been?"

"Of course. Should we wait or go in to have a look?"

Suhonen turned right at the next corner and started circling around the block. It would attract less attention than flipping a U-turn on a residential street. Joutsamo didn't get a response, because Suhonen's phone rang. It was his fiancée, calling to ask if and when he might be coming home. Suhonen said he didn't know. The call was a brief one, and Joutsamo chose not to comment on it.

Suhonen returned to the situation at hand: "We can't hang out in the car on a residential street like this. We'd need to get a van or do it from one of the neighboring houses. Maybe we should just go have a look and see what there is to see, if anything."

"Yeah, but if we're going by the book, I suppose we ought to have some reason to believe that the suspect's in there," Joutsamo said. Once the prison had asked for the help of the authorities in hunting down Repo, the search had turned into a police investigation. "And we don't have a warrant to conduct a search of that house. Our job is to find the convict."

Suhonen grunted. "If you say so. You're the one who's always talking about studying to become a lieutenant, but we wouldn't be here in the first place if we didn't believe Repo could be in that house, now would we?"

He parked a few houses down from the target. "You know, I'm a 'probable cause' kind of guy," he continued, as they stepped out of the car.

"In what sense?" Joutsamo asked.

"Police ops, of course. 'Probable cause' is a pretty good foundation for any operation. If I have probable cause to suspect something, I can do whatever I want. All I need is to meet the criteria for 'probable cause.'"

Joutsamo laughed, but she also checked to make sure the bulletproof vest she was wearing under her sweater was on straight. Her leather jacket was open, and her gun was holstered under her arm.

"Go around the back?" she suggested.

"I don't think there is a back door. At least there wasn't one at that gang member's house, and this one looks the same."

"Are we going to ring the doorbell?"

"No," Suhonen said, revealing a small, screwdriver-like device he had in his hand.

"You have a jigger?" Joutsamo wondered. You could open a standard lock in a split second with a jigger, if you know how.

"Yup," Suhonen said. "Search warrant regulations state you can only force entry when circumstances demand. This way we won't be forcing our way, plus we won't need a repairman to fix the door."

Joutsamo would have been interested in finding out where Suhonen had gotten the burglary tool in the first place, not to mention where he had learned to use it, but Suhonen wouldn't have told her. Besides, there was no point entering the premises making noise, so she kept her mouth shut.

\* \* \*

Timo Repo was dreaming about the ferry cruise to Sweden. His dad was carrying two bottles of Coca-Cola to the table for the boys and Carlsberg elephant beers for the grown-ups. Everyone was smiling, but no one was saying anything. The young woman at the next table looked Timo in the eye. Repo recognized her as his wife, and she was smiling, too.

A shadow fell between them and quickly disappeared. It wasn't part of the dream, and Repo's eyes popped open. He couldn't see anything out the window, but he was certain that someone had moved under the streetlamp.

He cautiously got up. Was that rustling coming from outside? Repo snatched his gun and his coat from the coat rack. He wiped the floor with the sleeve of his black suit just in case any water drops had fallen from the coat, and then he slunk into the bedroom. There was a bullet in the barrel of his gun, but he decided to hide in the closet. This wasn't the time for a confrontation yet.

\* \* \*

Suhonen carefully twisted the jigger, now in the lock, from a small crank at its tail end. The device was designed to move the detainer disks into the same position as a key would.

It took Suhonen less than twenty seconds to open the lock. The door creaked slightly as Suhonen pulled it by the handle. Joutsamo winced. The noise was definitely loud enough for someone who was awake inside to have heard it, but had it been loud enough to wake someone up? Not necessarily.

Suhonen pulled out his Glock 22, crouched down, and entered first. He didn't linger in the doorway—the street light behind him effectively turned him into a silhouette target. He edged right and waited there against the wall for a moment. It was darker inside than it was outside, and his eyes needed a moment to get used to the dimness.

The house smelled like it had been uninhabited for a while.

The living room appeared empty. Suhonen carefully rose and advanced, hugging the wall. Joutsamo followed, silently closing the outside door.

Suhonen waited at the corner of the dining room while Joutsamo slowly crept ahead, circling around behind the sofa. It didn't take long before she had a view of both the dining room and the kitchen in their entirety. They were empty, too. Joutsamo gestured Suhonen onwards. The bathroom came first, and Suhonen quickly checked it.

There was only one room left. Suhonen pulled open the bedroom door. The detectives crouched down on either side of the doorway. The interior walls of the old house wouldn't offer much protection from bullets. Suhonen glimpsed in quickly. There were curtains in front of the windows, but they let in enough light for him to note the twin bed in the middle of the room. On the left wall there was a desk and on the right, a closet.

Suhonen rose and entered. Joutsamo followed.

"Empty," Suhonen said, holstering his gun. He flipped on the light switch next to the door.

* * *

Repo stayed as quiet as possible at the back of the cramped closet. The coats were in front of him, but he could still make out the strip of light between the closet and the floor. The old clothes were dusty, and the pungent funk of mothballs filled his nose. He felt like coughing, but he chased the thought from his mind. He was clenching his pistol tightly. The grip felt sweaty.

Repo heard a woman's voice, "Yeah, that would have been a little too lucky, finding him crashed out here on the bed."

Of course: they were cops, Repo thought. That made him momentarily reconsider the circumstances and the resolution he had come to in the closet. Maybe he should shoot after all. A burglar or two he might have been able to catch off guard, but police officers? There were at least two of them, but there might be as many as ten.

Yes, he'd pull the trigger. He wasn't going back to that cell.

"Too bad he isn't," answered a male voice.

"Should we have a look around?" Repo heard the woman ask. The footfalls approached and stopped at the door. She must have been standing right in front of the closet, because the strip of light at the floor dimmed.

Repo could barely breathe now. If the closet door opened, he would shoot.

"No one's slept in that bed. Those blankets are army-regulation sharp," the man said.

"Okay. I'm going to have a quick look at the desk and the kitchen. You take the living room."

The man paused. "What is it you want me to look for?"

"Photographs of Repo. Friends, names, anything that will help us with the case."

"Okay. There was some mail there in the entryway, but it's going to be Old Man Repo's."

The woman walked away, presumably toward the desk.

* * *

45

Joutsamo scanned the room once more. The home of a lonely old man. A lamp and a couple of books were on the nightstand. The book on top appeared to be the memoirs of a Finnish man who had served in the French Foreign Legion: *Trained for Pain, Trained to Die.* The bookmark was halfway through.

Several medications lay on the dark surface of the desk. Joutsamo recognized some from her Narcotics days as hard-core painkillers that junkies used as substitutes for heroin. There were also three boxes, which Joutsamo quickly rummaged through. It was old crap: commemorative coins and freebie promotional gear. No photo albums or address books.

Maybe they'd be in the closet? Joutsamo decided to check and started walking back toward it.

"Anna," Suhonen called from the living room. "Come take a look at this."

Joutsamo hesitated for a second, and then walked out of the bedroom.

Suhonen was standing at the TV, holding something in his hand.

"What is it?"

"Get a load of this," said the undercover officer, holding up the photo taken on the deck of the cruise ship. Joutsamo examined it in silence.

"The old man blacked out his son's face, but he still keeps it on display. Why? And in a spot like that?" Joutsamo asked, even though she already knew the reason.

"You want me to answer that?"

"No," Joutsamo said.

The father had disowned his son.

Suhonen was quiet for a moment. "Let's get out of here. We're not going to find anything."

Joutsamo continued gazing at the photo as Suhonen turned off the lights, first in the bedroom and then everywhere else. Joutsamo set the photo back down on the TV.

"The brother," Suhonen said, as he closed the front door behind him. "Let's go have a chat with him."

* * *

Repo decided to wait in the closet ten more minutes, but it stretched to twenty before he dared to crack the door. The gun was still in his hand. The air in the bedroom felt cool, and he emerged warily from behind the coats, pistol cocked. The bedroom was empty. Repo had expected one of the cops would have stayed behind to lie in wait for him.

He walked into the kitchen in the dark and turned toward the living room.

Repo jumped. He was caught so off guard he didn't even have time to raise his weapon. A thin man in a long coat was standing there in the pale light of the streetlamp, and for a moment Timo Repo thought he had come face to face with his father.

He could only see half of the old man's face, but that was enough.

"Well, well, look who's here," Otto Karppi said in a reedy voice, aiming a shotgun at Repo.

# CHAPTER 5
## MONDAY, 7:50 P.M.
## JORVI MUNICIPAL HOSPITAL, ESPOO

Takamäki raced into the spartan lobby of Jorvi Hospital, out of breath. Near the main entrance was an information desk with a few windows, but only one was open. A fifty-year-old woman was explaining something to a bored-looking guy in a lab coat.

Takamäki scanned the room, but didn't see his wife. Plenty of images had gone through his head during the drive: his unconscious son being transported by ambulance, a breathing tube down his throat, the X-rays and MRI of his head at the hospital, the suspected brain damage.

Takamäki's sweaty shirt was glued to his back, and his hands were trembling.

The conversation at the info desk seemed to be going nowhere fast, so Takamäki decided to take matters into his own hands. The floor was marked with stripes in various colors: black, red, orange, lavender. The lieutenant had spent plenty of time interrogating assault victims in hospitals, including Jorvi, and so he knew what the colors meant. Yellow led to Surgery, red to X-ray. Takamäki picked the yellow one.

The line led Takamäki down the corridor to a nurse's station. A few orderlies in white coats were leaning against the desk. One had ominous bloodstains on his lapels. The lieutenant momentarily considered pulling out his badge but decided against it.

"Hello," he said in a serious tone.

"Hey," was the expressionless response of one of the orderlies, a guy with a buzzed head.

"Jonas Takamäki was brought here a little while ago," he announced, his voice quivering.

None of the orderlies responded immediately. Takamäki wondered whether that was a bad sign.

"Sorry, we don't know names. You might wanna try the info desk, back where you came from."

"Umm, 16-year-old kid. Bike accident."

Buzz-cut glanced at his buddy. "Oh, him. Yeah, what about him?"

"I'm his father."

"All right. I can take you there."

Takamäki noticed a familiar-looking bicycle helmet that was split at the side. Ugly visions and some that were worse than ugly flooded into his head. "Is that his?"

Buzz-cut nodded.

"How bad is it?" Takamäki gulped, as the orderly stopped at a door.

"He should be in here."

The orderly knocked, and a woman's voice responded with an "Uh-huh?" Buzz-cut opened the door and let Takamäki in.

It was a normal hospital room. A nurse in a white coat was at the treatment table, and Jonas was lying on it. Takamäki saw his bloody shirt.

"This is the father," the orderly announced and walked out.

The nurse turned away from Jonas and gave Takamäki a friendly smile. "It's nothing serious," she immediately said. "Just a broken arm."

Takamäki sighed, and Jonas turned to look. Takamäki registered his son's relatively bright eyes. The kid was grimacing a little from the pain, but managed a grin.

Takamäki came over to the head of the bed and stroked his son's hair extremely tenderly; his hand barely made contact. "Hey, buddy. I'm glad you're okay."

"The helmet took the worst of the blow," the nurse said. "But there's still the potential for a mild concussion. The doctor will examine more closely in a bit. We're definitely looking at X-rays and a cast, though."

The nurse continued cleaning the wounds on Jonas's right arm.

"It wasn't my fault. I had a green light. He went through a red light."

"That doesn't matter right now," Takamäki said, still stroking his son's hair. "What's important is that it wasn't anything more serious."

\* \* \*

In the dark house, Karppi kept his shotgun trained on Repo at a distance of maybe ten, twelve feet.

"Were those your friends?"

"Who?" Repo wondered. He was still holding the Luger, but the barrel was pointed at the floor.

"Those two who just left."

"No," Repo grunted. "They were cops. Looking for me."

Now it was Karppi's turn to laugh. "You did hightail it out of that restaurant pretty fast. Is that what you came here to get?"

Repo gathered the old man meant the pistol. "No, but it was there in its old spot in the hatbox."

"Erik told me the story."

Repo wondered which story his father had told his neighbor. "The war thing?"

Karppi nodded.

According to the story, Erik Repo had been given the gun right after World War II, as a young man of fifteen, by an old vet who wanted Erik to safeguard it for him. Apparently it had been used to shoot more than a few Russkies—the rumors were that several Soviet commissars had been executed at close range. The vet had been more than happy to give it away, so it couldn't be traced back to him.

"This gun is the real deal," Repo said, activating the safety with his thumb and shoving the gun into his waistband. "But we don't need any more bodies."

"We sure don't," Karppi agreed, lowering the barrel of his shotgun to the floor.

The men stood across from each other in silence.

"You didn't get a chance to finish your coffee back at the restaurant. Would you care to now?"

Repo shrugged. "Maybe. But not here."

"Of course not. Those cops might come back. I meant over at my house. Might be a better place for you, anyway."

\* \* \*

Karppi poured the coffee. The cups were delicate and old fashioned, not mugs.

"Cream or milk?"

"No thanks," Repo answered. He was sitting at the dining table in his black suit. He had loosened his tie.

"You take it bald, huh?"

"What?"

"Up north they used to say if you drank your coffee black, you liked it bald," the old man explained.

Karppi's house was the same size as his neighbor's, but the decor was a touch more genteel. The difference lay in the dark furniture and the massive bookshelf that took up a whole wall.

Karppi sat down across from Repo. There were also sandwiches and mineral water on the table.

"You and your dad have some of the same features. He'd always sit the same way, a little hunched over with his arms across his chest."

The remark prompted Repo to sit up straighter and uncross his arms. Karppi laughed and tasted his hot coffee.

Repo glanced at Karppi's old-fashioned cell phone on the kitchen table. "Why didn't you call the cops?"

"How do you know I'm not about to?"

Repo didn't respond.

"Why did he hate you so much?"

Repo turned his gaze to his black coffee. "Why do you think?"

"Because of what happened back then."

"We never really talked about it, so it's hard to say. You never asked him?"

Karppi dodged the question. "Erik was a reticent man." He took a sip of coffee before continuing. "Why did you kill your wife?"

Repo didn't answer, and Karppi backed off.

"I was just asking. That photo on top of the TV always made me wonder." Karppi stood. "Why the hell did your dad keep it out? If you want to forget something, you don't keep a photo that reminds you of it in a prominent spot."

"He may have had his reasons."

"I suppose he did," Karppi said. He walked over to the kitchen cabinets and pulled out a folder. "I wasn't blessed with children, so maybe that's why I found it so intriguing. I don't think I would have been capable of that sort of hatred myself." He set the green folder down in front of Repo. "Here."

"What's that?" Repo asked, without touching it.

"I gathered a few papers that looked important from your father's home a few days after his death. Just in case burglars came to call."

Repo opened the folder. The documents that had once belonged to his father were neatly organized in plastic sleeves. The bank statements were on top. Repo skipped past them and browsed through documents regarding the house, paid bills, a passport, and other important-looking papers. There were about fifteen plastic sleeves. The second-to-last one contained cash, maybe three hundred euros, at an eyeball estimate.

"Take it. You must need money."

Repo fished the bills out and placed them in his breast pocket.

The final sleeve, clearly the fattest, contained letters. Repo pulled them all out and glanced at Karppi.

"I haven't read them."

Topmost were postcards printed in a child's hand. Someone else had written Erik Repo's address on them. One was from the Canary Islands. "Hi Grandpa! We're in the Canary Islands. It's nice and warm here. I've been swimming every day. Love, Joel." The postmark was January 2003; Joel would have been eight years old.

The coffee was cooling. Karppi watched closely as Repo scanned through the mail.

There were several vacation and Christmas cards. There was also a letter from Joel. Timo read it quickly. In it, the boy thanked his grandpa for the Christmas money. He had used it to buy a computer game. It also contained a photograph of a boy, about ten, smiling broadly in front of a Christmas tree.

Karppi caught Repo wiping a tear from the corner of his eye.

Timo stared at the photo for a long time. He hadn't seen his son in eight years because the child had been taken into custody and placed with a foster family, and Repo wasn't allowed any information about them.

"You can sleep on the sofa."

"I'm not sure that's a good idea."

"Where else are you going to go? It's comfortable enough."

Repo took a sandwich and reflected. In a lot of ways, running into Karppi was a stroke of luck—and would definitely make things easier.

# TUESDAY MORNING

# CHAPTER 6
## TUESDAY, 8:30 A.M.
## HELSINKI POLICE HEADQUARTERS, PASILA

Joutsamo yawned. They had searched for Repo until after eleven the previous night, after which she had biked home to Töölö. She hadn't slept properly, and a few hours later she had cycled back to Pasila.

"Good morning," Takamäki called from the doorway.

Joutsamo turned around. "Good morning. How's Jonas?"

"Broken arm and mild concussion. Kaarina's staying at home with him."

"Thank God it wasn't worse. Who was the driver?"

"Don't know. Took off."

"Hit-and-run, huh?" Joutsamo said.

"The Espoo Police Department is investigating."

"In that case, you'll never know," laughed the sergeant. She had worked in the Espoo PD Narcotics division before transferring to Helsinki Homicide.

"I don't know. It's not such a tough case. Happened near Sello. There are a ton of surveillance cameras around there."

"The Sello shopping mall, huh?" Joutsamo turned back to her computer. Takamäki walked over behind her to follow along as she looked up data from Homicide's list of surveillance cameras.

"There," Joutsamo said. "They've got two kinds of recordings. Some are stored for a week, but others just for twenty-four hours. Hopefully they've got the sense to go look at the images today."

"Could be that some eyewitness caught the license plate and they wouldn't even need photos," Takamäki said, before changing the subject. "Where are we with the escaped convict?"

"Suhonen and I were out looking for him all evening. Went to the father's house, but got nothing. Well, we did find out that relations between father and son probably weren't the warmest. The brother indicated the same about their relationship, too. After murdering his wife, Timo Repo was shut out by his family."

"Well, he can't make it on his own out there. He's going to need help. He probably doesn't have any money," Takamäki said.

"Suhonen and I were thinking the same thing. We agreed I'd go visit the Riihimäki police and check out those old preliminary investigation reports, see if maybe we can find some names there. Suhonen will work the prison angle."

"Good," said Takamäki. "Any new cases last night?"

"Nothing serious. A couple of assaults out east at Itäkeskus, but the precinct will handle them. Couple of cars disappeared, a few B&Es, nothing out of the ordinary."

"You need some extra hands to help you with the Repo investigation? I could free up Kohonen and Kulta. They've almost got the railway station homeless case wrapped up."

"I don't think so. Let's see how things start rolling here. If we find any names in the old documents or the prison, then maybe."

Takamäki walked to the door. "Okay. Let's have a status check at two."

"If the rat stays in his hole and doesn't move, it's going to be pretty hard to find him. Should we use the media to smoke him out?"

"We'll take a look at two." Takamäki thought for a moment. "What do you think, should I make sure the Espoo police picked up those images from Sello?"

"I'm pretty sure they've got it under control."

\* \* \*

Takamäki deleted an email from the National Police Board reminding staff of the communication guidelines, thanks to some hapless sergeant who had given a lecture at some school. According to the new, stringent regulations, no officer was to make a public appearance without a written request detailing the purpose and message of the visit delivered in advance to the National Police Board.

Takamäki couldn't get the Sello surveillance images out of his head; he had to call. The mall switchboard connected him to the head of security currently on duty.

A male voice grumbled into the phone, "Aho."

"Lieutenant Takamäki here," Takamäki said, intentionally omitting Helsinki Police.

Aho suddenly sounded like a security guard whose sights were set on the police academy: "What can I do for you, sir?"

Takamäki held a brief pause. "Something pretty simple, actually. There was an accident yesterday evening over on the side of the mall facing the railroad. A cyclist was hit by a car."

"Really? There wasn't anything in the papers."

"Well, the injuries weren't very serious, but now we're tracking down the driver, who fled the scene."

"So you're looking for surveillance footage."

"Right," Takamäki said. "There's a little uncertainty here as to whether someone has asked for it yet."

"Not today, at least," Aho said. "I've been here all morning, and of course I can check yesterday's log, too."

Takamäki could hear Aho tapping at his computer.

"Nope, the images haven't been picked up. I mean, no one has even requested them."

"So you have the footage?"

Aho backtracked. "I'm not sure about that. I'm just saying it hasn't been turned over."

Takamäki began to see why the guy hadn't made it into the police academy and probably never would. Nevertheless, he kept his voice as steady and relaxed as possible.

"You think you might have a minute, buddy, to check and see if you guys have the footage there? It happened around 7 p.m. yesterday on the railroad side of the mall. Of course I'd be particularly interested in any shots of the car."

"Of course. It'll take me a second, though. I can call you back."

Takamäki gave Aho his cell phone number, thanked him, and ended the call.

"What footage are you looking for?" Suhonen asked from the doorway. Takamäki hadn't noticed him. Suhonen stepped in.

"It doesn't have anything to do with this Repo case."

"With what, then?" Suhonen continued. His curiosity was piqued, because it wasn't every day that a lieutenant called and asked for surveillance camera footage himself. That was a job for subordinates.

"Jonas got hit by a car over at Sello yesterday. I'm just making sure they hold on to the shopping center's surveillance cam images."

"Hurt bad?"

"Nah," Takamäki answered. "Not too bad. Broke his arm. But the driver fled the scene."

Suhonen thought for a second. "Isn't that an Espoo police case? Or I mean, at least not yours?"

"Yeah, it's Espoo's," Takamäki admitted, before deciding to change to a less-awkward subject. "Why isn't Repo back behind bars yet?"

Suhonen smiled at his lieutenant's clumsy attempt to change the subject. "'Cause we haven't found him."

"You think you might want to do that?"

"Do you remember when you ordered me to attend that class given by the Security Police last summer?" Suhonen asked, sitting down in his favorite spot on the windowsill across from Takamäki's desk.

"What does that have to do with this?"

"There was this one army intelligence officer lecturing about military intelligence, and he had a PowerPoint slide that he flashed up on the screen. It was this matrix that said that the most important task of military intelligence is to determine the other nation's capability and intentions. That's what helps you assess threats."

"And?"

"Well, I've been trying to apply that matrix to Repo. Does this Repo have the capacity for wrong-doing? Okay, he killed his wife years ago, so theoretically the potential exists. Still, I'd estimate his capability as being pretty minimal."

Takamäki tried interjecting, "I wouldn't."

"Let me finish. What about his intentions? That's a trickier thing, because we don't know why he fled. It's still pretty hard to see it as a particularly planned escape. It seems to have been more of a momentary impulse. Repo doesn't belong to a criminal gang, so we can't conclude, for example, that he's off on some vendetta he was ordered to handle. That being the case, I would also assess his intent to commit wrong-doing as pretty

61

minimal. And since both factors are low, the threat assessment is also pretty low. The guy's a sheep."

Takamäki looked at Suhonen. He tried to keep his face serious, but a smile crept into his eyes.

"But guess what. You're not some major from military intelligence, you're a..."

Takamäki held a brief pause, and Suhonen stepped into the trap.

"I'm a what?"

"You're a shepherd. So get that lost sheep back into the fold, pronto."

Suhonen stood and saluted, raising a hand to his nonexistent cap.

"Yes, sir!"

At that moment, Joutsamo walked up to the door. "I'm headed up to Riihimäki now," she said, before registering the scene. "All riiight. No need to explain."

Joutsamo was sitting in a small, windowless interrogation room. The preliminary investigation report for the Repo case lay open on the brown tabletop. Someone had etched the word "Fuck" into the table. The stack of papers was surprisingly slight, not even half an inch's worth. She'd been reading the interrogation transcripts for an hour and was almost done.

The case appeared relatively simple. Repo had been drinking at home with his wife. The next morning the police had found Repo sleeping in his bed and his wife sprawled out on the floor next to the kitchen table. Her throat had been slit from ear to ear. There was a ton of blood in the photos. That detail alone told Joutsamo that the woman had lived for some time after the deed, because the heart had kept pumping blood out of the carotid artery.

Joutsamo jotted down *Cruelty = Murder?* in her notebook. She could of course verify from the verdict whether it was cruelty that tilted the sentence from manslaughter to murder, but it wasn't a priority.

In the first interrogations, Repo had vehemently denied the act. He claimed he had passed out in bed and didn't remember anything about what had happened. A week later he had changed his tune, when his lawyer had been present at his questioning. According to the transcript, at that juncture Repo had said, "I consider it possible that I killed my wife, because evidently no other alternatives exist. I do not consider the act murder, but manslaughter. There was no way it was premeditated, and the act was neither exceptionally brutal nor cruel."

It was plain as day from the statement that the lawyer had gotten Repo to confess to the deed. Joutsamo made a note of the lawyer's name: Mauri Tiainen. Repo had not offered any motive.

The Repo family had lived in an apartment building. The neighbors had been interrogated, of course, and said that occasionally loud arguing could be heard coming from their apartment. Yet no one had heard anything of the sort on the night of the murder. No one had seen anyone else entering or exiting the apartment, either.

Repo's fingerprints had been found on the murder weapon. The photo docket contained a photo of a serrated eight-inch bread knife with a black handle. The blade was bloody. Powdered fingerprints could be made out in the close-ups. Looking from behind, they were on the left side of the handle. Joutsamo paused to work out how Repo had been holding the knife. Based on the fingerprints, he'd been gripping it the way you would normally hold a knife when you're carving wood. Had the throat been slashed from the front or the back? There was no indication in the report. No DNA analysis had been conducted on the weapon, but the blood found on the blade matched the wife's blood type.

The court-ordered evaluation of Repo's mental health had also been appended to the papers. That gave Joutsamo pause, because a psychological evaluation was a confidential document, and the police didn't need it to do their work. Yet someone had delivered it to the police, and of course Joutsamo read it.

Repo had not been diagnosed with any mental health problems. His father, Erik, had been a career military officer, and the family had moved frequently from base to base. The mother had worked in the base kitchens as a cook. Timo had told the doctor about his parents' alcohol use, strict discipline, and corporal punishment, as well as continuous competition with his big brother, who was two years older.

"When discussing childhood memories, the subject often mentions soccer, which appears to have been of significance to him. This indicates that, as a child, he looked outside the home for approval he was lacking.

"The subject says that in the 1960s, his father was suspected of causing the death of a serviceman in a hazing incident. Even though Erik was found not guilty, the matter had caused substantial friction within the family. The subject describes his father as having increased his alcohol consumption and grown more withdrawn."

Timo Repo had ended up serving in the army himself. He hadn't made it into officer school, and had had to settle for the NCO academy. "The subject says he performed well at the institution he termed the 'rat academy.' Psychological evaluations previously conducted on the subject and medical reports were acquired from the armed forces for the purposes of this mental health evaluation. They do not reveal any issues related to mental health."

The evaluation indicated that Timo had met his future wife, Arja, at a bar in Helsinki in the early '90s. A one-night stand had led to a relationship and marriage in 1993. The wife had one childless marriage behind her. Repo had also told the psychiatrist that Arja and his father, Erik, had occasionally argued, because Arja had once belonged to the Communist Youth Association. Erik's needling had prompted Arja to look into his old hazing incident. Timo had felt caught between a rock and a hard place, and visits to Timo's parents had subsequently grown less frequent.

"The subject described his family life as normal. According to the subject, alcohol was consumed, but not to excess. The subject indicates that alcohol use did not lead to absences from work. In 1995, a child was born into the family, which, according to the subject, was a happy and anticipated event. Joel's birth was a cause for joy, but the same year had also been marked by grief, as the subject's mother died of cancer."

Interesting, Joutsamo thought. And yet the trip to Riihimäki hadn't advanced the investigation in the least. She hadn't found a single name in the papers that would have been useful in tracing Repo. No acquaintances, no childhood friends. Nothing.

Several things nagged at her, however. She found herself wondering about the bread knife and how Timo Repo had been gripping it at the moment of the murder.

Fifteen minutes later, she knocked on the door of Detective Lieutenant Johannes Leinonen. Leinonen had led the Repo investigation and given Joutsamo the preliminary investigation report to read.

"Come in," Leinonen growled. He was sitting at his computer. A brown sport coat hung from the back of his chair. Sixty and gray, he was heavy enough that the buttons of his white dress shirt strained at the gut.

"Thanks," Joutsamo said, returning the stack of papers to Leinonen.

"Find anything?"

"I have a couple of questions."

Leinonen gestured for Joutsamo to take a seat across from him. His office was just like Takamäki's and that of a thousand other police officers. The shelves were full of folders, and there were stacks of papers next to the computer.

"Shoot."

Joutsamo referred to her notes. "In the first place, why was it classified as a murder?"

"Did you take a look at those photos? That woman's throat was slashed wide open."

"Repo initially denied the crime, and then he confessed. But only to manslaughter."

"He had no choice," Leinonen said. "The case was cut-and-dried. The lawyer, whatever his name was, I think it was Tiainen, talked some sense into him. Into Repo. No point fighting a clear case... That's not going to help anyone."

"But it never reverted to manslaughter?"

"No, because the act was so brutal and cruel. The medical examiner estimated that the woman had been alive for at least several minutes after the deed."

"Were any reconstructions done?" Joutsamo asked.

Leinonen frowned and looked intentionally perplexed.

"What is it you're getting at? I thought you were looking for this Repo?"

"Were any reconstructions done?"

"No, nothing like that. The case was totally clear."

"Was her throat slit from the front or from behind?" Joutsamo asked, still thinking about the fingerprints on the knife.

"I don't know. Does it matter? His fingerprints were on the knife, and there was no one else there. I don't understand what you're getting at."

Joutsamo didn't reply immediately. "I'm just trying to get inside Repo's head and try to think where I might find him," she said after a while.

"Is this some new profiling thing, or?"

"Yeah. We're piloting it down in Helsinki Homicide," Joutsamo lied.

"How about that," Leinonen said. "More American BS, sounds like."

"It's a system developed by the Germans, as a matter of fact," Joutsamo said, her face deadpan. "The Hannover police got really good results with it. But back to where Repo was standing when it happened. We can deduce from the bloodstains that the wife was on her feet when she was killed."

"Well, he didn't remember anything about it, so I guess we'll never know."

Joutsamo rose. "Do you mind standing up?" she said, picking up a twelve-inch ruler from the desk. "This is the knife. Based on the fingerprints, Repo was holding it the way you would if you were slicing bread." She circled around behind Leinonen. "Look, if you're holding a bread knife like this, then your hand isn't naturally going to twist into a position where you could slit someone's throat from behind."

The lieutenant turned around and looked Joutsamo dead in the eye. "Well, it must have been from the front then."

Joutsamo raised the ruler and made a slashing movement at Leinonen's throat. "Pretty harsh way to kill your wife, eye to eye," she said.

"I'm sure there've been harsher ones."

"But the photos didn't show any injuries on her hands from blocking the knife."

"He probably surprised her," Leinonen said.

"According to the witnesses, they didn't hear any shouting coming from the apartment, and Repo wasn't mentally ill."

"Well, it was a cut-and-dried case anyway. Repo was the perpetrator. Appeals court confirmed it too, so there's no point trying anything," Leinonen said, annoyed. "Was there anything else? I've got some real work to do here."

* * *

The red walls of Helsinki Prison rose up before Suhonen. A bald guard in a blue uniform was walking in front of him. Suhonen knew the way, since he had been to the "Big House" dozens of times. He had left his gun and phone behind at the entrance.

The guard opened the door and turned right, toward a narrow stairwell. The administrative offices were upstairs. The second-floor corridor had been painted light gray and was lined by rooms on either side. Fifty feet ahead loomed the iron door that led into the prison proper.

The bald guy knocked on the door marked Warden.

"Come in."

The guard remained at Suhonen's side as he entered. The room was big—thirty feet long and fifteen wide. Most of it was taken up by a long wooden conference table that butted up against the warden's desk. Behind it sat a dry-looking forty-year-old in a gray suit. Saku Ainola, who had been promoted from assistant warden to warden a year ago, was an old buddy of Suhonen's.

"Hey there," Ainola said. "Give me a sec. I still have to deny a couple more leave applications."

"No worries," Suhonen said. There was a thermos on the table. Suhonen pumped coffee from it into a paper cup. Prison coffee contended in the same league as police coffee, gas station coffee, and hockey arena coffee.

It took Ainola three minutes, and after that he came over and helped himself to coffee, too.

"Annoying, this Repo incident," he began.

"Prison escapes always are."

"We didn't see this one coming. No indication at all that the guy was a flight risk. Several years of a life sentence behind him. Probably would have been allowed to take unescorted leaves in a year or two."

"What kind of guy is Repo?" Suhonen asked.

"Harmless. Caused no problems for years."

"But before that there were?"

"Not for us, exactly."

Suhonen knew that Ainola knew all the lifers. He read the court papers on all incoming convicts.

"Well," Ainola began. "Repo admitted manslaughter in district court but still got life for murder. Then in appellate court he denied the whole thing, but of course the sentence didn't change at that point, nor did the Supreme Court grant permission to appeal. After that, he began a massive but obviously futile round of appeals."

"Huh," Suhonen said.

"He sent appeals just about everywhere: the attorney general, parliamentary ombudsman, even to the European Court of Human Rights. Pretty surprised he didn't send one to the UN. Some reporter came here to meet him, but I don't think she ever wrote about it."

"What was his complaint?"

"That he was innocent and had been unjustly sentenced."

"You read the verdict. Was there anything to his appeal?" Suhonen asked. Ainola had graduated from law school.

Ainola shook his head. "Not a chance. The case was clear cut. And none of the appeals ever went anywhere. Bottom-of-the-stack stuff, the kind no one even takes a second look at."

"But the issue was specifically his innocence?"

"Yes, and then about the conditions here too, but once he had been labeled a habitual complainer, no one took those seriously either."

"Should they have?"

Ainola grunted dryly. "Of course. Conditions here are nowhere near to what the law dictates. A civilized nation is judged according to how it treats its prisoners, and on that measure, we're not a Western country."

"Not many are, if that's the criteria we're judging by."

"Did you read the interview with Fredberg, the new chief justice of the Supreme Court, in Sunday's paper?"

"Scanned it," Suhonen said.

"He's absolutely right that prison sentences don't do any good. At least if we have to keep working with the same amount of resources and an increasing load of customers," Ainola said.

Suhonen wasn't particularly interested in getting into a discussion on criminal justice policy. "Let's get back to Repo. How long did he keep up the appeals?"

"For a couple of years after the verdict. Then he suddenly stopped."

"Why?" asked Suhonen.

"I don't know. He just stopped. Maybe he realized it wouldn't lead to anything, anyway. Gave up or got tired of it. Beats me."

"What kind of meds was he on?"

"That's stepping into confidential territory, but he popped sedatives, like just about everybody else here," Ainola said.

Suhonen thought activists would have their work cut out for them if they tackled prison conditions, but evidently animals were a more sympathetic cause than criminals.

"Who did he hang out with?"

"He wasn't in any of the gangs. Mostly kept to himself. When you said you were coming, I also asked over in his block. They told me then that he talked to a dealer named Juha Saarnikangas. He got four years for possession of amphetamines, but was released in August, if I remember correctly."

Suhonen wrote down the name, even though he had heard of the guy before.

"What about Repo's phone calls or letters?"

"I checked the logs. No calls in months, years actually. Some record of letters being received. Probably had to do with his dad's death, for the most part."

Suhonen nodded. Another strikeout. "Let's go have a look at the cell."

"No problem, if you have a warrant."

"Are you serious?" Suhonen asked, but then dug out a search warrant from the inside pocket of his leather jacket. The only part that had been completed was Takamäki's signature—a lieutenant's approval was sufficient under Finnish law. Suhonen quickly filled in the rest of the information right there. For the crime, Suhonen wrote down "prisoner escape," since that was what they were investigating.

"Handy," Ainola said.

\* \* \*

Takamäki knocked on the door of the Sello shopping center surveillance room. The person to open it was a short, uniformed guard with a moustache. He also had a big nose, and his heavy-framed glasses completed the Groucho Marx impression.

"Aho?" Takamäki asked.

Groucho nodded.

"Takamäki from Violent Crimes Unit."

"Sure. I've seen you on TV before, too. Come on in."

Takamäki followed the security guard, who had called him back about the surveillance camera photos. Aho had offered to send them via email, but Takamäki didn't think that was secure enough.

The room, which was lit by fluorescent lights, contained a few lockers, a coffee machine, a microwave, and a fridge. A random selection of magazines was strewn across the table.

"Let's go into the surveillance room," Groucho Aho said.

The back room contained a dozen TV screens for the surveillance cameras. In some, the image changed every few seconds. Takamäki suspected that staring at them would give him a massive headache in no time flat.

Aho sat down at the computer. "You have a flash drive?"

Takamäki handed over his stick, which had more than 500 MB free, enough space for at least 200 premium-quality shots.

"I already went through and picked out the best ones," Aho said. "There's no video. It's one of those cameras that takes a shot a second."

The first image showed a boy in a helmet approaching the crosswalk on his bike. The wet asphalt gleamed; there was no one else in the picture. The pedestrian light was red. In the next shot, the light had turned green, and now the front tire of Jonas's bike was in the intersection.

"In this next one, you can see the collision," Aho said, clicking on to the third shot.

Looking at the photo turned Takamäki's stomach. Jonas was blurry in it, because he was toppling over onto the asphalt, but you could see his arm breaking the fall.

A gray car that looked like a Toyota had come from the right, and the front bumper was dead on top of the bike's front wheel.

"This last one is probably the one you'll find the most interesting."

In the fourth shot, Jonas and the bike are on the asphalt, and the car had continued about five yards from the place of impact.

The brake lights weren't on.

"I focused on the license plate," Aho said, showing the fifth photo to Takamäki. The letters and numbers were clearly visible, and Takamäki wrote them down in his notebook.

Aho copied the photos onto the flash drive and ejected it from the computer. "Good thing you came to get these today. They wouldn't have been here anymore tomorrow. These external camera shots are recorded over every twenty-four hours."

"You don't save them even if they capture incidents like this?"

"Of course we do, if we see something. I don't know why the guy on duty yesterday didn't notice the sequence on his cameras. The ambulance showed up pretty quick, too." Aho handed the flash drive to Takamäki. "Here you go."

"Thanks for your help," the lieutenant said, adding that he'd show himself out.

* * *

Ainola and Suhonen entered the third floor of the east cell block, where most of the murderers were housed. The latest cycle of remodels at Helsinki Prison, which was originally built in 1881, had lasted for years. With the shrubs and other improvements, the block was almost pleasant now.

The corridors were quiet, because the majority of prisoners were elsewhere. That suited Suhonen, because he had no interest in showing his face to criminals in a context where he could be directly connected to the authorities.

Ainola greeted the guard and said they'd be entering Repo's cell. Ainola fit his own key into the lock. As always in prisons, the iron door opened inwards. That way the prisoner couldn't use the door to blindside a guard.

"Be my guest," Ainola said, letting Suhonen enter first.

Suhonen immediately caught the distinct scent of old prison cell. It was impossible to eradicate, even if you washed and painted the walls and floors. The little cell reeked of sweat, shit, and suffering. Over the past century and a quarter they had been hopelessly ingrained.

The cell was six feet wide and ten feet long. High up on the back wall there was a tiny window. The bed was on the right and the desk to the left. A TV, an electric water kettle, and a few books were on the table. Suhonen's eye immediately registered one detail—not a single girlie pic. As a matter of fact, the walls were spotless—not a single stroke of graffiti, either.

Behind the table a shelf held more books and some papers. The bed was made.

"A life of modesty," Suhonen remarked, pulling on his latex gloves. This time it was more a matter of habit than need.

"Dream prisoner. These past few years, I mean."

"A loner?"

"For that reason, too."

Suhonen started from the table. The books were nonfiction. Two were about the history of the Roman Empire, both borrowed from the prison library. Suhonen shook the books so that anything inside would have fallen out onto the table. But there was nothing.

Suhonen wasn't about to start looking inside the TV. This wasn't a narcotics raid. He was seeking information on addresses or acquaintances: scraps of paper, letters, a calendar.

He stepped over to the shelf and scanned it rapidly. A slim stack of papers caught his attention, and Suhonen picked it up. It was the Court of Appeals verdict in Repo's case. The pages were worn at the corners, and the paper felt greasy. The interior pages were heavily underlined, and comments had been written in the margins in tiny letters. Suhonen thought for a moment and decided to bring the stack to Joutsamo. His colleague had the best sense of the case and might be able to glean hints from the scribblings.

Suhonen set the stack of documents on the table. He scanned down the shelves but didn't find anything of interest, only a can of Nescafé, a mug, a folded sweater, and a couple of DVDs. *Pulp Fiction*? Okay, not a bad choice for a prisoner. Suhonen opened the cases, but all they contained were the disks.

"Why are there DVDs here, if he doesn't have a player?"

"Are there?" Ainola said, stepping a little closer. Suhonen handed the cases to the warden. "Oh, these are from the prison library. The prisoners can also borrow a DVD player there, but it's probably already been loaned on to someone else. I'd better return these, too. Otherwise he'll lose his DVD privileges once you bring him back here to his cell."

"Su-ure."

"What do you mean, su-ure?"

Suhonen didn't answer immediately. He turned toward the bed. "These convict escapes are kind of like murder investigations. If the case isn't wrapped up right away, we work overtime until it's solved. Murders can take months, but there are dozens of detectives working on them, at least at the beginning. Now we're chasing down this ghost with a few guys, and we don't really have anything to go on. Searching a cell like this is pretty pointless. The problem is that even though the guy's a murderer, he's a complete enigma. We don't know anything about his friends, if he even has any. We're not going to get anywhere with his family. So it's a total crapshoot. Of course he might get caught at some DUI checkpoint or end up in the Töölö drunk tank, but that's more a matter of chance."

"Are you stressing out over this case?"

"Not especially. I'm just pissed off that in a way we're doing pointless work. Okay, it's not totally pointless. But if we have to start by figuring out who the guy is, it's looking like we're in for a long-distance relay."

Ainola shrugged. "Welcome to the team."

Suhonen laughed. "All we'd need is to find something good under that mattress." Suhonen lifted it up. The bed frame was empty.

There was a knock at the door, and Ainola opened. The chunky guard from the break room was standing there. "Forsberg's in the break room."

"Who's Forsberg?" Suhonen asked.

"Our lucky lottery winner," Ainola grunted. "Last time around, he won four plus a bonus number from district court: aggravated robbery, felony narcotics, aggravated assault, felony fraud, and, for the bonus, criminal intimidation."

"Oh, Foppa," Suhonen growled. The jack-of-all-trades had gotten his nickname from the famous Swedish hockey player. "I remember him. He was Repo's closest buddy?"

"They're not actually buddies," the fat guard said. "But he was in the next cell over. He might know something."

The guard led the way to the break room. Suhonen could smell a fresh pot brewing. There was nothing about Forsberg particularly reminiscent of his namesake, although maybe the hockey player also liked to lounge around in sweats—presumably not brown prison-issue ones, though. Foppa the Con was sporting a white T-shirt, thick-rimmed glasses, and a growing bald spot. He was about fifty.

Suhonen extended a hand and the men shook. "Suhonen, Helsinki Police."

The crook's handshake wasn't especially firm. As a matter of fact, it was limp.

"Forsberg," he answered in a low voice. "So whaddaya want?"

"I have a couple of questions," Suhonen said.

"What about?"

"Repo. I want to know why he took off."

"How would I know?"

"They say you knew him best."

"Pffft," Forsberg said. "Nobody knows anyone in this joint. Everyone's out for themselves. I couldn't give a shit what some other convict is thinking. Besides, he was a pretty quiet guy."

"Pretty quiet?"

"Yeah. Mostly hung out alone, didn't talk to me, even though we both worked over in the sign shop. Someone said that back when he first got here he was pretty bitter, but I couldn't tell."

"Who said?" Suhonen asked.

"Can't remember."

"Who else did he talk to besides you?"

"No one, really. Okay, maybe Juha Saarnikangas. He's one of those junkies, looks like a skeleton. You know, when he raises his arms, his watch slides down to his shoulder."

"Okay," Suhonen nodded. "I've heard the name."

"Well, he's not big time. At least not big time enough for a cop to remember him. A real skeeze."

Suhonen thought Forsberg didn't exactly appear to be a rocket scientist, either. "What did Repo do at night?"

"Mostly sat or lay there in his cell alone. Spent a lot of time in the library. Seemed to like electronics. Borrowed books on the subject. Oh yeah, he'd always go read the newspapers, too. Maybe it helped him keep up with what was happening on the outside. Or at least he thought it did."

Forsberg paused for a second and drank his coffee. Suhonen let the silence weigh and reached for his own mug.

"But Timo's no gangster. Corking his wife was probably an idea that just popped into his head when he was drunk, ha-ha," Forsberg grunted, looking at the grim-faced Suhonen. "Don't you get it? Corking, ha-ha, 'cause he shut her up and almost took her head off at the same time, ha-ha."

"Yeah, I got it, it just wasn't very funny."

Forsberg stopped laughing. "Well, can't help you any more. He'll probably show up at some police station in a couple of days. I think his old man's funeral just sent him off the deep end."

\* \* \*

Sitting at his desk, Takamäki was working on his son's accident. He had copied the surveillance camera images from the flash drive to his computer. He had momentarily considered taking prints home, but then had rejected the idea.

He had seen so many crime scenes and images of them that the photos were nothing more than a tool for him. They didn't convey any emotion or terror, just information from the scene. But his wife wouldn't be capable of viewing the surveillance camera shots in the same way. That's why it was better not to show them to her.

Takamäki had pulled up the DMV database and was hesitating as to whether or not to look up the owner of the car that had hit Jonas. Investigating the hit-and-run wasn't his turf; it wasn't even Helsinki Police turf. The Espoo police were supposed to take care of it. But license plate info wasn't confidential. Anyone could call a toll-free number and request information on any vehicle.

The lieutenant entered the license plate number, and the system indicated that the owner was an Espoo leasing company. A guy named Tomi Manner was registered as the lease-holder. Takamäki looked up more info on Manner; according to his social security number, he was thirty-seven years old. His address was in Espoo, in the neighborhood of Tuomarila.

Joutsamo was a whiz with computers, but Takamäki could navigate the basics pretty well. Manner owned a small private security company. Maybe he had fled the scene because he was afraid of losing his security company license. On the other hand, it would be even worse to get caught fleeing the scene, on top of hitting a pedestrian.

Manner's record showed a couple of old traffic citations, but he wasn't suspected or convicted of anything more serious. Takamäki started wondering how far he should go. It wasn't like he was conducting an investigation or anything. He was mostly just satisfying his curiosity.

So Takamäki pulled up Manner's license photo, too. The young Tomi Manner had a crew cut and a confrontational gaze. At the time the photo was taken, his cheeks were covered in dark stubble. To Takamäki, Manner looked aggressive, exactly like the kind of person who would flee the scene of an accident. The photo was almost twenty years old, but it still communicated arrogance. Maybe that was because Manner's jaw was tilted higher than necessary. Takamäki started getting the feeling he'd like to exchange a couple of words with the guy.

* * *

Repo was lying on Karppi's sofa. His eyes were closed, but he was awake. Karppi was reading some biography at the dining table. Since finishing their coffees, the men had barely spoken to each other. The papers and photos Karppi had given him were in a plastic shopping bag on the floor.

Thanks to his prison time, the position was a familiar one to Repo. He could lie for hours without thinking about anything or, if he felt like it, thinking about everything, Now, all kinds of things were going through his head: his father's death, the escape, meeting Karppi, and the things he wanted to do. Or not just wanted to do, but what he intended on doing.

The problem with thinking was that once your thoughts got out of the corral, it was tough to wrangle them back in. Arja came back into his mind. And the image wasn't that smiling, beautiful woman from the wedding photo, but Arja's lifeless, slightly yellowed face. It was impossible to read anything from the dead woman's expression, not even pain, despite the fact that the deep wound in her neck reached almost from ear to ear.

Repo could still remember waking up. The memories came back, no matter how much he wished they wouldn't. He was lying on his bed, and a man in a blue uniform was shaking him by the shoulder. He felt nauseous, and could make out the barrel of a pistol through his booze-blurred eyes. On with the cuffs and into the paddy wagon.

What happened next at the police station was like a nightmare. Repo didn't remember anything about Arja's death. The detective laid into him. "C'mon, admit it. Do you confess? Why don't you remember? Goddammit, stop wasting our time! Be a man and take responsibility for your actions."

In the end, Repo had taken responsibility, since there was no other alternative. Even his attorney had advised him to. The evidence was clear, but that slippery snake had promised him that he'd get convicted of manslaughter, and that he'd be out after sitting six to seven years of a ten-year sentence.

But the district court had sentenced him to life in prison. Repo remembered the verdict being read. It felt like he was a bystander—he was watching some random show on the TV bolted to the courtroom wall. He wished he could change the channel or even scream when the district judge said the words, "Sentenced to life in prison for the crime of murder."

And the same thing in appeals court, even though by then he had denied having committed the crime. He hadn't been able to imagine himself ever having been capable of it.

Like it did every time, Repo's head began to ache.

"Hey, Timo," Karppi said, shaking him by the shoulder, the same way the police officer had on that one day. "Were you sleeping?"

Repo could see the old man smiling.

"No."

"Really, now? Well, you should probably eat something anyway. I made fish soup."

Repo noticed the smell of the soup and figured that he had fallen asleep after all. He should have heard the sounds of cooking.

"Did you go to the store?"

"No," Karppi smiled. "Straight from the freezer."

The men sat down at the table. Karppi had set out bowls and spoons.

"*Voilà, le potage de poisson.*"

In addition to the steaming pot, two pitchers stood on the table. Karppi poured himself some cranberry juice, and Repo helped himself to water.

"You have any aspirin?"

"No," Karppi said. "I hate pills."

Both ladled soup into their bowls. Repo tasted it; it needed salt. There wasn't any on the table, and he didn't feel like asking for it.

"You really speak French?"

Karppi nodded. "I used to work there."

"Not the Foreign Legion?"

"Oh, no. I worked for the Ministries of Defense and Foreign Affairs. Finland used to buy weapons from France."

The topic didn't interest Repo, but he could imagine Karppi and his old man, Erik, having talked about it frequently.

"Listen," Karppi began. "Change of subject. How long were you planning on shacking up here? Shouldn't you head on back to prison to sit out those couple of years you have left?"

A couple of years? Repo thought. Eight behind and maybe six before parole. But he let it pass. "Don't worry about it. A day or two, then I'll be gone."

"Where?"

"Now, that's none of your business," Repo said coolly. "And I'd suggest you don't ask."

# CHAPTER 8
## TUESDAY, 2:50 P.M.
## HELSINKI POLICE HEADQUARTERS, PASILA

Takamäki hesitated for a moment but then picked up the phone. He called the switchboard at Espoo Police and asked to be connected to the Traffic Crimes Unit. After three minutes and two call transfers, Takamäki discovered that Espoo didn't have a unit that investigated traffic crimes, but a PSPCIU, or Public Safety Productivity Center Investigative Unit. Traffic accidents were its responsibility. Takamäki got the name of the officer investigating the Sello incident. The name Lauri Solberg was unfamiliar to him.

"Solberg," answered a male voice. Judging by it, Takamäki figured the Espoo police officer was about thirty-five years old.

"Hi, Kari Takamäki here," Takamäki replied in a friendly tone. He had gone back and forth several times as to whether he would introduce himself as a VCU lieutenant right from the start, but had decided to be plain old Mr. Takamäki, the victim's father. At least at first.

"Good afternoon," Solberg responded officially, inspiring formality in Takamäki's voice, too.

"I'm calling about the hit-and-run that took place yesterday at the Sello shopping center. You're the investigating officer, correct?"

"Correct. Are you a witness?"

"No, I'm the father of the boy who was hit. I was curious as to the status of the investigation."

Takamäki could hear the radio playing in the background as Solberg paused. "Preliminary stages. How's your son doing, by the way?"

Takamäki felt like swearing out loud. He understood that "preliminary" meant that nothing had happened with the case other than the patrol on the scene having had submitted its report. Solberg had doubtless received the report that morning, but hadn't done anything about it. He hadn't even called the hospital to check on the status of the injured victim.

"He's doing pretty well. Squeaked by with a broken arm."

"Glad to hear it."

Takamäki wondered if he should have lied after all and said Jonas had sustained a concussion. Would that have lit a fire under the Espoo investigator?

"Any information on the driver?"

"Umm...we're looking into it," Solberg said. "Of course."

"Were there any eyewitnesses?"

"Unfortunately, I'm not allowed to share any information about the case with you at this point. The police are investigating the matter, and it will definitely be resolved. The only thing you can do at this point is trust us."

Takamäki counted to five before responding. "Has any action been taken in this matter?"

"Of course. The responding unit wrote up its report, and I've been assigned to investigate."

"And what steps have you taken today in this case?"

"Preliminary investigative measures."

This time Takamäki made it all the way to ten. "So you've read the original report and that's it. In other words, nothing."

Solberg tried to pacify him: "Please calm down, sir." He sounded like he had spent time in the field and was seeking authority from the voice he had used to give orders to the public.

"I'm as calm as I possibly can be," Takamäki said, thanking his luck that the conversation was taking place over the phone.

"Good. Could you please repeat your name for me?"

"I'm Jonas Takamäki's father. Kari Takamäki."

Solberg was silent for a moment. "You mean the lieutenant from Helsinki Violent Crimes Unit? I thought there was something familiar about your voice."

"The one and only. Does it make a difference?"

"Not really. Except that I can tell you I have eighty open investigations on my desk. Today I've been conducting interrogations on three old cases, so maybe you can see why this case hasn't moved forward a whole heck of a lot today. The patrol that was at the scene didn't get a single statement from a witness who saw the vehicle's license plate. I was basically thinking I'd place an ad in the neighborhood paper and try to get some eyewitnesses that way."

"Why are you so forthcoming with Lieutenant Takamäki but not Mr. Takamäki?"

"A fellow policeman understands, a father wouldn't."

The response disarmed Takamäki. The investigators in charge of run-of-the-mill crimes had their hands full. When cases were thrown in the laps of overworked investigators without any preliminary work, most would remain shrouded in darkness, even if there initially had been some chance of solving them. No one had time to even perform the preliminary steps properly. With white-collar crime, the Metropolitan Helsinki Inter-Municipal Group had gotten to the point where they reviewed all cases together and categorized them as urgent or non-urgent. This allowed them to dedicate sufficient resources to the cases that demanded rapid responses. The same sort of classification would work with run-of-the-mill crimes as well. Using similar categorization, some precincts had achieved some positive results with misdemeanors, but it had required that the initial investigative steps had been conducted properly.

"Has it occurred to you that there might be surveillance camera images of the incident?" Takamäki asked.

"Surveillance camera images? From where?"

"The shopping mall, for instance."

"Are there?"

"I don't have any interest in getting involved in the case, but the images do exist. I have some good news and some bad news about them. The bad news is that the images are from exterior cameras that are erased every twenty-four hours."

"And the good news?"

"I went and picked them up. I have the photos."

Solberg thought for a second. "Under what authority?"

"Let's just say it was unofficial collegial assistance."

"So, the media's favorite lieutenant didn't trust his colleagues. He just had to go and solve the case all by himself," Solberg jabbed. "Helsinki Homicide Investigates Collision between Cyclist and Car in Espoo. Now that would make a good headline."

This time Takamäki silently counted all the way to fifteen. "Yeah, well, but isn't it a good thing that someone's actually investigating it? Are you interested in those surveillance camera images?"

"Sure, I'm interested, but this case isn't getting any special treatment just because a lieutenant's son is involved."

"I'm not expecting special treatment, but how about a proper investigation? I could drop off a flash drive with the photos around 5:30 this afternoon. I'm tied up with a case of my own here."

"Sorry, office hours end at 4:15, but give me a call tomorrow. I don't have any interrogations scheduled, and I might just have time to take a look at those surveillance camera images."

"Fine. I'll call you tomorrow," Takamäki said, and lowered the receiver. This time he decided to count to twenty, and out loud, before he did anything else.

Joutsamo walked in as he hit sixteen. "What's up? Are you meditating or something?"

"Seventeen, eighteen, nineteen, twenty," Takamäki recited.

"What's going on?"

"You know a cop at Espoo by the name of Lauri Solberg?" Takamäki asked.

"Doesn't ring any bells," Joutsamo said, confused.

"In that case it doesn't matter," Takamäki said, his voice now calm.

Joutsamo eyed her boss as he turned to his computer.

"Umm, Kari, the meeting's supposed to start now."

"Huh? Oh yeah, of course." Takamäki replied.

"Does Solberg have anything to do with Jonas's hit-and-run?" Joutsamo asked.

Takamäki stood up and walked past her. "Suhonen here yet?"

"Yeah," Joutsamo said, more perplexed than ever, following her lieutenant into the corridor.

The conference room was just down the hall. Takamäki could see Suhonen and Kulta in the corridor. The men were counting together out loud. "Nine... ten...eleven..."

"What the hell?" Takamäki wondered, before he saw Kohonen doing chin-ups from a bar rigged up in the conference room doorway.

"Twelve," Kulta counted, but Kohonen seemed to be slowing down. "One more!"

Kohonen strained at the bar, trying to pull her chin up to it. "No...problem," she huffed, as her face turned the same shade of red as her hair.

"You got it, you got it!" Suhonen encouraged.

Kohonen struggled, and finally managed to complete chin-up number thirteen.

"Only thirteen, huh," Kohonen panted on the floor. "I ought to be able to do the same fifteen as Suhonen here."

"How many does the lieutenant have in him?" Kulta asked.

Before Takamäki could answer, Joutsamo intervened.

"He just made it to twenty over in his office. Now let's start this meeting."

* * *

Salmela was sitting in his rusted-out Toyota van in the Hakaniemi public market parking lot. He had backed the van up so that the rear was toward the brick building.

Whereas the finer folk did their shopping at the Market Square at the southern harbor, Hakaniemi Square had traditionally been a working-class marketplace. This history still lived on in the labor unions that kept watch over the square from the surrounding office buildings. And red flags flew in honor of the working man every Mayday, when crowds of thousands gathered at the square before their traditional parade through Helsinki's streets.

Salmela had no political convictions, but he did believe that taking from the rich was just fine. And the same went for the poor, too.

Kallio, a neighborhood of grim apartment buildings, rose behind the square on one of the city's highest hills. Its apartments were small, mostly studios or one-bedrooms. It had been a distinctly working-class area for decades, but was now headed down the same path as New York's SoHo. First students and artists displaced the working class, and then the rich bought up housing that was conveniently located close to the city center. The hundred-year-old Market Hall behind the van was solid but attractive, and the area's working-class spirit had been preserved in the interior. Salmela didn't care for the place, though. The red brick façade reminded him too much of the exterior of Helsinki Prison.

The market was closed, and Salmela was eyeing the grim view. Everything was gray. Couldn't they put a fountain in here or something? Salmela clearly remembered the days twenty years ago when he and his buddies used to roll drunks in the area.

Salmela leaned forward far enough to check the giant Pepsi-logo clock on the building to the left: 3:02 p.m. The asshole was late, even though Salmela had sworn him to be on time.

The criminal eyed the cars in the vicinity, looking for any indications of a police presence. An overly curious, circling gaze, a man sitting alone in a parked car, or a supposedly random loiterer were danger signals.

An old woman dressed in a black fake fur was walking her little Dachshund at the edge of the square. Salmela wondered whether she could be a police officer. Did the female undercover officers take theater classes or something to teach them how to act? He'd have to ask Suhonen about it someday in a nice roundabout way.

Goddammit, Salmela laughed to himself. Had he really gotten that paranoid? Oh well, better paranoid than in prison.

The Pepsi clock now showed 3:04 p.m. Salmela would wait two more minutes, and then he was out of there. At that instant there was a knock on the passenger window, and Salmela immediately regretted having stuck around. He could tell from the man's eyes that he was on something stronger than booze. The door was locked, and Salmela didn't feel like letting the emaciated junkie into his car. He gestured for him to come around to the other side.

Juha Saarnikangas looked like he was in pretty bad shape as he circled around the front of the van. His brown hair reached down to his shoulders and probably hadn't been washed in a week or more. His green army jacket looked foul. He also had a nasty-looking scar on his cheek that Salmela hadn't seen before.

Salmela rolled down the window. "What's up?"

Saarnikangas's heroin-decayed teeth turned his smile into a grimace. "Hey, man. Good to see you."

"No, it's not. What's so urgent?"

"I've got some really good stuff for you," Saarnikangas said, trying to maintain the smile.

"Sorry," Salmela said tersely. "I'm not buying anything. Shop's closed."

Saarnikangas's expression grew serious. "Hey, hey, come on, man! You don't even know what I'm selling."

Salmela pulled a cigarette from his pack and listened, mostly out of pity. He used to buy all kinds of stolen goods from Saarnikangas, but not anymore.

The junkie continued his spiel: "I've got a Compaq 6220 right out of the box. Retails at more than a grand!

I'll give it to you for a hundred."

Salmela blew smoke into Saarnikangas's face.

"All right, fifty. Please."

"I'm not buying."

"Come on, thirty... Fuck, man, I need some dough."

Salmela's interest was actually piqued by the time they got down to thirty, because that was almost nothing for a laptop. Juha must be really desperate.

"Look, asshole, you said you had something important to tell me. Not that you wanted to unload some junk."

Salmela started up the Toyota.

"Come on, man, at least give me a smoke," Saarnikangas begged.

Without saying a word, Salmela rolled up the window and drove off. He heard a thunk as Saarnikangas kicked the side of the van, and he could see the junkie giving him the finger in the rear-view mirror. If there hadn't been any bystanders nearby, he would have stopped the van, gotten out, and beat Saarnikangas's ass. Instead, he just flicked on his blinker and turned south out of the parking lot. The ugly complex belonging to the Federation of Trade Unions rose up at the end of the street.

Salmela was annoyed that he had wasted his time on Saarnikangas. The question crossed his mind of whether his son, who had been shot a year ago, would have been in the same condition if he had lived. The prognosis had been similar.

\* \* \*

There were no windows in the conference room. Takamäki, Suhonen, and Kulta had mugs of coffee; Joutsamo had tea. Kohonen wasn't there, she was busy writing up a report for an old case. The team had reviewed the original Repo file and concluded that the exercise hadn't been very productive. They had invested a decent amount of effort in the process but had achieved nothing. Tracking an escaped prisoner was clear cut— you either succeeded or failed, and this time the results were pretty evident.

"The guy'll get caught in some raid sooner or later," Suhonen said. "It'd be nice to get a real case, so we could do some real work."

"All right, now," Takamäki said. He wasn't sure how serious Suhonen was, but he could sense a level of frustration. The danger was that it would spread to the others.

"Looks like all we have is this Saarnikangas," Kulta said. "It's the only name in this case. I talked again with the guard who allowed Repo to escape, but he didn't have anything new to give me."

"Has anyone been back to the father's house?" Takamäki asked. "He's got to be sleeping somewhere... If he doesn't have any friends, then let's check the old places one more time."

"We can go by there again," Joutsamo said. "But this looks like it's headed for passive investigation pretty fast. No point dedicating much more effort to it."

Takamäki tried to drum up enthusiasm. "We're not giving up just yet. There's one trick we haven't tried yet."

"Give it to the papers?" Joutsamo guessed.

Takamäki nodded and read from a handwritten draft. "The headline reads 'Helsinki Police Seek Tips on Escaped Murderer.'"

Kulta smiled. "Not likely to make it to press in that format."

"It's not supposed to," the lieutenant retorted. "The rest goes more or less like this, 'On Monday morning, Timo Repo, serving life for murder, escaped from his father's funeral...'"

Joutsamo interrupted, "Do we have to say that he fled from the funeral?"

"Let me respond with another question," Takamäki said. "Why should we keep it a secret? It's not significant in terms of our investigation, and we have to give them some details. If we send out a press release with no details, the papers will ignore it, which means we won't get any response."

"Okay."

"Anyway, this goes on to say that Repo left the Restaurant Perho and headed toward downtown Helsinki. Since then, police have not received reports of any sightings, and are now asking the public for help. Then there's a description of him."

"Aren't you going to send a photo?" Joutsamo asked.

"Not yet," Takamäki said.

"Why not?"

"It might get us another round in the media a couple days from now if this one doesn't work. I did put here at the end that Repo was convicted of murdering his wife in Riihimäki in 1999. The police do not consider Repo particularly dangerous."

"Why does it say 'particularly dangerous?'" Kulta asked.

"Should we put 'completely harmless?'" Takamäki retorted.

"Somewhat dangerous, potentially dangerous, a smidgen dangerous?" Kulta mused.

Takamäki grunted. "I can drop the 'particularly' if we all agree that the guy isn't dangerous."

"Yeah," said Suhonen. "The thing that still gets me about this case is, why did  he check out? He's already got eight years behind him. There's gotta be some reason, and that's still the big mystery here."

"The reporters will probably ask that, too," Kulta reflected. "And don't tell them 'No comment,' either."

Takamäki chuckled. "I won't. I'm perfectly capable of saying, 'We don't know.'"

"And then their next question will be, how do you know he's not dangerous if you don't know the motive for his escape?" Joutsamo added.

"Well, that's why I have 'particularly dangerous.'"

Now it was Kulta's turn to grunt. "Okay, leave the 'particularly' in."

"Did we have anything else?"

"I've got a deck of cards over in my desk if anyone's up for a round of poker," Suhonen said.

"Texas Hold'em," Kulta suggested.

Takamäki stood before Joutsamo got the words out. "I don't know if it means anything, but when I went through his papers up in Riihimäki, something about the case started to bother me."

"What?" Takamäki asked.

"I don't know, but at least the fact that it was considered a cut-and-dried case right from the start. Doesn't seem like the detectives even tried looking into any other alternatives."

"Ainola over at the prison reviewed the paperwork and said Repo definitely was the perpetrator," Suhonen said.

"I'm not saying I have any facts to back me up. I just have a feeling that things aren't exactly the way they should be."

"They all think they're innocent," Kulta said.

Takamäki looked at Joutsamo. It wasn't like her to raise something like this if there was nothing to it.

"Well, try and think, maybe it'll come to you. We'll see at that point. I'll send this out to the media and let's go find this Saarnikangas, see if he can tell us something. Let's keep our eyes and ears open, people."

* * *

The clock on the fourth-floor editorial offices of *Iltalehti* read 3:34 p.m. Times from around the world were supposed to be displayed by a row of clocks, but according to them, the time in London, Tokyo, and Los Angeles was the same as in Helsinki. All that was left of New York was the sign; the clock itself had disappeared.

Marja Juvonen was playing solitaire on her computer in the rear corner of the quiet newsroom. Her thoughts, however, were on the previous night's party at the Lux nightclub. Her headache wouldn't let her forget, even though 600 mg of ibuprofen was keeping it at bay.

The large editorial offices were crammed with desks and computers. Juvonen had managed to get a corner spot where her back was against the exterior wall, so none of the bosses could take her by surprise—unless they'd rent a crane and check her computer screen through the window behind her back.

There was another good thing about her spot. It was as far as possible from the editorial office refrigerator, which had been nicknamed "the haz," for hazardous waste disposal. One of the graphic artists had once wrapped crime scene tape across its door.

Juvonen considered going for a smoke, but the broken ventilator in the smoking room drove her crazy. It crackled and popped nonstop. Generally speaking, the editorial offices were fetid. Up on the sixth floor, in Ad

Sales and Accounting, things were completely different: tidy, clean, and spacious. Why do those brown-nosers in Ad Sales have it better than we do, Juvonen wondered as she clicked away at her computer.

Her operating system didn't include any built-in games, but Juvonen had plenty of online games in her bookmarks. The thirty-four-year-old reporter had originally worked for a small-town paper, but a summer internship had been her ticket to getting a permanent job at *Iltalehti*, one of Finland's largest tabloids. She had started her career with a byline of "Marja Juvonen," but after coming to *Iltalehti*, she had started using the more pompous, pseudo-international "Mary J. Juvonen." Mary J. hated the crime reporting she had gotten stuck with. She would have preferred arts and entertainment, but one incident had blocked her career in the entertainment field.

Mary J. didn't try to hide it, though. Just last night she had told her life story again to someone at the nightclub, although she didn't remember who. "So I fucking said to him, 'Who do you think you are?' And he said, 'An artist.' And I said, 'My neighbor's Great Dane drops five pounds of art hotter than yours on my doorstep every morning. So let's try again: So, who do you think you are?' And the asshole called the editor-in-chief and that was it for working in the arts, ever. So here I get to shovel shit at the crime desk while those MBA assholes sip rosé at record company parties."

"Mary Jane!" Her managing editor was shouting at her from the news desk, fifty feet away.

Juvonen jumped slightly and reflexively clicked away her game, revealing her emails.

"Yeah, whaddaya want?"

"How's your hangover? Still feel like someone dropped a jug on your head?" Managing editor Ragnar

Johansson was bellowing loud enough for everyone to hear.

"Who do you think you are? My jugs are bigger than that ridiculous little peashooter you have," Mary Jane retorted.

"We need a front-page story." This time, fifty-year-old Ruthless Ragnar shouted so loudly that the dozen or so reporters in the room lifted their heads. "We're not going to sell any papers by reporting that the prime minister wants to raise pension contributions. I want some real news. That crap-rag is going to splash some scandal, and our papers'll be left behind on the racks."

Juvonen registered the epithet Johansson used to refer to their primary competitor, *Ilta-Sanomat*. It was a good measure of his state of mind. If Ruthless Ragnar was in a good mood, the *Ilta-Sanomat* was a "neighbor" or "our dear adversary." "Crap-rag" and "toilet paper" were neutral expressions. In bad moments—which were frequent—the epithets were truly malicious, and Ragnar was a verbally gifted man.

Juvonen glanced at her email to see if she'd find a lifesaver there. She noticed a press release from Homicide lieutenant Takamäki and clicked it open. The headline read, "Helsinki Police Seek Information on Escaped Murderer."

"Hey, Ragnar," Mary Jane called out. "Is an escaped murderer good enough?"

Johansson chuckled theatrically. "Goddammit, is it good enough? You're gonna save my day again. We'll go with that if nothing better turns up. A murderer stalking a new victim. Front page and we'll get a full spread out of it, if not more. Mary Jane, Välkki, and Karhunen, get over here, let's take a look."

The editorial meeting began thirty seconds later. Ruthless Ragnar was in his element. He boasted an impressive record: of the ten highest-selling front pages of all time, six were his. None of the other managing editors had matched his achievement, but they all thought Ragnar had just been lucky in terms being on duty when big news broke.

The bravado of a moment ago had shifted into a businesslike enthusiasm. Mary was allowed to sit in the empty chair at the table in the middle of the room, while Välkki and Karhunen, both thirty-year-old men in cardigans, stood.

"Mary, who is this escapee?"

"I'm not really sure. Timo Repo, fifty years old. Killed his wife in the '90s."

"He didn't just kill her if he's doing life, he murdered her."

"Yes," Juvonen agreed. "Right you are."

"Okay, let's start from the spread. Välkki will look into this Repo's background. Who he is."

Bespectacled Välkki nodded and left. There wasn't much time left in the day, and he had to find out which district or appeals court had sentenced Repo to life.

Johansson turned to Karhunen and his receding hairline. "Karhunen, I want a piece on someone who knows this Repo. Let's get a human angle on this. Välkki will probably pull up the verdict. If necessary, call every name on it. Also check all the media archives. Do we have photos of him? Of his wife's relatives? Can we find anyone who was at the wife's funeral? Who's afraid of him?"

Karhunen rubbed his forehead and went back to his computer.

"And Mary Jane," Ruthless Ragnar smiled crookedly. "From you I want a piece on the police search—no, make that a manhunt! Drama, pictures," Johansson said, painting a spread-wide headline with his hands. "'Police

Hunt Dangerous Fugitive.' Nah, that's boring. Come up with something better. Action, danger, fear!"

Mary J. quickly browsed through the eight-line press release she had printed. She'd milk a spread out of it no problem, but the photos looked like they might be a little trickier.

\* \* \*

Takamäki was sitting at his desk. His phone rang as soon as he ended the previous call. The female crime reporter from *Ilta-Sanomat* had been the first to call, but Sanna Römpötti from Channel 3 TV News came in second. It had only been four minutes since the release had been sent out.

"Hello," he said in an official tone.

"Hey there, Takamäki," said Römpötti. She had been a crime reporter for about twenty years, and had made the leap to TV news from *Helsingin Sanomat* newspaper a few years ago. "Römpötti here."

"Hi," Takamäki changing to a friendly tone.

"Prison escape, huh?"

"Yeah, but it's not that fascinating. We've been looking for him for a couple of days, just can't find him anywhere. That's why we're going to the media with it, see if the public can help us out," Takamäki explained. He didn't think an escapee no one had ever heard of would break the TV news threshold.

"Okay," Römpötti said. "I'll check back."

"Sounds good," the lieutenant replied, and the call ended.

Takamäki's phone rang again. "Hello."

"Juvonen from *Iltalehti*. It's Takamäki, right?"

"Good guess."

"Great," Juvonen said. "About Repo. Who is he?"

Takamäki thought for a second. Römpötti may have been recording the call, but Juvonen definitely was. Every word he said could and probably would appear in tomorrow's paper, or probably on their website yet that evening. "Timo Repo is a prisoner serving life who has escaped. He was convicted of murdering his wife."

"So it's a real escape, not some unauthorized leave?"

"Yes. The incident has been recorded as prisoner escape, per Chapter 16 of the Penal Code. Penalties include a fine or at most a year's prison sentence. The Prison Department requested the assistance of the police."

Juvonen paused for a moment, and Takamäki guessed she was taking notes.

"At most a year's imprisonment, so it doesn't meet the criteria for a wire-tap warrant?"

"No, but we don't have a phone number to listen in on either. Otherwise we'd give Repo a call and ask him to come on down to the station."

"How dangerous is he?" Juvonen asked.

"We don't consider him to be particularly dangerous."

"What does that mean?"

Here we go, Takamäki thought. "He was convicted of murder, so in principle he can be considered dangerous. But we're not aware of any factors that would make him particularly dangerous."

"Why did he flee?"

Goddammit, Takamäki thought, trying to keep his voice steady. "We haven't had the opportunity to question him, so we don't know. Yet."

"Does this Repo belong to a criminal gang?"

"According to our information, no, he does not."

Juvonen quizzed Takamäki further about the escape. Takamäki told her about the funeral, the coffee and sandwiches afterwards, and Repo's flight.

"Huh. Doesn't it annoy the police when the prison authorities let prisoners escape like that?"

"Well," Takamäki measured his words. "The prison authorities do their job and we do ours. It's not any more complicated than that."

Juvonen laughed. "Okay, so the search is on, then?"

"Yes."

"Where?"

"I'm not going to reveal that now."

"But raids are taking place?"

"Of course we continuously conduct searches of residences in cases like these," Takamäki said, a little tiredly.

"The SWAT team is on the move?"

"We haven't called them."

"But you will if necessary?"

Takamäki considered how he could answer this one. If he said no, he'd be lying, because of course the SWAT team would be used if a dangerous situation arose. If he answered yes, the following sentence would appear in the paper: "The police are ready to call in the SWAT units," which was an overstatement. But Takamäki didn't want to lie.

"If necessary, of course, they'll be called in."

"Could we come along and get some footage of a SWAT operation?" Juvonen tossed out.

"No."

"Just thought I'd ask."

"Was there anything else?" Takamäki asked.

"Yes," Juvonen answered. "A photo of this Repo? Just email it over."

"No can do," Takamäki said. "We decided we're not going to distribute it yet."

Juvonen was irritated. "What the hell? Why not?"

Takamäki paused for a moment. "If I say no, it means no."

"Are you serious? You don't want to catch him even just a little bit?"

"This is the decision I made in this case. I don't need to justify it to you."

"Who do you think you are?" Juvonen continued. She was upset that there would be a huge gap in the photos now. "We'd print it in the paper for free. Next time you guys can buy ad space when you want us to help you find someone."

Takamäki smiled. Mary J. Juvonen hadn't changed a bit. "All right, talk to you later," he said, and hung up.

# CHAPTER 9
## TUESDAY, 5:10 P.M.
## TOPELIUS STREET, TÖÖLÖ, HELSINKI

Repo was standing at a bus stop on Topelius Street, watching the traffic headed toward the Women's Hospital. He was still wearing the black suit and the gray coat he had stolen from the restaurant. He had taken an old-fashioned cap from Karppi's house and pulled it down over his forehead.

Darkness had already fallen. Half a dozen people were waiting at the bus stop. None of them appeared interested in him. His father's documents were in a plastic bag, as was the Luger, now wrapped in newspaper.

Bus number fourteen thundered up and everyone else boarded, but Repo just kept waiting. He wasn't interested in buses. What he needed was a car.

Karppi didn't have one, so Repo was going to have to get one by other means. He had concluded that he didn't have the know-how to steal any of the cars parked near Karppi's place, so he needed not only a car but the key to it as well. Repo knew how to jack an old-fashioned Saab 99, because all you needed to do to start them was to yank off the lock mechanism and stick a screwdriver into the exposed screw. Saab 99s, popular in the '70s, were extremely rare these days, though.

Repo had left Karppi's house an hour ago and travelled to Töölö by bus and tram. He had been standing at the stop for about ten minutes, but not a single suitable person had shown up yet.

One of the cars headed in the direction of the Women's Hospital braked, and the driver smoothly backed his Nissan into a parking spot. A man of about sixty in a blue peacoat stepped out and took a gym bag from the trunk. This guy might work, Repo thought, and started following him.

The man in the peacoat walked across the street toward the Töölö swimming pool, which was located in the basement of the Occupational Health Institute. It was ten yards or so to the door. Repo noted the sticker indicating surveillance cameras and held his head down so the brim of his cap shaded his face. A dozen or so stairs led downwards.

The man in the peacoat was about five yards ahead of him and was standing at the cashier by the time Repo made it through the lower-level door. He felt the pool's warm, chlorine-laden air, but he kept his coat on, and didn't even remove his cap.

The entrance to the cashier was perched on a little balcony, and Repo could see the swimming pools down below him. The cashier gave the man in the peacoat some sort of card.

Repo stepped up to the counter. "Hi. I'd like to go for a swim."

"Well, you came to the right place. Four-sixty, please," said the cashier, a brunette with a long face.

Repo handed the woman a five-euro bill from the money Karppi had given him, and she gave him the change and a piece of plastic the size of a credit card.

"I'm sorry. Is this a key, or?" Repo asked. The last time he had been to a public swimming pool, the cashier had given him an old-fashioned metal key for his locker.

"Never been here before? No worries," the brunette explained. "Use that card to get through the turnstile. Just swipe it across the reader and the turnstile will let you through. You need a fifty-cent coin for the locker. Drop it into the slot inside the door and that'll release the key. You'll get your money back when you leave."

The system sounded complicated to Repo, but everything seemed to have moved in that direction in the last eight years. Just like the card system in the buses, but luckily he had still been able to pay the driver with cash.

"Got it, I guess," Repo said. He went to the turnstile but couldn't see the man in the peacoat anymore. He was probably already in the locker room.

Repo swiped the card across the reader and was allowed to pass. The first door led to the women's locker room, the next two to the men's. Repo took the middle door. The locker room smelled like a strong cleaning agent and was relatively empty. It contained four or five rows of lockers about thirty or so feet long. There was no one in the first row.

In the second row, there were two older men getting dressed. They were discussing the politics of the '70s. Repo heard the names Sorsa and Sinisalo, the social democratic and communist bigwigs of the era.

Repo continued down past the rows of lockers. He didn't find the man in the peacoat until the last row. He had already hung his coat in his locker and was taking off his sweater. Repo walked past him and made a mental note of the locker number: 78. Repo rounded the corner, opened a locker and hung his coat inside. He stood there, as if absent-mindedly waiting for something.

Five minutes later, Peacoat Man sailed past Repo naked. He was carrying his swim trunks and towel in his hand.

Repo waited another minute before putting his coat back on. He walked back to the rearmost row and up to locker 78. He quickly scanned the area. There was no one around. He drew a spike from his pocket and pulled the door back with his fingers as far as the lock would give. Repo slid the screwdriver-like tool in through the crack and forcefully pressed the tongue of the lock inwards. The lock struggled for five seconds, and then gave with a snap.

Repo pulled the locker door open.

The man in the peacoat had tidily hung his clothes on the hooks, and Repo hastily searched the coat pockets for his keys. He removed the car key from the ring and pressed the locker door shut. He also tried to twist the tongue of the lock back far enough that the door wouldn't open by its own weight, otherwise someone could steal the guy's clothes, too.

You couldn't tell from the outside that the lock had been forced open. The entire process had taken about thirty seconds.

Repo put the car key in his pocket and calmly walked out of the locker room. The brunette at the register gave him a vaguely surprised look, but he mumbled something about a meeting that had slipped his mind.

Once outside the building, Repo made a beeline for the car. It took him a second to figure out that he needed to open the doors remotely. He sat in the driver's seat and thought for a moment before starting up the engine. He hadn't driven in eight years. He checked the emergency brake. It was off. Gas, clutch, brake, turn signals. Repo pressed the clutch to the floor and tested the gear box by shifting from gear to gear. It all started coming back to him.

He turned on the ignition and nosed out into the traffic. The clock on the dash read 5:20 p.m.

Pulling the first shift on the tip line, Joutsamo had forwarded the incoming calls to her desk phone. She was browsing through media websites, and, based on what she saw, most had quickly picked up Takamäki's release. The majority had used the headline "Murderer Escapes." The articles were pretty sparse in terms of content. So far, none of the newsrooms had found Repo's photo in their archives. It was unlikely that they would have sent photographers to cover the original court case anyway.

The two first calls had come from known troublemakers, who always called the police with their so-called "info." The phone rang a third time. Joutsamo's phone had a display that should've revealed the number of the caller, but now it read "Blocked." She turned on the recorder.

"Helsinki Police Department, Violent Crimes Unit," Joutsamo answered, marking the time of the call in her notebook: 5:47 p.m.

"Hello," said the caller, her voice tentative.

"Hello," Joutsamo responded.

"I just heard about that prison escape on the radio," the woman continued, her tone now more animated. "They read the description, and a man who looks just like that just went into that building."

"What building? Where are you?"

"I'm here in Bear Park. The address of the building he entered is 18 Fifth Street. I followed him into the stairwell, and it looked like he climbed up to the top floor, or maybe the second to the top."

"You didn't follow him any further, though?"

"I didn't dare to, because it looked to me like he pulled a gun out of his pocket right there in the stairwell.

I'm not positive, but that's what it looked like."

"Good. Do you know Repo from before?"

"What?" the woman gasped. "How would I know a convicted felon? He just looked like the description. He was walking through Bear Park with this evil glare in his eyes."

"Could I get your name, please?"

"Not a chance," the woman huffed.

"Why not?"

"You'll try to put me on the witness stand. I thought long and hard about whether I should even call, but I figured it was my civic duty."

"Well, thank you," Joutsamo said, ending the call and the recording. She wondered whether the press release could produce results so rapidly. The description was generic enough to fit many men, of course, but the caller seemed sane enough. Joutsamo wondered where Repo would have obtained a gun.

Joutsamo walked down to Takamäki's office, where the lieutenant was just pulling on his overcoat. "You headed out?" Joutsamo asked.

"Yup, I figured I'd spend some time with the family for a change."

"Okay, we're going to go see if there's anything in a tip that just came in," Joutsamo smiled.

"What tip?"

"A helpful member of the public called in and said that she saw a man matching Repo's description entering a building on Fifth Street."

"Is that so?"

"And she said she saw a gun, too."

Takamäki looked intently at Joutsamo. "Reliable?"

"I really don't know. But for the time being, it's the only thing we got. I was thinking Suhonen and I would go check it out."

"What did she say about the weapon, word for word?" Takamäki asked.

Joutsamo checked her notes. "The caller thought the man pulled a gun out of his pocket in the stairwell."

"And who is this member of the public? Did she give her name?"

"No, because she thought she'd end up a witness."

"Are there any known PTs in the building?" Takamäki asked. Apartments whose residents were known to be dangerous were registered in the Potential Threat database.

"No."

"I wonder what's there, then?" Takamäki said, taking his coat off. "Okay, let's bring in a few SWAT men to help out. No point fooling around if it really is Repo and he has a gun. The guy could be desperate. I'll take the lead from here and call in the SWAT team. You and Suhonen head right over just in case he moves, assuming it is him. Kohonen's still here, isn't she?"

"Yes," Joutsamo said.

"Kirsi can check who lives in the building. Brief her quickly before you go. Let's shoot for," Takamäki glanced at his watch, which read 5:52 p.m., "entry by 7:00 at the latest, but as soon as SWAT can spare us the men."

\* \* \*

A caravan of three SWAT vans rolled out from police headquarters at 6:45 p.m. Takamäki was sitting with Turunen, head of the SWAT team, in the lead vehicle. His phone was in hand as the van turned north up Nordenskiöld Street at the Neste gas station. The evening gloom had deepened from gray to black.

Eight SWAT officers had fit into two vans; the third one was for transporting the target. The vehicles weren't using their emergency lights.

Takamäki returned his phone to his pocket.

"Joutsamo said that the situation at the scene remains the same. No sign of the target."

Takamäki and Turunen had had a quick pow-wow in Takamäki's office, during which the lieutenant had filled the SWAT leader in on the case. Turunen had classified it as a routine search.

Before the railway underpass, the caravan turned right onto Eläintarha Road and headed toward Töölö Bay. When they got to the Helsinki Street intersection, Takamäki looked at the illuminated fountain in the bay and the downtown's gleaming city lights behind it. The thought crossed his mind that he really should be at home.

He snapped back to reality when Turunen started giving orders to his men through his headset. "We don't know the exact apartment of the target, but it's probably on the fifth or sixth floor."

Turunen rattled off names and tasks. The men were assigned floors and duties. The only one Takamäki knew by name was Saarinen, who was in the second van. He had heard a story about the Jack Bauer look-alike: one day after work, the SWAT guys had decided to spend the evening at a sauna, relaxing and drinking. Saarinen had begged not to come, saying he had promised his wife he'd go home. Eventually the other guys talked him into it, and after making the other guys promise to be quiet, he had called his wife. As he vigorously slapped his palm against his leather jacket, Saarinen explained to her that the SWAT team had gotten an urgent assignment in Oulu, and he was just walking into the helicopter. After the twenty-second call, they had headed off to the sauna.

Turunen gave out more orders. "Takamäki and I will cover the exterior of the building. Be aware that two homicide detectives are also on the scene: Joutsamo and Suhonen."

The adrenaline gradually began to rise in Takamäki's veins, too. He instinctively checked that his own Sig Sauer was in his coat pocket. He had originally gotten the Swiss-German pistol from a guy he knew at the Equipment Office. The Sig Sauer was smaller than the standard police-issue Glocks.

The van turned right at the corner of the Brahe Soccer Field toward the Kallio fire station and Fifth Street. They were only a couple of minutes from the target now. Takamäki called Joutsamo and informed her that they were approaching. He and Turunen had agreed that the operation would begin immediately upon arrival.

A tram was shuddering along in front of them, and the trip seemed to take forever. The Kallio fire station appeared on the right and Bear Park on the left. They had called Fire and Rescue and arranged to have an ambulance at the ready as a precaution.

Cars were parked in front of the building, but Turunen calmly double-parked the police vans in front of the entrance, as the street was plenty wide. The other vans pulled up behind Turunen.

The SWAT men had heavy bulletproof vests, helmets, and Heckler & Koch MP5 submachine guns.

"Okay, Saarinen, let's do this," Turunen said.

The hooded police were moving single file toward the door of the building when the first flash went off, immediately followed by a second, a third, and a fourth. Takamäki registered a photographer and a cameraman.

And then he recognized Mary Juvonen standing behind them.

Takamäki knew there was no point interfering in the photographers' work. That would only get you a scowling shot in the papers. He walked up to Juvonen. "You sure made it here quick."

Juvonen was wearing a black wool cap and a Burberry coat.

"Yeah, some woman called in a tip that Repo might be found here."

"She did, huh?"

"Yeah," Juvonen said. "So Repo's not particularly dangerous?"

"Come on, knock it off."

The SWAT team had entered the building, and the photographers were following. Takamäki gave Juvonen a stern look.

"The stairwell is a police operation zone. No photographers allowed. Who's going to tell them?"

"That's your assessment, huh?"

Takamäki nodded. "If he's in there, anything could happen."

Juvonen could tell from the lieutenant's tone that now was not the time to mess with him.

Juvonen raised her voice. "Hey, guys. Let's not go inside. We'll wait out here."

"You sure, Mary?" the photographer asked from the doorway.

"Yup. We'll do it this way this time. If they find him in there, then they'll bring him out this way in any case," Juvonen said with a glance at Takamäki, who nodded.

Takamäki went back and joined Turunen at the van. The photographers and the reporter stayed obediently on the sidewalk.

"Goddammit," Turunen said. "How the hell did they get here so fast?"

"The reporter said they got a tip from some woman."

Turunen shook his head. "Is that so? I'll bet you a beer we don't find him here."

"Fine, if you'll bet there are going to be five columns' worth of photos of your guys in tomorrow's paper."

Turunen wasn't particularly amused, but he smiled anyway. "Make it six and you're on."

Joutsamo walked up to the van. Suhonen had noticed the flashes and had stayed back in their car next to Bear Park. "You organize a press conference already?"

"I'm pretty sure someone else did," Turunen replied.

"Turunen, you have a camera in your van?" Takamäki asked.

"Of course."

"You mind getting it?"

It took Turunen thirty seconds. "Here," he said, handing it to Takamäki. "I already turned it on. Just point and press that red button. The flash is automatic."

Takamäki walked fifteen feet from Juvonen and the photographers and suddenly took a photo.

Juvonen's reaction was immediate: "Why'd you take a picture of us?"

"It's always a good idea to get a record of those present at a crime scene," Takamäki grunted, managing to turn around right before the photographer rapid-fired his flash.

"What's that going to be used for?" the cameraman blustered, annoyed that he hadn't captured the incident on tape.

* * *

Twenty minutes later, the SWAT men had checked all of the apartments in the stairwell and emerged without Repo. The *Iltalehti* photographers recorded their exit, but none of the masked men answered the reporter's questions.

The SWAT team marched over to the vans and prepared to leave. Juvonen followed, with the photographers at her heels. Their target was Takamäki, who was stepping into the lead van. Suhonen had already vanished from the scene, and Joutsamo was in the SWAT van.

"Takamäki!" Juvonen yelled from ten yards away.

The lieutenant climbed into the van and considered for a moment whether or not to reply. In the end, he rolled down the window.

Juvonen made it up to the door of the vehicle. The photographer immediately took a couple of pictures.

"Didn't find him?"

"Did you see him?"

"No."

"Look, Juvonen, get a grip. Don't mess with us," Takamäki said in a severe tone.

"Who do you think you are?"

"This isn't going to end here," Takamäki said, rolling up the window. Turunen popped it into gear, and the van jerked forward. Joutsamo said that she had recognized Juvonen's voice as that of the person who called in the tip, confirming Takamäki's suspicions.

Juvonen looked at the police vans cruising past Bear Park and turned toward her photographers. Both of them had heard the exchange. "Well, back to the newsroom. Nothing else is going to happen here. We'll get a spread out of this."

\* \* \*

Repo parked his newly-acquired car at a soccer field parking lot in Hakunila, a neighborhood in the suburb of Vantaa. There was a grass field next to the lot, but the junior team was training farther away on the gravel field, near a dome scrawled with graffiti. It was already dark outside, and the field's lights created a yellow glow.

Repo stepped out of the car, closed the door, and clicked on the lock. His driving skills had quickly come back to him.

Wearing his gray coat and black suit, the escaped convict walked toward the soccer field. At the end of the parking lot there was an old wooden cabin that functioned as the locker room. The weather was the best possible for soccer practice—about forty degrees, no rain. The forecast on the radio had promised that the temperature would drop and tomorrow it would sleet or snow.

There were about fifteen boys on the field, half of whom were wearing yellow vests over their sweat jackets. The team was evidently having a scrimmage.

"No, no. Remember distances," shouted a wavy-haired man in a parka. Repo guessed he was about forty. He was wearing a black beanie, like all the players.

The vests appeared to have the upper hand, and they drove the ball inexorably toward the sweatjackets' goal. A few parents were standing on the sidelines chatting, but from ten yards away Repo could only make out a word here and there.

He searched the field for a familiar face, but couldn't find it. In their matching soccer sweatsuits and beanies, the boys all looked the same.

Those parents are probably talking about hockey, Repo wondered. At least that's what the words he heard—lines, checking, hitting—sounded like. On the other hand, they could have also been talking about prison.

No one paid any attention to Repo.

The vests—more prison slang—were outplaying their opponents, and scored again. One of the boys faked out a defender near the sideline and centered the ball in front of the goal, from where another player headed it into the back of the net.

A dull clapping echoed from the coach's leather gloves. He called out to the winger, "Great fake and center, Joel!"

Repo startled. Joel. He took a closer look at the boy and recognized the features from the photo Karppi had given him. The face wasn't as round as it used to be, but it was his Joel, no doubt about it.

The coach continued shouting out the pitch: "Markku, that header was just like Ronaldo! Nice goal! Okay, kick off from midfield."

The goalie angrily kicked the ball into center field, where one of the vests snagged it out of the air.

Repo heard one of the sweatjackets complaining to the coach about the teams: "All the best kids on the same team. This is totally unfair."

Joel jogged up to the middle of the field. Repo watched every step.

"Fair and fair. Stop complaining, Leevi," the coach said, blowing his whistle. The game continued.

Repo watched Joel's every move. In his day, he had played Division II soccer himself and knew a lot about the game. But that didn't make any difference now. He didn't look where Joel was positioned or whether his touches were clean. He wasn't interested in whether Joel knew how to tackle properly, or whether he led too much with the soles of his feet.

Repo simply watched his son, mesmerized. He felt like running out onto the pitch and hugging him. Telling him how proud he was of him. Tears rose to his eyes as he understood what he had lost.

Repo clearly heard the words when one of the parents standing next to him said to a man in a green ski cap, "That Joel *of yours* is definitely the best player we've got. He's not going to be hanging around here too long before they move him up."

The words cut Repo to the quick. That Joel of yours. *Of yours.*

The boy was *his* Joel, not anyone else's. He wasn't that green-capped guy's Joel. Repo felt like shouting, but he knew he couldn't.

Eight years earlier, Joel was a tow-headed toddler he had taken to the soccer fields dozens of times to kick the ball around. Where had the years gone? Repo knew the answer all too well: prison. And for no reason. His wife was dead. His mother was dead. His father was dead, and his son was gone. What did he have left? Nothing.

Repo wondered how Joel would react if he walked out into the field and told him he was his real father. Could they still have a life together?

What would his life be like if his wife were still alive? Once again, thinking hurt too much.

Repo saw now that coming here to stand at the sidelines had been pointless. His son wouldn't recognize him. What had he been thinking? That Joel would run up to him, stop, and say, "Dad?" That they'd hug and walk off into a new life together? Repo chuckled to himself. The boy wouldn't remember him, and probably wouldn't even know his name. The guy in the green beanie was his dad now. Not him.

Repo took a final look at the man in the green cap. Take good care of my son, Repo silently told him, and headed toward the car he had stolen. Where had his life gone?

"What are you going to do about Juvonen?" Joutsamo asked. Takamäki, Suhonen, and Kulta were also sitting in the austere conference room at police headquarters in Pasila. Someone had drawn a big question mark on the flipchart.

"What do you think I should do?" Takamäki asked.

Joutsamo was incensed. "Nail her to the wall. That was a really dirty trick."

"What's the crime?"

"I don't know, but you can't mislead the police like that."

Takamäki was silent for a moment. "Resisting police authority. It includes false reports. As I recall, the maximum is three months in jail."

"That's not going to get you a search warrant for her phone," Joutsamo noted.

"Don't need it. Let's call her in for questioning and confiscate it. That'll let us check the numbers called," Takamäki said. "But we also have to think about costs and benefits here. It's not in our best interest to create a rift with the media."

"That's not what we're talking about, hopefully," Joutsamo said. "No one else in the media behaves that way. They always want photos, but we're going to be screwed if this is how they're going to start acquiring."

"Or was it just a one-off overstepping of bounds?" Takamäki wondered out loud. "Happens to police, too."

"Were you guys planning to continue this conversation on media ethics much longer?" Suhonen yawned. "If we can get back to the case... I think the key is figuring out why Repo took off."

"You have any ideas?" Joutsamo asked.

"Some ideas, but not too many facts."

"Maybe he's offed himself?" Kulta suggested. "Was so shocked by his old man's death that he flew the coop and ran into Töölö Bay. At least that would explain why we can't find him."

"If he wanted to, he could've killed himself in prison," Joutsamo said.

"But if it was the funeral. Temporary insanity."

"Give me a break," Joutsamo replied. "When we went to the old man's house, there was a photo where Timo Repo's face had been blacked out. They weren't close. But I bet you're on the right track, that the dad's death has something to do with the motive for the escape."

"Okay, theoretically it's possible that he had been planning to split for a while, but this was his first chance," Kulta said.

"He could've got himself sent to a hospital, if he faked it well enough," Joutsamo noted.

Kulta wouldn't give up. "Revenge? Bitterness?"

"Toward whom?" Suhonen continued. "He stopped filing appeals. Guys like that are psychologically wired so that if they're bitter about something, it snowballs and they start seeing conspiracies everywhere. If Repo was spinning out of control, the guards would have noticed something. It would've showed somehow in the pen, overall edginess or continuous bitching. But he's been a total sheep ever since he gave up appeals," Suhonen said. "He wasn't cracking. We're missing something here."

"Or not," Kulta reflected. "It could just all be in his head. Something no one else can understand."

"But even that would have been evident in the pen."

"What if he hasn't changed? What if he's been screwed up the whole time, but was able to hide it?" Joutsamo suggested.

"All of these lead back to the suicide theory one way or another," Takamäki noted. "A desperate man commits a desperate act, and because we don't know why, we assume the only answer can be suicide."

"There's not always an explanation in cases like these," Kulta said. "Sometimes a human life hangs by an extremely slender thread."

"But if we go back to the act itself," Joutsamo began. "His wife's murder."

Takamäki waved a hand. "Not right now. Let's go back to it tomorrow. Suhonen, you have anything going on tonight?"

Suhonen shook his head. He never had anything going on that would've taken precedence over work.

"Find Saarnikangas. That's the only name on the outside that has come up. Being a junkie, he's probably on the move at night, even if Repo stays holed up. That might lead us somewhere."

"Maybe," Kulta said.

"You got any better ideas?"

"No, I just don't think it's a very strong direction."

"It's not," Takamäki admitted. "But it's the only one we have."

"We could go check the old man's house again," Joutsamo suggested. "Mikko and I could drop by."

"Oh, we could, could we?"

"Yes," Joutsamo smiled.

"Sounds good," Takamäki said, standing and flipping over the sheet with the question mark.

Takamäki quietly opened the front door of his house. It was a little before nine o'clock. He figured Jonas might already be in bed. Kaarina wasn't, though. She was sitting at the kitchen table with her laptop.

"Hey," Takamäki said softly.

"Hey," Kaarina answered. Takamäki detected a coolness in her voice.

"How's it going?"

"Fine. Nice you could make it home so early."

Takamäki took off his coat and hung it up in the entryway. The lower floor of their townhouse contained a kitchen and a living room. The three bedrooms and a sauna were upstairs. The house had been built around 1990, and had suffered serious water damage a few years back.

"There's food in the fridge if you're hungry."

Takamäki sat down at the table. "Not really," he replied, browsing through the day's mail. Nothing important: the latest issue of *Technical World*, a bank statement, some bills, a couple of ads.

"How's Jonas?"

"What about him?"

"How's he doing?"

"Not great. I gave him some ibuprofen that ended in a huge string of zeroes."

"The samples you got from work?"

Kaarina nodded. She was a head nurse at the municipal hospital.

"He's sleeping now. He did ask for you a bunch of times earlier this evening."

Takamäki felt bad. He should have been there to answer his son's questions. "What did he want?"

"Mostly he was interested in whether the entire hockey season was gone thanks to his arm. I didn't know the answer."

Takamäki felt a pang of regret. "He should have called me."

"You've told the boys time and again that they shouldn't call you at work. I'm assuming that's why he didn't want to bother you."

"Well, the season probably isn't totally gone yet. It'll be six to eight weeks, I'd say. Or guess."

"Jonas probably would have liked to hear that. But there's no point waking him now. His arm was really sore, and he had a hard time falling asleep."

Takamäki went over to the fridge and took out a beer.

Kaarina couldn't resist needling him: "There's food in there, too."

Takamäki didn't bother answering; he popped off the cap with the opener on the fridge and drank straight from the bottle.

Kaarina turned back to her laptop for a moment, but then interrupted herself. "Who hit him?"

"Don't know."

"The Espoo Police must be looking into it."

"Yeah."

"No one from there has called me. Did anyone call you?"

"I called the investigator," Takamäki said. "As a matter of fact, I dropped by Sello and picked up the surveillance camera images."

"Why? Shouldn't the Espoo Police take care of that?"

"They should, but I thought I'd make sure it happened."

"Can you see the hit-and-run in the pictures?" Kaarina asked hesitantly.

Takamäki nodded.

"How bad did it...?"

"There were a few stills. You can see the collision and the car's license plate number."

"So he'll get caught?"

"Possibly. You can't make out the driver."

"Whose car is it?" Kaarina asked.

Takamäki took a swig of his beer. "I don't know. Let's allow the Espoo Police to do their job."

"Well, they don't sound very efficient, since they haven't even questioned Jonas about the incident yet, and you had to pick up the photos."

"The investigator's pretty busy. I promised I'd take him the photos tomorrow."

\* \* \*

The green Volkswagen Golf turned onto the Tuusula Expressway, as sleet slapped into the windshield.

"Have you ever played boardless chess?" Kulta asked Joutsamo. He was at the wheel.

"What?"

"Boardless chess. Chess without a board and pieces. Let's give it a shot," he suggested, turning off the highway. They still had a mile or so to go. "I'm white, so that means my pieces are in squares one and two. You have seven and eight."

"Huh?"

"I'll make the first move. Pawn from D2 to D4."

Joutsamo smiled. "OK, knight...ummm, B8 to C6."

"Good," Kulta said, slowing down. He let an old woman cross the road. "Pawn from E2 to E3."

Joutsamo tried to picture the chessboard. "Knight from E6 to B4. Have you played this before?"

Kulta kept his eyes on the road. "Once with Suhonen. We got to the third move before we started arguing about where the pieces were."

"So let's quit while we're ahead," Joutsamo said. "Turn right up there."

Kulta spun the wheel, and the car curved onto the street where the deceased Erik Repo's home stood.

"It's that one," Joutsamo said, and Kulta eased off the gas. The sides of the road were again lined with parked cars, but Kulta managed to crank the Golf into a space so tight Joutsamo wouldn't have even bothered trying to squeeze into it.

The officers stepped out of the car, and Joutsamo tugged up the zipper of her black coat. She fumbled around in her pockets, but didn't find her hat or gloves there.

"Queen from D1 to G4," Kulta said.

"That's a dumb move," Joutsamo answered. "My knight is going to move to C8. Check. And then I'm going to take your rook."

The streetlights bathed the yard in a yellow glow, but the wooden house itself was dark.

"Bet you a coffee that this trip is a complete waste," Kulta said, not waiting for a response.

The detectives started walking toward the house. Joutsamo tried looking for signs of forced entry, but there was nothing visible. At the gate, she took a quick look inside the mailbox. It was empty. A black garbage can stood next to it in a small wooden shelter. She looked inside that, too: also empty.

"No sign of Repo in there?" Kulta joked, continuing on to the house. He peered in through the window first, but didn't see any movement in the dark interior. He took the windows to the left; Joutsamo took those to the right. They met at the back of the house, both of them shaking their heads.

"I think I won that coffee," Kulta said.

"I never bet you," Joutsamo protested, looking over at the house next door.

"An espresso will work, too."

"Let's go talk to the neighbor," Joutsamo said. She started circling around to the front yard the way Kulta had come.

"What neighbor?" Kulta wondered, following her.

"The one who was just watching us out of that window."

Kulta looked at the neighboring home, but the window facing them was dark.

"Wow. X-ray vision, huh?"

"You get it with your sergeant's stripes. You should apply for those brass classes, too. Plus, think about who's emptying Repo's mailbox. They deliver the neighborhood paper three times a week here, as I recall."

The pair returned to the street and headed toward the neighbor's house. Joutsamo checked the name on the mailbox: Karppi. The house gave the impression of belonging to an elderly person or couple.

The windows were dark, but Joutsamo was certain she had seen movement. Of course it could have been nothing more than a cat walking across the windowsill.

Joutsamo rang the doorbell. No answer. She rang again. Nothing.

"Agh," Kulta grinned, reaching under his coat and pulling out his Glock from its holster on his belt. "Deadbolt's not on, so all we need to do is give the lock a little tickle."

Joutsamo sighed.

"No?" Kulta said, twirling the gun around and giving the door a couple of sharp raps with the butt. He called out in a commanding tone: "Police! Open up now! I repeat, Police. Open this door immediately!"

Kulta smiled when he could hear movement and the sound of footfalls inside. "I get at least a double espresso for this."

"Except if whoever's inside has a heart attack, in which case you'll get an indictment."

Rustling could be heard from inside. Joutsamo recognized it as the sound of an old-fashioned chain. The door opened, revealing an elderly, gray-haired man in a brown sweater. He looked scared and immediately took a couple of steps backwards.

"Anna Joutsamo from the Helsinki Police Department," Joutsamo announced, showing her badge. "This here is my colleague, Mikko Kulta."

"From the same firm," Kulta quipped.

"You're police officers."

"That's what we just said," Kulta said.

Joutsamo thought the jab was unnecessary and clearly missed its mark. The old man didn't catch it.

"You were watching us from the window a minute ago. Did you think we were criminals?"

The man grunted. "This place is swarming with them. Last summer, two houses were emptied on this street alone. The residents were on vacation and everything of any value was taken."

"Do you live alone?" Joutsamo asked.

The man realized he hadn't introduced himself, despite the fact that the officers had. "Right, of course, I'm Otto Karppi, and yes, I live alone. My wife died years ago." He didn't extend a hand, though.

"Well, we're not investigating break-ins right tonight, we're interested in whether anyone has been over at Repo's house during the past couple of days."

"Why are you interested in that?"

"Why don't we ask the questions here," Kulta growled.

"I'm just interested because I've been managing my old friend's affairs."

Kulta corrected him, "Those of the deceased, you mean."

The corners of Karppi's mouth turned up in a slight smile. Joutsamo immediately saw how Karppi had lured Kulta into a trap. Now the old man knew that the police knew that Repo was dead, and of course it was easy to draw conclusions from that. His body might be old, but there was still plenty of spark running through that brain of his.

"Okay, let's drop the games. You know why we're here," Joutsamo said. "Of course we're looking for Erik's son Timo, who ditched his escort at the restaurant."

"That's obvious," Karppi said, smiling a little more broadly now. His teeth were badly yellowed. "Haven't caught him yet?"

"No," Joutsamo answered.

"Well, I haven't seen him here, and no one has been to Erik's house since the day before yesterday, which is when I think you visited there last," he said, smoothing and tidying his sparse hair.

"Do you have any information on where we might find Timo Repo?" Joutsamo asked.

"I don't know him at all. We met at the funeral, but that's the extent of it."

"You were there?"

Karppi looked irritated. "I just said I managed my old friend's affairs."

"I have one more question, just to verify," Joutsamo said. "You've been emptying Erik Repo's mailbox. Have you found anything inside that would help us in locating the escaped convict?"

"Not really. It's mostly just ads these days."

"All right," Joutsamo said, digging a card out of her pocket. "If you spot any movement at the neighbors' or if Timo Repo contacts you, please call the number on this card."

Karppi took the card. "Good-bye."

"Good-bye," the officers replied, turning back toward their vehicle. Karppi closed the door, and Joutsamo could hear the rustling of the chain from a few yards away.

The detectives returned to the car, and Kulta climbed in the driver's seat. Joutsamo gazed at the quiet street and asked Kulta, "If he saw Suhonen and me the first time, why was he afraid of us this time?"

"You guys didn't talk to him. He didn't know you were cops."

"He didn't know, but Karppi isn't dumb. He was there when the escape took place at the restaurant, and I'm sure he understood that the police would be looking for the escapee at his father's home."

Kulta started up the Golf. "Where to?"

Joutsamo continued her train of thought. "There was something fishy about that. Why would he be afraid of us or hide from us?"

"Everyone's afraid of the police," Kulta laughed. "But maybe he knows more than he let on. And he didn't even offer us an espresso." Kulta steered the car onto the street. "Would he hide Repo in his house?"

"It's possible, of course."

"Should we start staking out Karppi's place?"

"No!"

"Why not?" Kulta asked.

"You could come and sit here in the car, but think about it. Karppi was old man Repo's friend, and the father and son didn't have a close relationship. I don't think he was close to Timo Repo at all. But he was hiding something from us. If we can't find Repo by tomorrow, then we'll come by and talk to him again."

* * *

A little after 9 p.m. Suhonen was driving northwards on Sörnäinen Shore Drive in his grimy old Nissan. He had chosen to take his own car rather than the usual department Peugeot. Traffic was almost nonexistent. He left the concrete colossi of the Hakaniemi housing complex behind on the right and the tall apartment buildings of Kallio on the left. He passed the gas station and continued toward the Eastern Expressway. He was driving 55 mph, even though the speed limit was 45.

As Suhonen passed a taxi he glanced at his phone, lying on the passenger seat. The thing pissed him off. Suhonen remembered the early '90s, the good old days when mobile phones didn't exist. What bliss! You could work at your own pace, all you had to do was produce results. And on top of it all, it had been a Finnish company that had introduced the mobile phone to the world. Now proletariats around the world had cause to despise his little homeland for helping to create the 24/7 work culture.

But work wasn't what was eating at Suhonen at the moment. His fiancée, or more like his soon-to-be-ex-fiancée, had called and wondered what was keeping him. In Raija's opinion, he should be on his way home.

Suhonen and Raija, who worked at an insurance company, had moved in together under the condition that work might keep Suhonen in the field after hours from time to time. Which would, of course, be balanced by extra time off now and again.

Lately Suhonen had been getting the feeling that the arrangement was no longer satisfactory to Raija. She

132

thought Suhonen should apply for a supervisory position; he'd make more money, his work load would be easier, and he wouldn't end up in risky situations anymore.

This is what Raija had been nagging him about over the phone earlier. In return, Suhonen had suggested that she could get a late-night shift at McDonald's, and then they'd work the same hours. Raija had hung up on him.

Suhonen grabbed the phone from the seat and pressed the green headset twice. The phone dialed a number that Suhonen had already tried a few times. A woman's voice announced in a cool tone, "The number you have dialed is currently unavailable."

Goddamn Salmela. The guy had changed his number without telling Suhonen. They'd have to have a talk about that.

Suhonen sped past the first few exits. He was headed for Kontula, to a couple of bars where Saarnikangas was a regular. It seemed like there were an infinite number of them. Suhonen had already gone through the bars in Kallio and Hakaniemi without finding the guy.

The speed limit climbed to fifty, and Suhonen slowed down. He tried to calm himself—he should never let his emotions interfere with his work. He turned on the radio: Ari, the latest *Idols* winner, was singing his bubble-gum hit, and Suhonen clicked it right back off.

\* \* \*

Joutsamo was sitting at her desk, tapping away at her computer. The portable TV on Kulta's desk a few feet away was on. Kulta had already gone home, as had Takamäki. The only ones left in the office were Joutsamo and Kohonen.

The sports highlights program wrapped up, and a current affairs show began. On the screen, a grave-looking Sanna Römpötti was explaining that the topic of this evening's episode of *Hot Seat* was justice. The guest was Aarno Fredberg, chief justice of the Supreme Court. In line with the show's format, Römpötti got right down to business: "Chief Justice Fredberg, you said in a newspaper interview last Sunday that prison sentences don't do any good. What would you propose as an alternative?"

The question was tough enough that Joutsamo paused to watch.

Fredberg was coming up on sixty and his appearance resembled a corporate attorney more than a Supreme Court judge, who weren't known for always being impeccably coiffed or wearing the latest suit from Hugo Boss.

"The alternative is clear. Take fires, for example. If they started occurring with significantly greater frequency than they do today, it probably wouldn't make sense to increase the number of fire stations, but rather to look into the causes of the fires."

Römpötti pressed him. "But fires are very different from felonies."

"I wouldn't say so. In both cases, the issue is some type of a societal disruption. Fires are often a matter of technical flaws, and it's easy to impact, say, the fire safety of TVs. And although a lot of research has been conducted on it, the human mind is a more complex phenomenon."

"What would you like to change?"

"Criminal justice policy needs to be opened up to broad-based discussion. Nowadays we apply this fire station model to crime by increasing resources for law enforcement and prosecutors, like they're always doing in America. This leads to an increased amount of prisoners, escalating the cycle of marginalization."

"Isn't that a bit disingenuous? Isn't ending up in prison one of the end points of a cycle of marginalization?"

"You're right. As a matter of fact, you're right at the heart of the matter. Prisons don't rehabilitate anyone. Prison doesn't act as a deterrent for people who commit crimes. It's crucial to understand this. We have to change our focus now. People can't be allowed to end up in circumstances that lead them to commit crimes in the first place."

Joutsamo listened, her mouth agape. You could have expected this from some leftist politician, but had the country's chief judge gone insane?

Römpötti continued her battery of questions. "So if a wino runs out of booze, and he's about to burglarize a store to obtain more alcohol, society should provide a place where he can get booze for free."

"For example. Although it might be preferable to try and influence matters in such a way that we don't have winos, if that's the word you want to use. There are a good ten thousand people caught up in a cycle of incarceration. Let's give them a free place to live, substance abuse treatment, and, for instance, a sheltered job. Let's anchor them in life."

Joutsamo thought the other way around—from the victim's point of view. People shouldn't end up in situations where they become the victims of crimes. Evidently the permissive criminal policies of the 1960s were making a strong comeback.

"Sounds like a pretty utopic agenda," Römpötti remarked, setting her pen down on the desk.

"Because it hasn't been attempted yet," Fredberg answered.

"Who will pay for it?" the reporter asked. Funding was always a critical factor.

"A day in prison costs 125 euros, a month 3,800 euros, and a year 45,500 euros. When you add the costs of law enforcement, prosecutors, and judges on top of that, you easily get to a figure that's twice as high. And this sum multiplies exponentially when you include the other costs of crime, like damage to property and insurance payments."

The reporter tried to interject, "But..."

"Please don't interrupt," Fredberg growled, giving Römpötti an angry look. "We have almost 150 prisoners serving life sentences now. With each of them doing 12–14 years, the costs of incarceration alone are 550,000–640,000 euros per prisoner. With that kind of money, you could prevent the majority of homicides from ever happening. And if someone tells you any different, they're lying."

Römpötti tried again, "But..."

Sitting at her screen, Joutsamo wondered how the chief justice would happen to be able to pick out in advance those particular individuals in whose lives it made sense to invest half a million euros.

"I already asked you, please don't interrupt! Society should prevent crimes from taking place in the first place, or if we want to think realistically, decrease them significantly. An inmate is imprisoned for an average of a little under ten months, so 7,000 convicts are released from prisons every year. One in three starts off homeless, 60 percent have substance abuse problems, and one-fifth have serious mental health issues. This is the target group we should concentrate on first."

"So commit a crime, and you'll get money, a job, and a place to live," Römpötti said, but she didn't let Fredberg respond. "Let's move on to the next topic."

The reporter glanced at her papers. "We reviewed your twenty-six-year history at the Lahti District Court and the Kouvola Court of Appeals, as well as your last four years in the Supreme Court. Now this number may not be completely accurate, but according to our information, you've participated in handing down at least 36 life sentences for murder. Do you believe that those people could live normally as part of our society as well?"

"Perhaps you've misunderstood me. The majority of our homicides take place among alcoholic men. If we could get to the point that violent situations didn't arise among them, the number of murderers would decrease. As a matter of fact, the model that I presented earlier came to me when I was thinking about this specific group of convicted individuals. Now, it's the role of the judge to ensure equal protection for everyone under the law. But whenever a crime takes place, society has failed."

"So no one needs to take responsibility for themselves? Society will take care of everyone's problems?"

"Yes, it would be to everyone's advantage. There wouldn't be criminals or victims of crimes. Of course I understand that we also have the mentally ill, but they belong in mental hospitals. For professional criminals, we would of course still need the heavy machinery at society's disposal, but not as extensively as we use it today."

"So we'll basically turn these people into aquarium fish," Römpötti said.

"We need to think about how we want to use our money. Parking enforcement is being privatized at a rapid rate. Why couldn't traffic enforcement also be privatized? Do we need to train police officers for two years so they learn how to read vehicle speeds from a radar? I don't think so. A private company would do it more efficiently, saving the police resources for more serious problems."

To Joutsamo, Fredberg's proposals seemed dangerous. As a judge, the guy obviously had experience in criminal cases, so what he was saying couldn't be considered complete hogwash. But privatizing traffic enforcement? Joutsamo's thoughts were interrupted by the sound of her desk phone ringing. The judge and the reporter kept talking as Joutsamo answered.

"Helsinki Police Department, Anna Joutsamo."

"Hi, this is Mauri Tiainen, attorney at law."

"Hello," Joutsamo said. She couldn't immediately place the name, but it did ring a bell. Before the attorney could continue, Joutsamo remembered. Tiainen had been Repo's district court representation.

"Yes, I don't think we've met, but I represented Repo, this escaped convict, in district court."

"I know," Joutsamo rapidly responded. The guy sounded like he was about fifty, even if the agitation in his voice made it difficult to judge.

"So why wasn't I informed?" the attorney demanded.

Joutsamo was stunned. "About what?"

"The escape, of course."

"Umm...and why would we have informed you about that?"

"Because that was what was agreed with the Riihimäki Police. Wasn't it in your records?"

"You're speaking with the Helsinki Police Department. We don't know anything about any such arrangement."

"Goddammit!" Tiainen snapped. "That's just wonderful!"

Joutsamo lightened her voice a touch. "It's unfortunate that the arrangement wasn't communicated to us, but why should the police have informed you about this incident?"

"Because he vowed to kill me."

"Timo Repo?"

"Of course. After the murder conviction in district court, he was really upset and said he'd kill me the first chance he got. From my perspective, that chance is now."

"Hasn't it been eight years since then?"

"That guy's so nuts he definitely won't forget. In the early years of his incarceration, he sent me repeated letters about his threat. I took them to the Riihimäki Police, but they just said they couldn't do anything about it, because Repo was already doing life. A life sentence isn't going to get any longer because of a few death threats."

"Why would he want to kill his own lawyer?"

"Well," Tiainen squirmed. "His wife's homicide was a completely unambiguous case, but Repo didn't remember anything about it because he was so drunk. I suggested to him that he confess, and we'd try to get it lowered to manslaughter. In that case, Repo might have gotten a six-year sentence, maybe. But the district court viewed it as murder and slapped Repo with life. That sent him over the edge."

"Okay," Joutsamo replied.

"Then the Court of Appeals upheld the murder conviction, so in that sense no injustice took place at district court."

"But he was upset with you for advising him..."

Tiainen interrupted. "Upset is putting it mildly, but you've got the picture."

"So he didn't want to confess?"

"Hard to say. Repo was pretty messed up back then. He didn't know what to do, and I thought it was the smartest decision in that situation. There was no reason to contest the case. He would have been convicted regardless."

"So it was a clear case?"

"Absolutely clear-cut," Tiainen said. "I've handled about thirty homicides over my career and in this instance there was no uncertainty about the perpetrator. The only open issue was that Repo didn't remember anything about the act."

"Why did Repo kill his wife?"

"Agh, I don't remember. Or as far as I remember there was no reason. Maybe they had an argument," the lawyer guessed. "Which is exactly why I'm going to take a weeklong vacation somewhere! Preferably abroad."

"Do you have any idea where he might be?" Joutsamo asked quickly.

"Haven't the foggiest."

"You don't know or remember who he was hanging out with back then?"

"Not a clue. He was being held as a suspect at the Riihimäki jail, and that's where we met. We didn't discuss friends, and hopefully we don't have any mutual ones."

"Well, just so you know, according to our information, Repo settled down after a couple of years, and neither the guards nor the other prisoners had heard about any vendettas."

"Well, why did he escape then?" Tiainen asked.

"We don't know."

"Exactly. That's not going to get me to cancel my vacation plans," the lawyer huffed.

Joutsamo asked Tiainen to be in touch if Repo tried to contact him, and he promised he would. The call ended right as Kohonen walked into the room.

"I think I'm going to head out. These thirteen-hour days are killing me."

"Go ahead. I was also thinking I'd leave pretty soon, as soon as I get a chance to talk to the lieutenant on duty about Repo."

Kohonen put on her blue parka. "Did you notice the report in the system? A car was stolen in Töölö in a pretty unusual way."

"Nope. How?"

"Someone broke into a locker at the swimming pool and took the keys from the coat pocket. The car disappeared from in front of the pool, but the wallet was left untouched in the locker."

"My first instinct is insurance fraud. The owner's behind on the payments and had to get rid of his wheels."

"I don't know, but it's a new approach, anyway."

Joutsamo thought for a moment. Of course the MO would fit Repo. He was not an expert at stealing cars, so it would be easier to take the key than to look for a car without an ignition block and try to hotwire it. "When did this happen?"

"I don't remember exactly, this afternoon or evening."

Joutsamo nodded. Probably wasn't Repo, but if it was, he already had an hours-long head start. Plus, the car's license plate and description had already been sent out to all units, so Joutsamo didn't need to take any action. Of course tomorrow she could ask the responding patrol if they had gone to the swimming pool and retrieved a surveillance camera image of the thief.

"Hey," Joutsamo said to Kohonen. "You wanna go grab a drink at the Hotel Pasila bar?"

"I thought you were never going to ask. As long as we don't talk shop or get pony-faced."

Joutsamo's curiosity was piqued. "Pony-faced?"

"Well, right after I had turned eighteen, I was at the disco with a bunch of my friends from the stables. We had been there drinking all night, and then I noticed this really familiar-looking person standing in front of me. I tried to walk around her, and bam!—I slammed into the mirror face first and shattered it to bits," Kohonen grinned.

"Okay," Joutsamo laughed. "No getting pony-faced. I want to get your views on this old murder conviction of Repo's."

Takamäki drove his Toyota station wagon into the small, empty, tree-ringed parking lot in the Helsinki suburb of Espoo. There were no houses nearby, but several dumpsters of various colors stood in the clearing. Not everyone had bothered to throw their trash inside; some lay on the ground, too.

The thermometer read 35° F, and the sleet had eased off. Takamäki turned off the engine. He hadn't been able to sleep; the Sello surveillance camera images had been eating at him. He had to see if he could find the car based on the address.

Takamäki turned on the Toyota's dome light and examined the images of Jonas's accident in the weak glow. He made a note of the point of contact between the gray car and the bicycle, in front of the front left tire.

Takamäki climbed out of the car and locked it. Other than the sounds of his car locks clicking, Tuomarila was completely quiet.

Takamäki looked around again. Tahko Lane began across the street from the parking lot. He crossed the street and started climbing up the dirt road.

Tuomarila was a residential area located between downtown Espoo and Finland's wealthiest municipality, Kauniainen. Takamäki remembered having come to look at an apartment here years ago, but his family had ended up a few miles closer to Helsinki, in the Espoo neighborhood of Leppävaara.

According to the address info, Manner, who had the lease on the car that hit Jonas, lived on Tahko Lane. The online maps showed his house as being located just below the crest of the hill. The neighborhood was a mix of single family houses and townhouses. Takamäki assumed that Manner lived in a single family house, because the address didn't include any letters or apartment numbers.

At its foot, the slope rose steeply. Takamäki remembered the area as having been much more forested and sparsely populated, but it had since been built up into a townhouse slum. Takamäki grunted as he passed a posh brick complex that sloped back along the contours of the terrain. Okay, so maybe the neighborhood wasn't a total ghetto after all.

After a hundred yards, the grade eased off. Good jogging terrain, Takamäki thought. Over in Leppävaara they didn't have such long, steep climbs.

The address Takamäki was looking for gleamed from a cube-shaped lamp on the corner of a brick-red garage. The brick house had two stories and three big windows on the street side—they were dark. The streetlamp in front of the house illuminated the front yard, which consisted of the driveway and a handful of bushes. The acre-sized backyard looked like it was undeveloped and forested.

Takamäki continued past the house as if he were a local resident coming home on the late bus. He noted a blue BMW in the garage. Takamäki was disappointed, but a few more steps revealed another car on the far side of the beemer: a gray Toyota. The street light wasn't strong enough to illuminate the license plate.

Takamäki's pulse quickened. He walked far enough past the house that he couldn't be seen from the windows and glanced back once more. There was no one around. Takamäki slipped into the woods. He crouched down and listened for a moment. He was out of breath, but it wasn't the climb that had winded the habitual jogger.

Still crouching, Takamäki carefully edged past a large spruce. He saw the Toyota between the trees, about ten yards ahead. It was parked nose first in the garage, and Takamäki was to its right. He'd have to circle between the brick house and the garage in order to get a look at the left side.

Enough street light made it through the branches that Takamäki didn't have to move in total darkness. He stopped for half a minute to listen. Silence. The garage was open from three sides, and firewood had been stacked along the back wall. Takamäki crept closer, keeping low. A branch cracked under his foot, and he stopped. He smiled at himself, because there was no way anyone could have heard it. There weren't any security guards around.

He was now about five yards from the car. Luckily, the house had only one small window in the side facing the garage. Takamäki guessed it was a ventilation window for either a bathroom or a storage room.

Takamäki rose back up to a hunch and started rounding the garage to get to the car. A spruce branch scratched his cheek. He brushed the back of his hand against his face and noticed a drop of blood.

The brush reached right up to the edge of the garage. He was only a couple of yards from the car, but he'd have to get over to the left side. Touching the vehicle would be a bad idea, since it was a late enough model that it probably had some sort of alarm. Takamäki continued around behind the garage. The gravel crunched under his shoes. He glanced into the backyard. It looked open, but he couldn't make out the details in the dark.

Takamäki made it to the rear edge of the garage and warily glanced in. Still silent. The car was within arm's reach, but there was so little light that Takamäki couldn't tell whether or not there was a dent in it. He pulled out a flashlight and his cell phone. He opened up his camera app and gingerly stepped forward.

A powerful light burst on, momentarily blinding Takamäki. He expected some sort of alarm, but none came. The light was attached to the wall of the house at a height of seven feet. If it had an alarm, it was a silent one. Takamäki guessed it was equipped with a motion sensor, but the light was so bright he couldn't tell.

He put his flashlight back in his pocket and took two steps closer to the car. The light made photographing the car easier.

He could hear a dog bark inside, and based on the sound, the pooch was a big one.

Goddammit, Takamäki thought. He quickly bent down toward the car and saw a dent and scratches near the front tire. Some of the blue paint from Jonas's bike had even been left behind on the body.

Takamäki snapped two pictures with his cell phone. Then he heard the door open around the corner, in the front yard.

"Caesar, what is it?" said a man's voice. The dog barked a couple of times.

Takamäki made a rapid retreat behind the garage. For a moment, he considered stepping forward. In all likelihood, the guy was guilty of reckless endangerment, causing bodily harm, and fleeing from the scene of an accident. And the victim had been Takamäki's child. He had verified the facts he had set out to verify. But maybe the real reason was that he wanted to ask the guy why he hadn't stopped to help the victim.

Maybe the guy needed a lecture about taking responsibility.

Or maybe what he really needed was to get his butt kicked.

"Is it the foxes again?" Takamäki heard him say, and the dog barked a final time.

Takamäki cautiously backed up along the edge of the garage and behind the big spruce. Maybe this wasn't the right moment for a conversation.

"Caesar, quiet! I don't have time for this. Now go to sleep," the man growled and closed the door.

Takamäki's heart was pounding, and he stood still for a few minutes before backing deeper into the forest.

He stayed in the trees until he made it back to the quiet dirt road. He decided to take the longer route to return to his car, so he wouldn't have to walk past the house.

Maybe he should leave these gigs to Suhonen from here on out, Takamäki thought.

\* \* \*

The Hurriganes' "Get On" was playing in the bar, but not as loud as Suhonen thought the seventies rock classic deserved to be. A tip he'd heard in a Kontula bar had brought the undercover detective to this dive in the run-down Puotila shopping center in eastern Helsinki. He had no problem hearing the conversation at the next table.

"Hey, did you hear about that guy in the Skulls?" said a rat-faced guy with a buzzed head and an Arsenal tracksuit. He took a long swig of his beer before continuing. "He had to play Russian roulette to be able to get out of the club."

His audience of one had a green sweater, a thick walrus moustache, and hair that fell down into his eyes. Suhonen also noted his large hands. Suhonen guessed his age was somewhere in the vicinity of forty to fifty, about ten years older than his buddy in the Arsenal tracksuit.

"And he had shitty luck. The dude pulled the Nagant's trigger, and of course he died. The rest of the Skulls got out of there, and the cops chalked it up as a suicide."

"There wasn't anything about it in the papers," said Moustache Man.

"'Course not, because the cops said it was suicide. They don't report cause-of-death investigations to the press," replied Arsenal Fan.

Suhonen could have stepped in and informed them that the story was a crock of shit. He had heard it three weeks ago and had, of course, checked all the suicides among known motorcycle gang members and hang-arounds for the past six months. There hadn't been a single one. Numerous suicides had been committed with handguns in general, but nothing indicated that the story was true. Suhonen was more inclined to believe that the gang had started spreading the tale themselves purely to reinforce their reputation.

"Those Skulls are totally nuts. You don't want to stick your nose too far into their business."

"Heard anything from Foppa lately?" asked Arsenal Fan.

"Visited him a couple of weeks ago."

"What about his old lady?"

Moustache Man grunted. "You should know..."

"I should know what?"

"How she's doing. You're over there all the time. Everyone knows that…"

Arsenal Fan went quiet. "Does Foppa know, too? I'm kinda tripping about that."

"I didn't tell him, and we didn't really talk about her anyway."

"Okay, good," the buddy replied, taking a swig of his beer.

Suhonen was drinking a Coke and considering his next move. The mention of Foppa's name gave him an opening. Suhonen made his decision quickly and rose with his glass. His odds were low, but sitting at the bar was starting to get old… There had been no sign of Saarnikangas. His dark mood suited his role.

"Hey, guys," he said without smiling, and sat down at their table. Arsenal Fan and Moustache Man looked at the intruder without saying a word.

"You were talking about Foppa. I know him."

Neither one said anything until Moustache Man figured it was best to announce, "So do I."

"Good," Suhonen said. "That's what it sounded like a second ago."

"Were you eavesdropping?"

"No," Suhonen replied, his voice clearly softer. "You guys were talking loud enough for half the bar to hear. Not smart."

Moustache Man eyed Suhonen intently. "Where do you know Foppa from?"

"Did time in the same block."

"Which one?"

Suhonen felt the urge to smile, but it didn't suit his role. Moustache Man had tossed out a control question.

"East block, third floor."

"What were you in for?" Arsenal Fan asked, a little shyly. Suhonen figured he was wondering whether the stranger had heard the story about him taking care of the wife.

"Occupational mishap. Two years, two months for aggravated assault. Got caught on a surveillance camera I didn't know about."

Arsenal Fan and Moustache Man nodded sympathetically, but clearly a little uncertainly.

"Who are you looking for?" Moustache Man asked.

"How so?" Suhonen's tone was so coy that the other two could tell he was definitely looking for someone.

"An enforcer like you in a neighborhood pub. Drinking a Coke. You think we're stupid?"

"I don't think you're stupid. And this Coke is warm. Suikkanen," Suhonen said. His motivation was clear: by introducing himself first, he brought himself to the same level as his drinking buddies.

"Suikkanen." Moustache Man savored the name. "Never heard."

Suhonen flashed a cold smile. "You're not supposed to have."

"Yugi," Arsenal Fan said, extending a hand.

Moustache Man eyed his buddy coldly, and Yugi pulled his hand back. Moustache Man introduced himself: "Eki."

"Nice to meet you," Suhonen said, giving another smile.

"I'm going to ask repeat the question, if you don't mind," Eki continued. "Who are you looking for? Who's in trouble?"

Suhonen stroked his chin. "No one would be in trouble if everyone just paid their debts."

Arsenal Yugi and Moustache Eki were silent. Both were pleased that neither had any debts to speak of. The enforcer in the leather jacket seemed like a bad guy, one you didn't want to spend a whole lot of time around.

"Juha Saarnikangas."

"Juha?" Yugi let slip. Eki gave his friend an evil look. Now there was no point denying it, even if they wanted to.

"They said in Kontula he might be here."

"How much does he owe?" Eki asked.

Suhonen shrugged. "It's none of my business."

"What is your business?"

"Finding him."

"And then what?" Eki asked.

"Now, that's none of your business."

"Why would someone send a torpedo like you after some small-time junkie? That's a pretty stacked deck."

"You want to join in?" Suhonen asked, looking intently at Eki. "Would it be more even then?"

"I'm not too fond of your tone."

"You don't have to be."

Yugi had taken a swig of his beer and now managed to get a word in. "I don't give a shit about the guy. He stole a wallet from some twelve-year-old kid in Tallinn Square once, goddammit. I was having a drink and happened to see it. It was completely out of control, and I ran the clown down. When I brought the wallet back to the kid, who was bawling his head off, the cops were there, and I had a hell of a time explaining what happened. Luckily they believed the kid that I wasn't the one who took it. In the end they even thanked me."

Suhonen nodded. "Touching story. But where can I find him?"

Yugi continued, "He was here about three hours ago, but he shot up in the john, and the bouncer threw him out. Got banned from here for a month, for a change. I think he's crawled back to some hole for the night. I doubt he'll be out again."

"What hole?"

"I don't know. He's got some bitch here somewhere nearby, but he's always hanging around the Itäkeskus Mall parking lot in the morning, checking to see if someone left their car door unlocked and their stuff inside. That's where I'd look for him if I had to."

"And would you?"

"I won't," Moustache Man said quickly.

Suhonen ignored Eki's response. "A C-note if you tell me where to find him."

"I don't have to do anything else?"

"All I need is to know where I can find him."

Eki tried to curb his buddy's enthusiasm. "Think for a second about what you're getting mixed up in."

"I'm not getting mixed up in anything except helping someone give the idiot what he deserves."

"You're drunk," Eki said, standing up. "Sorry, I'm not interested in this conversation anymore."

Suhonen gave Moustache Man a hard look as he rose.

"No worries. I already forgot," Eki said, heading in the direction of the bar.

"Good," Suhonen growled, writing down the number for his off-the-record line on a scrap of paper he found in his pocket. The prepaid phone couldn't be traced back to the police.

\* \* \*

Joutsamo saw a knife. Not some gleaming dagger; just a rusty old all-purpose Mora. She realized she was in an empty, windowless room. A lone light bulb dangled from the ceiling. A second knife fell from somewhere, and then a third. Soon the floor was covered in knives. They reached up to her ankles, her knees. Joutsamo wanted to run, but she couldn't move.

She woke up in a sweat. She had kicked off her blanket and was sprawled in bed in her T-shirt and underpants. She looked at the red lights on her clock radio: 3:32 a.m.

She lay there for a moment, breathing. The windows of her one-bedroom Töölö apartment gave onto the large interior courtyard. The curtains were drawn, but yellow light from the yard gleamed in through the gap.

Her nightmares had returned. Joutsamo wasn't able to predict when they came, and it made going to bed unpleasant. Violence had been stored to her mental hard drive. At times Joutsamo wondered whether she should go back to Narcotics or transfer to other duties. But something about violent crimes fascinated her. Maybe it was that evil was so unpredictable. People committed senseless acts for such trivial reasons. Joutsamo had always been interested in the motives behind a crime, especially if one was never found.

Joutsamo rubbed the sleep from her eyes and her thoughts cleared. There was a direct cause for her nightmare—the Repo case.

Kohonen and Joutsamo had sat for a couple of hours in the half-empty bar at the Hotel Pasila, sipped three ciders apiece, and talked about the old Repo murder case without reaching any conclusions. Something about it bothered her, and Joutsamo couldn't put her finger on it. But now she couldn't sleep.

She got up and walked into her kitchenette without turning on the lights. She wet her hands under the faucet and splashed water onto her face in the dark. It refreshed her, even though she had only intended on rinsing away the clammy sweat. She grabbed the electric kettle, ran some water into it, and put it on to boil. She found a mug in the cupboard and picked out a teabag from the package next to the kettle.

Joutsamo sat down at her two-person table. There was a laptop at the other spot and old newspapers on the chair. The three-foot-wide window had a view of the neighboring building, now dark. It had about a hundred windows, and only two of them had lights on. Everything looked so peaceful.

Suddenly Joutsamo realized what had been bothering her about the Repo case. It was a question to which there had been no answer. Joutsamo was irritated that the problem was so elementary—she should have seen it right away at the Riihimäki police station while she was reviewing the reports.

The wife had been lying in the kitchen with her throat slit, and Repo had been passed out in the bedroom. So who had called the police? The preliminary investigation reports didn't contain the answer.

# WEDNESDAY MORNING

Takamäki walked down the VCU corridor toward his office. He yawned and thought that the whole building could use a thorough renovation. Sure, police stations were supposed to be uninviting, but not this cold.

Joutsamo recognized the rhythm of his gait and stepped out of the team room to greet him.

"We need to talk," she said. "Now."

"Good morning to you, too," Takamäki replied, continuing past her toward his office. Joutsamo fell in behind him. "We catch our escaped convict yet?" he asked, without looking back.

"No," Joutsamo answered.

Takamäki made it to his office door. "Any hot tips?"

Joutsamo followed her boss. She was carrying a stack of papers. "Nope."

Takamäki hung his overcoat on a hanger next to the door. A dress shirt, tie, and sport coat for impromptu appearances hung on another. Takamäki was wearing the blue Norwegian fisherman's sweater his wife had given him the Christmas before last. He sat down at his desk. Joutsamo was still standing in the doorway.

"Well?" Takamäki gestured for his sergeant to sit.

"Let's start from the tip."

"So we have something?" Takamäki said, reaching down to turn on his computer.

"Well, sort of. A car was stolen from the Töölö swimming pool yesterday evening."

157

"A car was stolen from the pool?" he looked up at Joutsamo.

Joutsamo grunted. "The keys from the locker and the car from outside. An intriguing method, and Kohonen went over this morning to get the surveillance camera image." She handed the print to Takamäki. "Take a look at the clothes."

Takamäki examined the image shot at the pool cashier. The camera was at the ceiling, and the brim of an old-fashioned cap shaded the man's lowered face. His clothing, on the other hand, was clearly visible in the color photo. He was wearing a gray trench coat, and a dark suit was discernible underneath. He was carrying a plastic bag. Takamäki nodded. "That's our man. At least possibly."

"This guy entered the building right after the man whose keys were stolen and exited more or less immediately. The lock had been broken."

"What else did he take?"

"Nothing. Just the car key. According to the victim, the car key had been on the same ring as his other keys, but they were still intact."

Takamäki took another look at the surveillance camera image.

"So he wanted a car. Are there any other cameras on Topelius Street? Did he know this man, or why that specific car?"

"Doesn't appear to have any connection. The victim doesn't have a criminal background, just your average joe."

The computer demanded a user ID and password from Takamäki; he complied.

"Two conclusions that would point toward it possibly being Repo. One: he doesn't know how to steal a car.

Two: he doesn't have friends who'd steal one for him. So he's on his own."

Joutsamo nodded. "That's what I was thinking, too."

"Why the Töölö pool? Is it the best place in terms of where he's staying now, or just somewhere he's been before? Somehow it seems an MO like that would demand a familiar milieu, at least familiar enough that he had used the lockers at some point and realized that it would be possible to pull off there."

"Hmm," Joutsamo said. "I don't know. Those locks aren't exactly theft-proof at any pool."

Takamäki handed the photo back. "In any case, we're a good twelve hours behind. Car hasn't been found?"

"No. Of course an APB was sent out immediately, but no reports yet. Too bad that the victim's phone was in his coat pocket, not the glove compartment. It would've been easy to position it."

Joutsamo was right. A car theft was grand larceny, and they had reason to suspect Repo. Now they could use more stringent measures, like wiretapping, if they only had a potential target to apply them to.

Takamäki kept thinking out loud: "But he's in Töölö? If you draw a one-mile radius around that pool, it contains tens of thousands of residents."

"Not one of whom seems to know Repo," Joutsamo added.

"Why would he want a car?" Takamäki said.

Joutsamo shrugged. "Had to move. Is it possible he had some hideaway somewhere nearby where he holed up right after the escape for twenty-four hours? And now he had to get moving."

"In any case, he might be anywhere now. The car indicates a longer trip."

"Exactly. The Border Guard has been alerted about the car, but let's see what we can do here in town."

"If he's driving out of the country, I'd guess he'd head north and cross over into Sweden. Did he ever work there? Does he have any other connections to Sweden?"

Joutsamo shook her head. "No foreign contacts have come up, Finnish ones either. We don't know. This is one nasty manhunt."

"We've definitely had some easier ones," Takamäki admitted, opening up his email.

"Kulta and I dropped by his father's neighbor's place, and something's going on there. We'll probably swing by again today," Joutsamo said.

"Heard anything from Suhonen yet?

"Sleeping. He sent a text message that he was out chasing Saarnikangas down all night, but no luck. Promised to come in this afternoon."

"Okay," Takamäki said.

Joutsamo tossed the day's *Iltalehti* onto Takamäki's desk. "Which takes us to item number two, which is also the number of the page where you'll find the article—in addition to the front page, of course."

The lieutenant looked at the front page. The lead headline was about some TV celebrity's drunken shenanigans. He didn't recognize the name, but he was sure that his wife and sons would. Takamäki wasn't interested unless the guy committed a violent crime or ended up the victim of one. According to the headline, all he was guilty of was being a sloppy drunk. At the bottom of the page, in clearly smaller print, it read "Murderer Escapes." The lieutenant turned the page and was blasted by huge letters stretching across the spread: "SWAT Team Hunts Down Dangerous Convict."

In the main photo, armed and helmeted men were entering a building. It was a six-column shot—Takamäki realized that he now owed Turunen a beer. There was a balloon across the photo: "*Iltalehti* along for the raid." Takamäki briefly scanned the article, but it didn't offer any new information. A shorter piece featured a photo of Takamäki and a few of his comments. The set also included Mary J. Juvonen's commentary, where she criticized the prison authorities for their laxness. The police took a beating as well, for not immediately releasing the news about the fugitive's escape and holding back Timo Repo's photo.

"What about the other papers?"

"Blurbs, single column."

"Well, this'll give them a jolt to join in our manhunt," Takamäki said. At that moment, his phone rang; it was a blocked number. Takamäki glanced at Joutsamo before growling hello.

"Römpötti here, hi."

"Hi," Takamäki answered. He knew the TV reporter well. "Look, I'm in kind of a rush right now."

"This won't take much time," Römpötti replied, clearly annoyed. "Next time you invite reporters and photographers along on your raids, can you give me a call, too?"

"That's not exactly how it went," Takamäki said defensively. "But we can talk about that later."

"So Repo's still on the lam?"

"Yep," Takamäki replied. The call ended with Sanna Römpötti promising to call back.

Takamäki lowered his phone to the desk. "And now the other reporters think we've been giving *Iltalehti* preferential treatment."

"Oh, shit," Joutsamo said.

"I'm betting Skoog can handle this *Iltalehti* case for us. I think he'd actually enjoy it. Knowing our deputy chief, he'd probably initiate a criminal investigation into Juvonen's actions."

Joutsamo laughed. "Resisting police authority? That's pretty nasty, but I don't have a problem with it. On to item number three."

"How many of these are there?"

"This is the last one."

"Well?"

Joutsamo briefly considered how to formulate her words. "There's something strange about that Repo murder case."

Takamäki looked his best investigator in the eye. "Tell me."

"I can also write you a memo, but last night I realized what's been bothering me about it the most."

"Is that why you have those bags under your eyes?" Takamäki asked.

"You've got some pretty nice ones yourself. And where'd you get that scratch on your cheek?"

"All right, continue," Takamäki replied, before the conversation got off on the wrong track.

"I read the reports, but nowhere does it say how Repo's wife's murder came to the police's attention. All that was written in the reports was that a patrol went to the scene."

"It could have been some neighbor, couldn't it?"

"A neighbor would have called the police if the sounds of arguing or other noise would have been heard coming from the apartment. But no one heard anything or reported anything of the sort."

"So in your view, a third person was at the scene who left and anonymously called it in to the police. And this third person has never been found."

"Everyone considered the case so clear cut that no one was interested in the third person, or just to be safe, let's say the potential third person."

"That also sounds like an issue we might want to take upstairs to Skoog."

"You think we should dig a little deeper?"

Takamäki nodded. "I trust your instincts here. When you have time, write up a memo about the investigation reports and the verdict, and we'll talk about how to proceed from there. Was there anything new in the night-shift reports?"

Joutsamo shook her head and stood. "Some residential B&Es, assault and battery at a grill, petty theft at a grocery store, and about twenty pounds of dynamite went missing from a residential construction site. Nothing out of the ordinary."

Takamäki nodded and Joutsamo exited. Thefts of explosives didn't happen every day, but they were by no means unheard of. Evidently construction crews stole them from each other. This conclusion was based on the fact that the stolen explosives were rarely recovered.

After Joutsamo left, Takamäki thought for a second. He picked up his phone and took another look at the two photos he had shot the previous night in Tuomarila. He pulled the Sello surveillance camera images out of his desk drawer. Neither shot was particularly high quality, but it was the same car. The license plate alone confirmed that.

Takamäki had talked with Jonas that morning. His son remembered the car having been green, but he'd been confused about other details, too. According to Jonas, he had been in a hurry to get home because he was supposed to go to hockey practice. The only problem was, Jonas's team didn't practice on Mondays. He didn't remember the trip to the hospital at all. The doctor had ordered him to stay home from school at least until the end of the week.

Takamäki lifted the receiver of his desk phone and tapped in Lauri Solberg's number. The Espoo investigator answered right away. Takamäki asked if he'd have time for Takamäki to bring the photos by today. That suited Solberg. Takamäki also told him that his son didn't remember the events clearly. Solberg still wanted to talk to the boy, and Jonas would have to bring the medical reports along to the interview, but they could agree on a day later.

"By the way," Solberg said. "I don't want to talk about those surveillance camera images over the phone, but just out of curiosity, is the vehicle a Toyota?"

"Yeah."

Solberg read off a license plate number that stunned Takamäki into silence.

"Yeah, that's a match," Takamäki muttered.

"That Toyota burned last night in the parking lot at the Espoo ice arena."

"Burned?" Takamäki wondered.

"Yup," Solberg said smugly, pleased to have caught the lieutenant off guard.

"What time?"

"Why?" Solberg asked, but continued nevertheless. "The fire department got the alarm at 5:53 a.m. Someone in the neighborhood called it in. Of course we were in contact with the lease holder. An Espoo resident by the name of Tomi Manner, who said he noticed the car had been stolen when he came home late last night from a business trip. Says he would have reported it missing this morning."

"Interesting," Takamäki managed to say, before asking a question to which he already knew the answer. "Who owns the car?"

"An Espoo leasing company."

The first thought to pop into Takamäki's head was that Manner had torched the car so he couldn't be traced to the hit-and-run, but on the other hand, since Jonas hadn't been badly injured, it wouldn't have gotten him more than a fine. Then again, Manner didn't necessarily know about the extent of the boy's injuries. The next thought was insurance fraud. Something bizarre was definitely going on with the car, especially since he had seen it last night at Manner's place with his own eyes. But he wasn't about to tell Solberg that. At least not yet.

"Hello," Solberg said. "You still there?"

"Yeah."

"Well, this could be insurance fraud or something related to your son's hit-and-run, so I sent Forensics out to check his house in Tuomarila. Manner's story might not be a total crock, because preliminary information indicates that someone other than Manner had been moving around in the vicinity of the garage where the vehicle was parked."

Takamäki reflexively wiped his cheek with the scratch on it. He wondered whether he had smeared blood somewhere or left fingerprints behind. What about footprints? He had been wearing Nike running shoes, thousands of pairs of which had probably been sold in Finland. He didn't have anything to hide, but still he decided to not say anything to the Espoo police officer. "Okay, I'll call you this afternoon to set up a time to bring those photos over."

"Sure. And, oh yeah," Solberg added. "Nice shot of you in *Iltalehti*."

Takamäki ended the call, and his phone immediately rang again. It was Deputy Chief Skoog, ordering Takamäki and Suhonen to attend a noon meeting. Evidently the topic was important, but Skoog didn't want to discuss it over the phone. What would Homicide be getting lectured about this time?

* * *

Joutsamo stepped into the office of Detective Lieutenant Leinonen at the Riihimäki Police Department. The big-bellied sixty-year-old was sitting at his computer again, and his brown sport coat hung from the back of the chair, just like during Joutsamo's previous visit. He was also wearing a white shirt again, too. Maybe it was even the same one, because Joutsamo caught a pungent whiff of sweat.

"Well, what is it this time?" Leinonen growled. Joutsamo had called in advance to announce her visit. Before Joutsamo could get a word out, the gray-haired lieutenant continued, "Haven't found him yet, huh?"

"No," Joutsamo smiled. "We're trying hard."

Leinonen laughed. "I'm sure you are. I read about the raid in *Iltalehti*. Do you guys down in Helsinki have to use the papers to handle all of your work?"

Joutsamo was on the verge of giving a snappy response, but changed her mind. There was no point escalating the tension. She just stood there in the doorway, since Leinonen hadn't asked her to sit. "Listen, one question did come to mind."

"What's that?"

"Who informed the police that Repo's wife, Arja, had been killed?"

"Huh?" Leinonen rumbled. "I can't remember, and I don't have time for this shit."

"You didn't seem to have time for it during the investigation either," Joutsamo continued. "Tell me, how did the police know to enter the apartment?"

Leinonen didn't respond immediately. "What exactly is it you're getting at?"

"Think about it. According to the preliminary investigation reports, none of the neighbors heard any sounds of arguing or fighting. The police go in and find the wife dead and Timo Repo passed out on his bed. Neither one of them called the police, that's for sure. So who did?"

"Well, someone definitely did."

"I agree," Joutsamo said. "So it didn't occur to you guys to figure out who that might be?"

"Hell, how would we have figured that out? Besides, it was a cut-and-dried case."

Joutsamo spoke in a needlessly sardonic tone: "All cases are cut-and-dried if that's the way they're investigated."

"Aha, so now you're exporting your Helsinki BS out here to the provinces. You guys are worse than those arrogant *besserwissers* at the NBI. Don't you go trying anything now, missy."

"I'm not trying anything, I'm just asking."

Leinonen turned back to his computer. "Well, the answer is that it's been eight years since that woman's murder, and I don't remember. Believe it or not, we actually have more recent cases to work on."

Jackass, thought Joutsamo. Actually more than that, a stupid jackass, because he wasn't capable of admitting to himself that he was a jackass. "One more thing."

"Oh, you're still there. I was hoping you had disappeared."

"Tell it to your fairy godmother."

Leinonen responded with a mocking smile. "So what else did you need, missy?"

Joutsamo felt like smiling back, because whenever men started calling her "missy" she knew she had won.

It was a sign that they couldn't come up with any rational justifications.

"I need your signature on this."

"What is it?"

"We need Timo Repo's DNA, and it presumably exists in the forensic evidence. According to the report, the evidence includes at least Arja Repo's shirt and trousers, the knife, and Timo Repo's blood-stained shirt."

Leinonen laughed arrogantly. "You're wasting your time, missy. It's been eight years. It's probably been destroyed."

"No, it hasn't." Joutsamo said calmly. She brought the paper over to Leinonen's desk. "I called your evidence clerk. The box is still there on the shelf."

"It is?" Leinonen sounded genuinely surprised. "Well, if you want those old rags and the knife, you can have them. I guess there's probably still the kid's stuffed animal, too. There was also some blood on that."

Leinonen scratched his name on the document indicating transfer of the forensic evidence to the Helsinki Police Department. Joutsamo thanked him and left.

She was slightly—only very slightly, when it came down to it—ashamed of the fact that she had been forced to lie to the lieutenant. A DNA sample had already been taken from Repo in prison in early 2007, when new legislation had enabled samples to be taken from all felons. Presumably Arja Repo's blood and maybe Timo Repo's blood would turn up in the evidence, but would it also contain DNA from some third party?

## CHAPTER 13
## WEDNESDAY, 9:50 A.M.
## MALMI, NORTHERN HELSINKI

Repo was lying on the couch, staring up at the ceiling. In prison, that had mean either ugly concrete or the bottom of an upper bunk. In Karppi's home, the ceiling was made of wood that still showed the grain and the knots, although the material had darkened over the years.

Repo had returned to the house in the middle of the night and tried to enter as silently as possible with the keys he had borrowed from Karppi's coat pocket. He had slept for three hours, but then his thoughts had infiltrated his dreams.

Time went by slowly lying on the sofa, but it had gone by slowly in his cell, too.

Repo heard the front door open. He could feel a current of air. Repo waited for the door to squeak or creak, but it opened silently.

The escaped convict wondered if he should turn his head or just keep staring at the ceiling. What difference did it make? None, presumably. Repo had left the stolen car a couple of hundred yards from the house. He knew he'd need it again. A large shoulder bag was on the floor at his feet.

Someone had entered. The footsteps were light, so the intruder wasn't a police officer. Repo heard the old man's voice.

"Where have you been?"

Repo closed his eyes for three seconds and sat up on the sofa. "I went out for a couple of beers."

"Don't lie to me!"

"Lie or not, it's none of your business."

"As long as you're staying here, it is."

"You won't have to worry about that for long," Repo said. His exhaustion had taken the form of physical pain, and he had to lie back down.

"Where were you?" the old man insisted.

Repo didn't answer.

"The police were here looking for you," Karppi continued.

"Here?"

"Your dad's house and here, too. Asked if I had seen you."

Repo was now sitting up again. "Well, had you?"

Karppi shook his head. "No. Not yet."

"Not yet?"

"Not yet."

Repo stood, because there was no way he was going to get any sleep now, thanks to the ornery old man. And he wouldn't have anyway. Maybe he'd better make some coffee.

Karppi moved over so he was standing in front of Repo, blocking him from going into the kitchen.

"I was thinking I'd make some coffee."

The men stood there, face to face.

"Listen here. I've helped you because your father wanted me to. He asked me in the hospital, on his deathbed, to help you if you came here. Well, I've done that."

Repo looked at Karppi. "He asked you to do that?"

Karppi nodded.

"Thanks for the help, then."

"He also told me some other things."

"I need coffee," Repo growled, gently thrusting the

old man out of his path. The escapee continued toward the kitchen.

The infuriated Karppi raised his voice and circled around in front of Repo: "You will not push me around in my house!"

"Take it easy," Repo said, passing the other man without touching him.

Karppi huffed, but took a couple of steps backwards. Repo turned and ran water from the tap into the coffee pot. Two, three cups would do it. The coffee was in the cupboard, and Repo eyeballed roughly the right amount as he poured it into the filter.

Repo turned and noticed that Karppi was crouching down at the end of the couch, where he had left his shoulder bag. Repo marched into the living room. Karppi rose. The couch stood between them.

Karppi looked Repo in the eye. "What is it you're planning on doing?"

"I'll say it one more time: it's none of your business."

"Where'd you get that?" Karppi asked, glancing into the shoulder bag. "Tell me."

"Found it in town," Repo said. He started circling the couch from the right.

Karppi took a couple of steps left. Even though he leaned against the couch as he moved, his voice remained forceful. "Timo! You're doing something I don't want to be a part of; as a matter of fact, I don't even want to know about it."

"So stop asking then," Repo said from the foot of the sofa. Now he was closer to the bag.

"I'm asking for your own sake. You're planning on doing something evil."

"In prison, you have time to think about all kinds of things," Repo said, taking a step toward the old man, who was now standing about ten feet away.

"I think we need to call this game off right now," Karppi said, picking up his cordless phone from the table. "I'm going to call the police and tell them what's going on before you can do anything irreversible with that."

"Life is irreversible," Repo said, lunging at Karppi.

"Stop!" cried the old man. "Wait."

Repo stepped closer and Karppi stepped back. Karppi looked at his phone and typed in 000 before he realized that the emergency number had changed; it was now 112 everywhere in Europe.

Karppi raised his hand from the phone just as Repo came within arm's reach. His right hand grabbed for the phone.

"You're not calling anyone."

"Stop! Listen!" Karppi, terrified, stepped backwards. Repo's palm smacked the old man's shoulder hard. Karppi lost his balance and fell. He tried to break his fall with his hand, but his head cracked against the corner of the oak dining table.

A voice came from the phone: "112, what is your emergency?"

Karppi felt a blackness filling his head. He could see the ceiling, and the pain gradually faded. He tried to talk, but was incapable of making a sound. He heard a rattling in his breath, and then the blackness ended too.

What Repo saw was an old man sprawled on the floor with a bleeding head. Karppi's mouth was agape, but he was silent.

The woman's voice repeated: "112, what is your emergency?"

Repo raised the phone from the floor, "Sorry, it was a mistake."

He gazed at the old man from a distance of a couple of yards. The pool of blood slowly began to grow.

"Sir, is there an emergency?"

"Everything's fine," Repo said. "My kid was just playing with the phone. Sorry," he managed to say.

"All right, sir." The operator ended the call.

Repo bent over and felt Karppi's throat for a pulse. There wasn't one. Goddammit, he swore. He stood and rubbed his face. Why did this have to happen? He hadn't intended for things to go this way. He hadn't wanted to kill Karppi. Repo wanted to shout that it had been an accident. This wasn't supposed to happen!

He tried to calm himself, but he couldn't. He looked into the dead man's gaping eyes. Why did Karppi have to try to resist him? It didn't make any sense. Why had he come to the old man's house in the first place? You should never mix others up in your business, but that's exactly what he had done.

Repo couldn't stand looking at the body, so he went and took a sheet from the old man's bed. The fugitive spread it across the corpse. A corner of the sheet was immediately soaked in blood.

Repo stepped back over to the couch and sat. He was tired, but he wondered whether the woman at emergency response believed him. Did she think everything was all right, or were an ambulance and the cops already on their way? Repo picked up his bag from the floor and pulled out the Luger. He was exhausted, but he couldn't stay here.

God-fucking-dammit. What just happened? And why? Why did things always have to turn out this way?

## CHAPTER 14
## WEDNESDAY, 10:20 A.M.
## KALLIO NEIGHBORHOOD, HELSINKI

Suhonen was at home in his one-bedroom Kallio apartment, lying in bed in his underwear. He wasn't asleep, but he didn't have the energy to get up either. He had made it home around four, and Raija had left at seven without saying a word. Suhonen had tried to give her a kiss, but she had just walked out.

I could get up in a bit and make some coffee, Suhonen thought. Or maybe he'd wait until the noon meeting that Takamäki had sent him the text message about. Suhonen ruminated about breakfast, but couldn't decide: cold cereal, granola, hot cereal, sandwich? Maybe he wasn't hungry yet; he had dropped by a 24-hour deli around three and chowed down a double-sausage meat pie.

Suhonen rubbed his face-stubble. His hair felt greasy, too. He needed a shower.

His phone rang. Suhonen could tell it was his off-the-record phone and rushed into the entryway to dig it out of his jacket pocket. The phone displayed the caller's number, but Suhonen didn't recognize it.

"Yeah," Suhonen answered.

"Is that Suikkanen?"

"Yeah," Suhonen said. He was standing in front of the mirror and could see all his scars. He turned his back to the mirror.

"Hey, man," answered a male voice. "We met at the bar yesterday. Yugi."

Suhonen remembered Arsenal Fan. "Yeah, what do you want?"

"You promised me a C-note for that clown Saarnikangas."

"Where is he?"

"Right here in my kitchen. I found him at Itäkeskus Mall this morning and brought him here. Tied him to a chair."

Fuck, thought Suhonen.

Yugi continued, "He says he doesn't have any money. I can take care of him for you for five grand. No one will ever hear from him again."

"No!" Suhonen said emphatically. "I need to talk to him."

"Can I take care of him afterwards?"

Suhonen felt like being the man from Del Monte and saying *yes*. Because the world would doubtless be a better place if Saarnikangas weren't in it and Yugi were behind bars, but unfortunately that wasn't an option. "Where do you live?"

"Eastern Helsinki," Yugi said and gave Suhonen the address.

"I'll be there in fifteen minutes. Don't touch him."

Yugi's voice sounded disappointed. "Okay. He's in pretty bad shape, though. Shivering and whining, says he needs a fix."

Suhonen ended the call and swore. He went into the bathroom and took a zip-lock bag from the medicine cabinet that contained several packs of drugs. He dug out three packs, wrapped a rubber band around them, and put them in the inside pocket of his leather jacket.

He had to keep Saarnikangas coherent. He retrieved an ancient light blue Nokia cell phone from his nightstand drawer and inserted a prepaid SIM card into it.

* * *

Ten minutes later, Suhonen parked his car on Manor Road. The building's balconies protruded from its brown stucco wall in the style of the '60s. It was only three stories tall, but it had several entrances. Suhonen mused that in the US such buildings had been built upwards, while in Finland they had grown horizontally.

He got out of the car and walked to the door leading to Yugi's stairwell. He pressed the buzzer, and a few seconds later the lock clicked.

Suhonen took the elevator up to Yugi's floor and checked on the landing to make sure that his Glock was within easy reach. Suhonen didn't actually think he needed the weapon; the gesture was primarily directed at Yugi, just in case he was watching through the peephole.

Suhonen pressed the doorbell and the door popped open.

"Hey," Yugi said. There was a victorious smile on his face and a touch of fear in his voice.

Suhonen handed over two fifties to Yugi, who was still wearing the same Arsenal tracksuit. "Where is he?"

"In the kitchen."

"You lead the way."

Yugi led. The apartment was grim, with hardly any furniture. On the way, Suhonen glanced into the bedroom, where there was only a mattress, no bed. The living room was the exception, containing a sofa, a thirty-two-inch flat-screen TV, DVD player, Xbox 360 console, and three piles of movies and games on the floor.

Yugi hadn't lied; Saarnikangas was sitting at the kitchen table, with his hands tied to the chair behind his back. Suhonen had seen the mug shot taken of Juha during his last trip to the clink, but he probably wouldn't have recognized this crater-faced skeleton from it. His cheeks were hollow and his brown hair matted. He was wearing a brown T-shirt so splotchy that Suhonen wondered if it had originally been white.

"Here," Yugi announced.

"Good. Untie him."

Yugi was visibly disappointed. No doubt he wanted to watch Suikkanen rough up the poor junkie. He unknotted the laundry line. Saarnikangas tried to say something, but couldn't get form the words.

"Did he have a coat?" Suhonen asked.

"Yeah," Yugi said, stepping over to the balcony door. "I had to put it outside, because it smelled so fucking bad."

He retrieved the coat and handed it over to the quivering druggie.

"I hope you get what you deserve."

"All right, let's move," Suhonen said, pushing Saarnikangas in front of him. Despite the brief airing, the army jacket reeked like a disgusting blend of dirt, dog shit, and puke.

In under a minute, Suhonen and Saarnikangas were out of the apartment. Yugi came to the door. "Hey, Suikkanen, don't you think I deserve some thanks?"

Suhonen pressed the elevator button and gave Yugi a cold stare.

"One. Never say my name in the presence of the target. Two. You already got your money."

Suhonen opened the elevator door and shoved Saarnikangas in. Luckily he was able to stand, so Suhonen didn't have to carry him. The junkie leaned against the brown wall as the elevator shuddered downwards to the floor. Suhonen dug a white tablet out of his pocket, peeled off the plastic, and handed it to

Saarnikangas. The junkie gave the man in the leather jacket a questioning look.

"Subu," Suhonen said.

Saarnikangas snapped the pill in two. He put half under his tongue and slipped the other half into the pocket of his jeans. Suhonen was sure he would shoot it. Subutex-brand buprenorphine had taken a firm foothold in the Helsinki drug market as the fighting in Afghanistan was cutting into heroin production. In France a Subu pill cost two euros; in Helsinki, twenty.

Suhonen quickly escorted Saarnikangas to the passenger seat of his car. Suhonen got in behind the wheel and headed out. He opened both front windows a good couple of inches so the worst of the stench would dissipate. The car clock read 11:09 a.m.

By the time they hit the Itäkeskus Mall on the Eastern Expressway, Saarnikangas had found his tongue.

"Who are you?"

"Does it matter?"

"What's up with all this? That Arsenal retard kept talking on and on about some debt."

"Forget the debt."

"But there's gotta be some reason for all this."

Suhonen pushed it up to fifty-five, passing a red Volvo with a ski rack. Traffic was heavy. "I need your help."

Saarnikangas didn't respond, he just looked at Suhonen. "He said your name was Suikkanen."

Suhonen eyed the gaunt junkie. The trembling had stopped.

"Look, Suikkanen, are you a cop?"

"How so?"

"No real gangster that looks like you would give a rat's ass about a speed freak like me. They would've let that Arsenal spaz take care of me. You're not from the

AIDS support center either, and I've never seen you at the needle exchanges, so that doesn't leave many alternatives."

Suhonen thought for a second. "I'm not a cop. Cops don't give junkies drugs," he said with a smile.

"There's a first time for everything. At least for me." Saarnikangas grinned. Suhonen wished the guy would have kept his mouth shut. A few teeth were missing, and the ones he had were in bad shape. "What do you want?"

"I'm looking for a friend of yours."

"Do I have any friends?"

"From what I've heard, you know this guy."

"Who?"

"Timo Repo."

Saarnikangas furrowed his skinny brow. "Repo? That sap who wrapped a pretty necklace around his wife's throat? He's still in the hole."

"Not any more."

"He skipped out?"

Suhonen nodded. "A couple of days ago."

They passed the Kulosaari metro station on the right.

"So where's this taxi headed?"

"You get to decide. If you promise to help me, I'll take you wherever you want, but if you don't I'll take you straight to police headquarters. You've got a big stack of unpaid fines on the books, and society needs you in jail to make good on them."

"So Repo escaped," Saarnikangas said.

"Does that surprise you?"

"A little. He was basically a nothing. Losers always stick together, and that goes for the joint, too. That's why we used to talk. Okay, so he's bitter, but I always thought he'd tough it out. If you've already done eight years of a life sentence, it doesn't make any sense to cut out."

"Why did he take off?"

"He had a chip on his shoulder a hell of a lot bigger than Lance Armstrong's, but he didn't really talk about it in recent years. You could sense a stifled rage in him. See, I'm a good judge of people. And sensing what they want."

Once they hit the end of the Eastern Expressway, Suhonen turned into the lane leading to Teollisuus Street. Police headquarters was more or less just down the road.

"Well, then you probably know what I want."

"Repo back in the pen."

"Right. You are good," Suhonen said. "So what's it gonna be? You decided where we're headed?"

"One more question. What do I get?"

"A pack of Subu," Suhonen said. That was seven tablets.

Saarnikangas tried to bargain: "Two."

"This isn't an auction. So, police headquarters it is."

Suhonen drove under the Sture Street bridge, and the smell of the coffee factory reminded him that he hadn't had his morning coffee yet.

"Okay, Okay. One's good," Saarnikangas said. "But I need a phone. Mine's...at the pawnshop."

Sure, thought Suhonen. Pawnshops didn't take phones. Suhonen dug the old Nokia 6110 out of his pocket and handed it to the junkie.

"What the hell is this? No one uses these anymore."

"That's why I happen to have an extra one," Suhonen replied. At one point he had bought a few from Salmela precisely for situations like this. "Do you have your own SIM card? Because there's a new one in there."

"What good is that going to do me?" Saarnikangas said, taking the phone's back cover off. He dug his old SIM card out of his inside pocket of his jacket and switched it into the phone. But somehow Suhonen's SIM card still disappeared into his pocket.

"So the deal is simple. If Repo calls you, you set up a meeting with him and you tell us. After that, you get..."

Saarnikangas shook his head. "No way. I'll get a rep as a snitch. I'll find out where he is and tell you. You guys grab him in a way that I don't get burned."

"That'll work," Suhonen said. The car was stopped at a red light at the end of Teollisuus Street. The Pasila rail yard was in front of them, and beyond it the forbidding office blocks of West Pasila.

"Where am I going to drop you?"

"How about the Neste station?"

"Done."

"But you gotta buy me a coffee. I don't have any cash. That Arsenal idiot grabbed me when I was collecting empties at Itäkeskus Mall. It's a pretty tight race out there every day, you know. The fastest one gets all the dough."

Suhonen pulled out a twenty and handed it to Saarnikangas. "Okay, I'll get your coffee."

"And a sandwich? I'm starving."

"I'm pretty sure that'll get you a sandwich, too," Suhonen chuckled, turning toward the service station.

"All right," said stony-faced Deputy Police Chief Skoog, glancing at his watch. About twenty detectives were sitting in the biggest conference room at Helsinki police headquarters. The room had windows giving onto Pasila Street, but the blinds were lowered and the curtains were drawn. It was right next to the canteen, and the smell of almond-baked fish was wafting in.

Takamäki and Suhonen were sitting side by side near the windows. On Takamäki's right sat Captain Karila, the brawny head of the VCU, and on Suhonen's left sat Lieutenant Ariel Kafka. Takamäki knew everyone: the head of Narcotics and three of his most experienced team members, a slate of Intelligence officers, and the higher-ups from Financial Crimes.

Takamäki's conclusion was clear: this time they wouldn't be discussing the seemingly endless launch of Skoog's intelligence-driven leadership model. Something bigger was in the works. Skoog's style rubbed folks different ways, but under his leadership the productivity of the Helsinki Police Department had risen noticeably.

Next to gruff Deputy Chief Skoog sat Jaakko Nykänen, who had recently risen to head of intelligence at the National Bureau of Investigation. Takamäki knew him well; he was one of Takamäki's former detectives. The detective with the Burt Reynolds moustache had taken a bullet in the neck during a Homicide shoot-out but had survived. He had been left with a hoarse voice as a memento of the incident. Nykänen had later signed up for lieutenant courses and ended up at the National Bureau of Investigation after a stint at Espoo Narcotics. Thanks to his recent appointment, he had been promoted to captain and had risen past Takamäki in the chain of command.

"Most of you probably know Nykänen from the NBI," Skoog drily noted, "so I'll turn the floor over to him. There is one thing I'd like to say, however. This meeting has been called because occasional overlaps have occurred, and we're trying to avoid such messes. In addition, we're starting a new model of cross-unit cooperation," Skoog said, before nodding in Nykänen's direction. "The floor is yours."

"All right," Nykänen began in his raspy voice. "This morning I talked to Espoo's Narcotics, Financial Crime, and Violent Crime detectives about this, and this afternoon I'm headed east to Vantaa. The issue is this."

Takamäki waited for PowerPoint slides emblazoned with the NBI logo or a handout, but Nykänen didn't have either.

"This is fresh stuff, but it's heavy. So let's see if we can get cooperation to work on a broader basis. For more than two months now, we've had a tap in this one narcotics case that leads all the way to the Netherlands. It's a normal hash case, and it's not the reason for this meeting."

Everyone listened silently. The Financial Crimes men had pen and paper in front of them.

"The target we've been tapping is one Jorma Raitio from Järvenpää. The name is probably familiar to at least some of you."

There was nodding, mostly among the Narcotics and Intelligence men. Takamäki had heard of the guy, too.

Just to be sure, Nykänen continued explaining Raitio's background. "Raitio is more muscle than the brains of the organization. Has had several years' worth of convictions for violent crimes and narcotics offenses. He's the link to this hash case, which is why we were tapping him. Four days ago, he received the call that's the reason for this meeting. A man, who at that point was still unknown to us called him and asked him to pick up a case of beer from the corner store."

The cops chuckled.

"Well, of course we applied for a warrant to tap this unknown number too, and in couple of days it turned out that there were three beer runs in the works. We don't know exactly what jobs are being planned here, but evidently three different groups are involved. We suspect that the caller is the coordinator of three simultaneous jobs in the greater Helsinki area. Raitio's the only name we are sure of, though."

"We have any information on the jobs?" asked the head of Narcotics.

"No. We're betting robberies. Might be jewelry stores, banks, or maybe an armored car, but I'm pretty sure the grocery stores are safe."

This sparked off another round of laughter.

"So our intent is to paralyze the entire group in the near future," Nykänen said. "We're seeking enough evidence to take them all down. We want convictions. At the same time, we want to prevent any criminal activity from occurring."

Takamäki thought Nykänen's language was needlessly militaristic, but that was the price of the War on Crime. Skoog looked pleased.

"Three simultaneous gigs," Karila thought out loud. "That's going to cause some serious chaos among the police forces throughout greater Helsinki."

"That's right," Nykänen said. "We wouldn't normally bother you with such lightweight intel, but there's something else. The man suspected of being the main coordinator is an Espoo resident by the name of Tomi Manner."

Takamäki's eyes almost popped out of his head. He was glad that no coffee had been served, because he definitely would have spilled it in his lap. Manner? The guy who ran over his son? Goddammit.

Nykänen continued, "Manner owns a small private security company, and of course we've researched his customers. The problem is that Manner used to be a mid-level manager at a national security company, which has several banks and jewelry stores as clients. Manner doesn't have a criminal record, just a few traffic infractions."

"So what does the NBI want from us?" asked the Narcotics chief, in his frank style.

"Nothing more than cooperation, actually. Let us know if you have any ongoing cases involving Manner. If you hear about any beer runs, let us know. The intention, of course, is to coordinate the case through the NBI, so we can prevent the robberies. Does the name Manner say anything to anyone?"

Takamäki thought for a second and decided not to mention the hit-and-run, but the car theft reported to the Espoo police was a matter of public record. He raised a finger.

"Kari," Nykänen said, and everyone turned to look at Takamäki.

"This morning there was a car theft reported to the Espoo Police, and this Manner is the victim. According to the report, his Toyota was stolen from his house last night."

Skoog cleared his throat. "Takamäki, what does this have to do with Helsinki VCU work?"

"It doesn't. Nykänen asked whether the name Manner said anything to anyone, and that's basically what it said to me."

Skoog's gaze was piercing. He'd had problems with Takamäki before, too.

Takamäki's boss decided it was time for him to intervene. "Takamäki's team has been tracking escaped murderer Timo Repo, so of course they've been monitoring car thefts."

"As we saw in the papers," laughed the Narcotics chief, and everyone joined in.

Now it was Takamäki's turn to give his boss a cold stare. He didn't need anyone defending him.

"Okay," Nykänen said. "I'm going to pass my cards around, just in case anyone doesn't have my mobile number. Call whenever."

As the rest of the group filed out, Takamäki walked up to Nykänen. "You have time to come over to the old unit for a cup of coffee?"

Nykänen glanced at his watch. "I'm in kind of a rush, actually. I've got to get to Vantaa."

"Jaakko, coffee, now," Takamäki ordered, as if Nykänen were still working in his unit. "I just have one thing I need to tell Skoog first."

Takamäki explained the *Iltalehti* incident to the Deputy Chief, who promised to take it upstairs for further action. Nykänen overheard the conversation, and he struggled to keep a straight face. Not that Nykänen approved of what the reporter had done. It was more the gravity with which Skoog approached the matter that made him smile. Skoog was receptive to Takamäki's idea of confiscating the reporter's phone as a warning.

Skoog inquired about the Repo manhunt, and Takamäki said they were doing everything they could. Takamäki didn't bring up Joutsamo's suspicions regarding the man's potential innocence. This was neither the time nor the place.

Then Takamäki grabbed Nykänen, and they headed down the corridors toward the VCU's premises.

"Jaakko," Takamäki said, stopping in the hall between closed doors. "I know you're in a rush, so I won't force coffee on you."

Nykänen looked relieved, because he was supposed to be at Vantaa PD in forty-five minutes, giving the same presentation for the third time that day.

Takamäki took out his cell phone and fiddled with it for a second. He pulled up one of the photos he had taken the previous night. Takamäki handed the device to Nykänen, who saw the dented front corner of a Toyota.

"What's this?"

"Manner's car."

"The one that burned?"

"Yup," Takamäki said.

Nykänen looked at Takamäki. "Who took this photo?"

Takamäki sighed. "I did."

"When?"

"Last night in Tuomarila."

Nykänen looked at Takamäki, eyes wide. "Okay, I'm not in a hurry anymore. Goddammit! Suddenly I feel like I could use a cup of coffee after all."

\* \* \*

Ten minutes later, Nykänen and Takamäki were sitting in Takamäki's office, hot cups of cop coffee in front of them.

"Why don't you start at the beginning?" Nykänen said.

Takamäki told him about Jonas's hit-and-run, the Sello surveillance camera images, the indifferent attitude of the Espoo police, his nocturnal verification trip into the wilds of Tuomarila, and his intention of dropping by Manner's and lecturing him about the morality of hit-and-runs.

"I'll be damned." Nykänen sighed heavily. "We've been racking our brains trying to think of how we could get a tap in that house and you just waltz in there in the middle of the night like some horny teenager."

"You guys should probably make sure that Caesar isn't home."

"Who's Caesar?"

"Manner's dog. I don't know what breed, but based on the bark, I'd say it's not too small."

Nykänen wrote down the dog's name. "Good to know. But the hit-and-run at Sello?"

"That's exactly what I was thinking during the meeting."

"Sello has plenty of banks and jewelry stores," Nykänen reflected.

"And armored cars drop by to pick up cash from the supermarkets and other businesses. But that's just a guess," Takamäki said.

"How does the car arson fit into the picture, then?"

"That's a bit of a mystery. Manner had told the Espoo Police a story about a business trip that he didn't return from until last night. We don't know if it's true or not. But it is possible that one of his colleagues had scoped out the escape route in Manner's Toyota and he didn't hear about the hit-and-run until his return. It'd be a good way to cover up his tracks."

"But why draw the police's attention if there's a big gig coming up?"

"An alibi for the car and for Manner?" Takamäki suggested. "If they've been staking out other targets in that car, then they can say that it's been missing for a couple of days. Because if three big jobs went down at the same time, it wouldn't take us long to start looking for connections from the targets' surveillance cameras."

"And had he reported it stolen earlier, he would've run the risk the whole time of the car being pulled over by the cops. Now they were able to scout out the fastest escape routes," Nykänen mused. "With jobs like that, the most important thing is to get the haul out of the getaway car as fast as possible."

"Who was driving it? Now that's an interesting question," Takamäki said, taking a sip of his coffee. He pulled out the Sello surveillance camera images from his drawer and showed them to Nykänen.

"Yeah, well, I can't make anything out from that, but it's probably Manner or one of his lieutenants."

"There's one more problem."

"What?" Nykänen shot back.

"A guy named Lauri Solberg over in Espoo is investigating this hit-and-run of Jonas's, and evidently this car theft of Manner's, too."

Nykänen looked thoughtful. "Solberg? Never came across him during my narc days."

"I think he's pretty new, but he knows I have these Sello photos."

"How'd come you're the one who ended up with those anyway, not the investigator from Espoo?" Nykänen asked.

"I went and picked them up from the Sello surveillance room. Espoo hadn't thought of that."

"Of course not." Nykänen was smiling, but he also rubbed his forehead. "Under no circumstances do we want this Solberg to start digging into Manner's car's movements around Sello, because Sello is now the first, and, for the time being, only potential target we know about. If Solberg lets Manner know that we're aware of his car's movements there, they'll drop the target immediately."

"Right," Takamäki said.

"We'll set up stakeout teams at Sello right away, and it'd probably be best for me to get in touch with either Solberg or his boss, and have them drop their investigation of that hit-and-run pronto. If necessary, we could have all cases involving Manner transferred to the NBI for investigation."

"Right," Takamäki repeated.

"Sorry. I wouldn't like it either if there wasn't even an attempt to find out who was driving a car that hit my kid, but I'm sure you understand."

Takamäki laughed. "Of course I understand, but hopefully I don't have to explain it to my wife. Because she'd ask what the police's priorities are: property that's covered by insurance, or physical injuries sustained by a human being? In any case, I'll leave it in your hands."

\* \* \*

The sleet had started coming down again. It was colder now, and the flakes formed a layer of slush on the asphalt. Repo was walking along Malmi Curve toward the Kirkonkylä Road bridge that spanned the train tracks. He glanced backwards again, but the only person there was the woman pushing a dark blue baby carriage who had been there ten seconds before.

Apartment buildings rose to his right, and the train tracks ran to his left. Repo had wondered what to do. He couldn't stay in Karppi's house. The old man's death was an accident, but of course no one would believe him. No one had listened to him the first time, either.

He had left Karppi's house and left the car on the street there. Maybe that was a mistake, but he wouldn't go back now.

Repo knew that he was innocent of his wife's murder. Understanding that had taken him a couple of years. There's no way he would have been able to slit Arja's throat.

On the other hand, he was sure that he wouldn't have been capable of killing Karppi either, but it had still happened. Repo cursed the old man. Why did he have to go sticking his nose into Repo's business? Everything had been set, but now it was all a huge mess again.

Repo switched the bag over to his other shoulder and glanced backwards once more. Pain and exhaustion. Of course he had gotten used to it, but before he could go on, he had to get some sleep to clear his head. There was a headline about an escaped murderer on the front page of today's *Iltalehti*. Maybe his photo was in there too, so Repo didn't dare to buy the paper.

A few hours' sleep in some quiet spot and then the final preparations. After that he'd be ready. Where? Train, hotel, bus... Repo tried to come up with a quiet place, but couldn't think of anything suitable. Repo arrived at the intersection and noticed an ad for the Eurokangas fabric shop on the light post.

Eurokangas? That had been Juha's nickname in the joint. He didn't know anyone else who could help him. Maybe Saarnikangas—that was the guy's real name— had a place where he could get a little sleep. Convicts were supposed to be loyal to their friends; that's what Repo had understood.

He had taken Karppi's cell phone and money, which of course made him a robber-murderer, but that didn't matter now. Repo pulled out a small notebook from the breast pocket of his black suit and flipped to "Eurokangas."

\* \* \*

Takamäki was having lunch in the canteen at police HQ. Beef soup was in his bowl, milk filled his glass. Suhonen was sitting at the same table. Takamäki had tried to ask him about his relationship with Raija, but no dice. The undercover detective evidently didn't feel like talking about it—he had just grunted something that the lieutenant hadn't been able to make out.

It was coming up on one o'clock already, and there was plenty of room in the canteen. A few patrol officers in uniform walked in and over to the counter.

Takamäki's phone rang, and he saw that the caller was Joutsamo. "I'm eating, but tell me," he answered.

"Some of us have time for lunch, huh?" Joutsamo said.

"Well?"

"I dropped by Karppi's place on the way back from Riihimäki. Thought I'd just ask him a few questions."

"And?" Takamäki stopped eating. He glanced at Suhonen, who began listening. "Did Karppi say anything?"

"No. And he never will."

"Dead?" Takamäki said.

"Killed, I'd say. I went in, and he was lying there in the living room. There was a major fracture at the back of his skull."

"Dead, back of his head bashed in," Takamäki repeated for Suhonen's benefit. "Classic blunt object?"

"Or corner of a table. I didn't stay to investigate, so I wouldn't contaminate the scene any more than I already had."

"But Karppi hadn't slipped?"

"It's possible, of course, but in that case I'd be interested in knowing who covered the body with a sheet."

"Okay, Okay," Takamäki said. That was cause to suspect homicide, and the covering of the body indicated that the perpetrator knew the victim. "When?"

"Looked fresh. I felt his diaphragm, which already exhibited signs of rigor mortis. I'd guess an hour, two at most."

"Any signs of Repo?"

"Can't say. I checked the body and got out of there. I called in a patrol unit and thought I'd check out the vicinity. Of course I also called into the Emergency Ops Center, so the search is already on, but could you get Forensics over here? Vallesman Road," Joutsamo said, followed by the precise address.

Takamäki promised to call Kannas. The manhunt for escaped convict Timo Repo would turn into a high-profile case the moment the media caught whiff of Repo's being implicated in Karppi's death.

Suhonen heard the whole story, since Takamäki called Kannas next and explained what had happened.

"Pretty bad," Suhonen said, once the call ended. He had finished his lunch. Takamäki's soup had cooled in the bowl.

"Yeah. Changes things."

"Did Repo want to get back at Karppi for something? He was his dad's neighbor. Could there have been some schism between them?" Suhonen reflected. "Money? Some old grudge?"

Takamäki thought Suhonen was asking the right questions. "Let's not jump to any conclusions. Let's see what Forensics turns up. We're not even certain that Repo has been inside Karppi's house."

"Wanna bet?" Suhonen asked.

"No," the lieutenant replied. "I want to eat my cold soup."

Takamäki managed to take two spoonfuls before his phone rang again. Suhonen smiled.

It was Solberg from the Espoo Police.

"Can you talk?" Solberg asked, like he normally did.

"Eating lunch," Takamäki replied in a tired voice.

"Then I can probably bother you for a second," Solberg said aggressively.

Takamäki disagreed, but he still answered, "Well?"

"Those surveillance camera images—when are you going to get them to me, and why the hell can't you just email them?"

Goddammit, Takamäki thought. How was he going to explain this one?

"What's the status of the forensic investigation of that car and the house?"

There was a momentary silence at the other end.

"How about you let me ask the questions. This is a crime being investigated by the Espoo Police, and you're in possession of evidence we need. No doubt you've acquired those images lawfully, so it would be best if you'd deliver them here before we need to turn this into a bigger deal than it is."

Takamäki tried to calm him. "Listen, Solberg. Don't forget to breathe."

"Are you fucking with me? If you want, I'll get a warrant from my lieutenant, and we'll come over to

Pasila right this second."

"Take it easy. You might not be grasping the whole picture here."

"I'm grasping it perfectly goddamn well. There's something sketchy about this Manner case, and I'm going to get to the bottom of it."

Takamäki strongly doubted Solberg's ability to do so, especially since he wasn't going to be allowed to get involved. He tried to think of a way to calm the guy down. He glanced at Suhonen, who was pretending to concentrate on his coffee but was listening to every word.

Takamäki came up with a solution that would at least buy him some time. "I'll bring the photos in an hour, if nothing acute comes up in the manhunt."

"I'm glad you're coming to your senses," Solberg said victoriously. "I'll wait."

Takamäki didn't bother telling him he'd be waiting for a long time; he just hung up. Then he looked at Suhonen, who gestured at the coffee cup in front of Takamäki.

"That's still hot," Suhonen smirked.

Takamäki tasted his lukewarm soup and decided to leave the rest.

"That was that guy from Espoo I was telling Nykänen about."

Suhonen nodded. "Somehow I figured."

"The guy's incorrigible. Hell, how can I explain something to him that I'm not allowed to talk about? He'll probably suspect some conspiracy if he's told to drop the case."

"I know the type," Suhonen said, still smiling.

Takamäki gave his grinning subordinate a questioning look.

"He's just like you," Suhonen said.

Takamäki was stunned. "But when I..."

Suhonen laughed out loud.

"Goddammit," Takamäki said, joining in the laughter.

"But Suhonen, remember that we have an escaped convict on the loose who we have cause to suspect of another homicide."

Suhonen couldn't stop laughing. "And a few beer thieves to find, too. It's not easy being a criminal investigator. I should probably transfer to the Auto Theft unit."

\* \* \*

The forensic investigators were wearing white paper overalls. There had been no need to discuss tactics, because Joutsamo had pronounced Karppi dead. Kannas had ordered a slow approach, which meant that the body would be examined last.

The scene had been photographed starting from the door, and afterwards the investigators had started combing the floor inch by inch. Joutsamo's footprints had been taken too, so they could later be distinguished from those of any potential suspects. Kannas knew that Joutsamo's DNA sample was already in the database, so it would also be possible to look it up later. Joutsamo had said that she had only touched the door, the sheet covering the deceased, and the deceased himself.

Kannas had seen hundreds of old people's houses like this, usually in cause-of-death investigations where no crime was involved. In those instances, the investigation was significantly easier. The police showed up and did a superficial examination of the scene. The house was only investigated more thoroughly if the medical examiner decided there was any ambiguity involved.

A couple of younger investigators were combing the floor. Kannas' knees were in such bad shape that he left the floor work to others. He dusted powder on the door and looked for prints. When he found them, he used tape to transfer the print to paper. Then he documented the precise location where he found each print.

Many death scenes smelled atrocious, with papers, garbage, bottles, and moldy food piled up to the investigators' ankles in addition to the decomposing body. This was different: very tidy, even if the decor was heavily indicative of the fifties. The family had probably been established and the furniture bought back then. Old people weren't big on change.

Kannas moved inside after finishing the door, once the techs crawling along the floor had moved onward. The area around the light switch was usually good. This time was no exception. The problem here appeared to be that the majority of prints that he had found so far resembled each other. In all likelihood they were from the deceased. Of course he couldn't say for sure yet, because even the dead had ten fingers, with a different print on each one.

The techs put the strands of hair and other items they found into zip-lock bags and documented the exact spot where each had been discovered.

This is going to take hours, Kannas thought. But there was no rush. Least of all for the deceased, who was the customer in this case. Kannas liked doing the dead one last service. If someone had taken another person's life, the living should do everything in their power to figure out who the killer was.

The techs had split up. The one on the left circled around toward the living room while the other one continued on toward the body. They should probably take a break soon. Working on all fours was hard on the knees and the back. If anyone knew that, Kannas did. The tech who was closer to the body had about ten more feet to go.

If there was evidence of the killer in the house, Forensics would find it. That had been clear from the start. Tying their findings to suspects was Takamäki's team's job.

## CHAPTER 16
## WEDNESDAY, 4:57 P.M.
## HELSINKI POLICE HEADQUARTERS, PASILA

The meeting had been set for five. Kannas had promised preliminary results by then. Suhonen entered the conference room, where Takamäki, Joutsamo, and Kohonen, the pull-up champ, were already waiting.

"Wow, you're on time," Kohonen said.

Suhonen grinned and made some remark about showing up late usually paying off, because meetings normally began with pointless chit-chat. He joined the others around the gray table-top.

"Didn't find him out in Malmi?" Suhonen asked.

Joutsamo shook her head.

"That Riihimäki thing," Joutsamo began, giving a Takamäki a glance. "We can probably talk about that for a second before we begin the meeting proper."

Takamäki was amenable to the suggestion.

Joutsamo gave the background. "So about that case where Repo got life. Something about it just doesn't click. The entire investigation aimed solely at Repo being the only possible perpetrator. And I think there's something really wrong there."

"Brief explanation," Takamäki said.

Joutsamo raised her thumb. "One. The act was extremely cruel. Repo's wife's throat was slit from the front in such a way that the killer saw her face."

A forefinger rose up next to Joutsamo's thumb. "Two. None of the neighbors heard any fighting to speak of that night."

Middle finger. "Three. They weren't troubled alcoholics, who had gone off the deep end; it was a family with a young child where both of the parents had jobs."

Ring finger. "I've read all of the preliminary investigation reports and court verdicts, but nowhere is there a mention of a possible motive."

Joutsamo's pinky rose last of all. "And on top of all that, you take into account that the police were informed of the homicide by some external party while the woman was lying dead in the kitchen and the husband in all likelihood passed out in bed. The call didn't come from the apartment. In other words, something stinks here. And I'd say pretty bad." Joutsamo's gaze circled her colleagues, seeking support, but no one responded immediately. "Well, at a minimum. it wasn't a clear-cut case like that asinine lieutenant in Riihimäki claimed."

Kohonen glanced at Takamäki before jumping in. "I agree. There's something weird about the case. It doesn't add up."

Suhonen shrugged. "Of course you're more familiar with the paperwork, but the truth is that the motive in those domestic violence cases can be incredibly minor. Something the other person said or did two months earlier that's been eating at the killer. Then when they get enough liquor in them and they're not thinking so straight, it just happens."

Joutsamo looked at Suhonen. "But who called the police?"

"What time did it happen?" Suhonen asked, continuing without waiting for an answer: "Where did the wife work? Was she supposed to be somewhere at some time, and someone who knew her called the police?"

Joutsamo laughed. "That's pretty..."

Suhonen interrupted her. "If you're fixated on that innocence theory, that's just as bad as the Riihimäki police being stuck on the guilt theory, but you have to understand that this thing isn't based solely on the police investigation. Both the district court and the appeals court found the guy guilty of murder."

Kulta came in. "Sorry, couldn't get off the phone."

Takamäki rubbed his face. Discord was the last thing he needed in his team.

"I think Anna's approach in that old case is something we should definitely follow up on, but only once Repo is back in prison."

"Okay, I'll write up a memo," Joutsamo said, but didn't bother to add that she had already sent the evidence she had got from the Riihimäki police station in for DNA analysis. The question she had posed to the lab was simple: whose DNA was on it?

"Karppi's death makes the hunt for Repo top priority," Takamäki continued. "Karila promised us more resources, as long as we figure out where we need them and can use them. The number one question is, do we have definite proof that Repo has been in Karppi's home?"

All eyes turned toward Joutsamo. "I don't know."

Big, burly Kannas appeared at the door. "Hey," he said with a smile. "Definite proof of what?"

Takamäki looked at his old patrol partner. "Glad you could make it."

"What do we need definite proof of?" Kannas repeated.

Before Joutsamo could say anything, Takamäki continued. "A simple question: has Repo been inside Karppi's home?"

"A simple answer to a simple question: yes."

"Can you elaborate?"

"But...I only give simple answers to simple questions," Kannas said.

Takamäki tried to smile, but it was forced. "Could you give us a little more information—explain in a little greater detail?"

"Fingerprints?"

"Yes," Takamäki said, in a tone of feigned friendliness.

Kannas sighed. "Of course. A fingerprint is a unique identifier made up of patterns formed on the skin of an individual's finger. They have been utilized in criminal investigations since the 1890s. The first fingerprint..."

"Not now," Takamäki interrupted with a smile. "Not now. Just give us the information."

Kannas glanced at the others and realized that it might be best to get down to business.

"All right. Let's fast-forward 120 years into Karppi's house. Timo Repo's fingerprints were found there in several locations. We can't tell when he was there or for how long, but he was definitely there. Prints were found on the dining room and kitchen tables, the couch's wooden backrest, the coffee maker, and in the bathroom. Based on this, we can deduce that he wasn't there just for a quick visit. And yes... Those prints can't be eight years old, because the house has been cleaned regularly. And, it's not likely that Karppi had sworn off coffee for that long, either."

"What can you tell us about the body?"

The mood seemed somehow tense, so Kannas decided to stick to the facts.

"The body is at the medical examiner's office, so they will provide more detailed analyses, but it was lying next to the dining table, and there was blood and hair on the corner of the table. A naked-eye estimate: I'd say the gray color of the hair matches the hair on Karppi's head."

"So he hit his head on the table." Takamäki said. It was more of a statement than a question.

"Yes, it's pretty rare for a table to hit someone in the head," Kannas jibed, but the joke flopped. "There were no substances on the floor that would directly indicate slipping. The deceased's medical history is unknown, so it's impossible to say whether he had a propensity for fainting or some other condition that could have caused the incident."

Takamäki looked at Kannas. "So at this point we know that Repo was inside the home at some point and that Karppi hit his head against the table for one reason or another."

"The cause of death will be revealed during the autopsy," Kannas said. "I'd estimate the time of death to be morning, maybe between nine and eleven. It's also possible that he had a heart attack and lost his balance and... Well, there's no point speculating. The guys are combing through Repo's dad's house now, and after that we'll take a look at that car Joutsamo found down the street, the one stolen from the swimming pool. They promised to call right away if the prints matched Repo's."

"Was there a cell phone or landline in Karppi's house?"

Kannas thought for a second. "There was a cordless phone in the living room, but we didn't find a cell phone."

"I'll find out whether he had one," Kohonen announced.

"Let's get the info on calls made from the landline just in case Repo used it," Joutsamo continued.

Takamäki thanked Kannas and added, "So the situation is that we have reason to suspect Timo Repo of homicide. Of course it's also possible that an outsider had been there, but Repo remains our main line of investigation. We'll decide on the classification of the crime once we have more facts, but as of now we're looking at murder."

The others nodded.

"And one more thing. Up till this point, our efforts have earned us an F-minus. Let's try and do a little better."

"What about the press?" Joutsamo asked.

Several reporters had asked about Repo's hunt that day.

"I'm still working on that," Takamäki said.

* * *

The wipers swept the sleet from the car's windshield. Suhonen was waiting at a red light at the corner of North Shore Drive and Maneesi Street. It wasn't an intersection per se; it was a pedestrian crossing signal. A revolving ad display circled lazily in front of a red-and-yellow brick structure dating from 1840, North Shore Drive 18. Liisa Park was on the right, and behind it stood the War Museum. Suhonen had read somewhere that this was Helsinki's *Jugendstil* architecture at its best.

No one picked up, and Suhonen tossed the phone onto the gray passenger seat. Goddammit, Salmela! Okay, it was possible that his SIM card could have expired by now.

The lights changed, and Suhonen stepped on the gas.

He hadn't felt like hanging around the station, where everyone seemed down about their zero-result manhunt.

When a case didn't move forward, police had too much time to think. That's when it was better to go out onto the streets and see if you could find something there.

Suhonen had been tooling around Kallio and Sörnäinen, hoping that he would accidentally run into a familiar face. Someone who would be able to tell him something. He had popped into six different bars for a coffee, and now he had to piss like nobody's business.

On the right, at the corner of North Shore Drive sand Kirkko Street, rose a handsome building with a tall, round corner tower. It was designed by Theodor Höijer in the 1880s. Suhonen had once staked out one of the sailboats in the nearby marina from in front of this residence and remembered the street-side plaque well. It stated that the lindens fronting the building had been planted by the ambassador of Imperial Japan in the autumn of 1943 as an emblem of the friendship between the peoples of Japan and Finland.

A little further up Kirkko Street stood the Ministry of the Interior. Maybe they'd let him use the bathroom if he flashed his badge. Then he'd be able to say that for once the ministry had offered genuine assistance to an officer in the field.

Suhonen's second phone rang. "Yeah?"

"Is that Suikkanen?"

"Is that Juha?"

"No, it's Scarlet Pimpernel."

"Huh," Suhonen growled. "What the fuck?"

"'Is that Juha?' sounded like code language, is all. My code name could be Scarlet Pimpernel from here on out."

"I'll give you a scarlet nose if you don't get to the point."

At the corner of Customs Square, Suhonen turned the car from the North Shore Drive extension onto

Alexander Street. He passed a low, one-story brick building on the right.

"I've got an address," Saarnikangas croaked.

"For Repo?"

"I think he's there."

"What is it?"

Saarnikangas cleared his throat. "Hmm, system's kind of shutting down here, short-term memory loss. Early onset of Alzheimer's."

"Stop using so much junk," Suhonen growled, turning his car onto Maria Street. On the right, up ahead, was Maria Street 9, which stood out from the street's other, older, more beautiful buildings. It was a corrugated metal structure built in the sixties. The only good thing about it was the Ace of Spades karaoke bar, the premier karaoke bar in Finland, where not just anybody dared to take the mic.

"Goddammit," Juha cried. "You just said what I was supposed to remember. Junk. You promised me a couple of packs. I need them."

"Once I have Repo."

"You don't understand," Saarnikangas said irritated. "I need it so I can pay this one guy. Plus a C-note."

"Money, too?" Suhonen said. He was sure that Saarnikangas was taking him for a ride. But he had a lousy hand, and it was best to check what Saarnikangas was holding. A few Subus and a C-note didn't make much of a dent in the state budget. "Okay," Suhonen said before the junkie could start elaborating.

"Okay? Like Okay-Okay?"

"Where are you?" Suhonen asked, his voice hard.

* * *

Sanna Römpötti and Anna Joutsamo were sitting in the second-story kebab joint at the Pasila train station.

"How is it?" the reporter asked.

"These always taste the same. Does this place belong to some bigger chain? Someone who supplies the lamb to all these restaurants?"

"I wouldn't be surprised," Römpötti said, plastic-forking chunks of meat from a pita swimming in garlic sauce.

"Listen," Joutsamo said. "The food here isn't the reason I wanted to meet you."

"Really?" Römpötti asked, although she had guessed what was on Joutsamo's mind as soon as she called.

"Repo," Joutsamo said.

"The escaped convict? What about him?"

Joutsamo hesitated again. She knew that with Römpötti she didn't have to say *You didn't hear this from me*, but the situation was still delicate.

"It's the original conviction. I read all the papers and spoke with the lead investigator from the old case, and at least to me, it feels like it's on really shaky ground."

"Innocent?" Römpötti asked directly.

"I'm not saying that, but it sparks some questions."

"Like what?" Römpötti asked, pulling a pen and notebook from her bag.

In ten minutes, Joutsamo repeated the same points she had brought up not long before at police station, and Römpötti jotted them down.

"This is a big deal," Römpötti said, once Joutsamo was finished.

"Don't you think? At least those are questions that should be raised."

"Yeah, especially since Fredberg, the current chief justice of the Supreme Court, was one of the members of the appeals court bench."

"Was he?" Joutsamo asked. Suhonen had brought her the copy of the verdict he had found in Repo's cell, but Joutsamo hadn't noticed Fredberg's name.

"Yes. For that TV interview I went through all of Fredberg's life sentence convictions. Of course we didn't analyze them the way you did. There were thirty of them, but I definitely remember the name Repo."

"I have the verdict. I'll have to check it out."

"Just picture the headline, Supreme Court Chief Sentenced Innocent Man to Life."

"Immediate resignation," Joutsamo nodded.

"Most definitely. How's the Repo case progressing, anyway?"

"Haven't found him yet, even though we've been working our butts off."

"Has he headed out of town?"

Joutsamo considered a moment before answering. "We have strong indications that he's here in the greater Helsinki area."

"What kinds of indications?" Römpötti fired back.

"Hey, we gotta have some secrets, too," Joutsamo chuckled. "No, it's genuinely information that I can't divulge without endangering the operation."

"Aww, I wouldn't tell anyone except a million of my closest friends."

\* \* \*

Suhonen found a small space in front of a red stucco building on Korkeavuori Street and parallel-parked his Peugeot in it. His urge to piss had disappeared after he dropped by the burger joint at Kasarmi Square. He hadn't ordered any more coffee.

Suhonen got out of the car and waited for the number 10 tram to rumble past. He leapt across the road, trying to dodge the puddles. The double towers of the neo-Gothic Johannes Cathedral rose before him. Saarnikangas had told him he was inside the hundred-year-old church. What the hell, Suhonen thought. At least it was a change from the endless smoky bars.

Suhonen leapt up two stairs at a time as he strode up to the double doors. The church was shaped like a cross, with the entrance at its foot. Suhonen had never been inside, but ten years ago at the station they had watched the televised service for the two officers who had been shot execution-style on Tehdas Street by an escaped Danish convict.

The church was bigger than it had looked on TV. The dark, ornate pews, heavy candelabras, and stained glass made the interior gloomy, even though the walls were pale. Five people appeared to be sitting in the hall. Four were at the front; one sat further back. Suhonen immediately recognized Saarnikangas's matted hair. The junkie was sitting near the central aisle.

Suhonen sat down next to him.

"Are you seeking redemption?" Suhonen whispered. "I am the way and the path."

Saarnikangas's eyes were tired. "Who're you, Jesus Crystal?"

"Listen, Juha," Suhonen said gravely. "If you want to check yourself into a clinic, I can get you in. Seriously."

Saarnikangas looked at Suhonen. "I don't think I'm feeling it... I tried once, but I cut out mid-treatment. It's not for me."

"Are you sure?" Suhonen asked. He didn't want to moralize and preach about a better life, because it wouldn't do any good. Juha Saarnikangas had an alternative, but the motivation had to come from himself, no one else. Suhonen knew a lot of junkies and crooks who had made it, but many more who had died.

"Check out that altarpiece," Saarnikangas asked. "Do you know who painted it?"

Suhonen shook his head.

"Ever heard of Eero Järnefelt?"

"Not on my list of APBs."

"Funny," Saarnikangas said, without smiling. "That was originally supposed to be Albert Edelfelt's painting *Bethlehem*, but he crossed swords with Melander, the architect. The architect won, and Edelfelt's work ended up a couple of years later in a church in Vaasa as an altarpiece titled *The Shepherd Kneels*."

Saarnikangas looked at the tall, narrow painting of three men and a horse gazing up at the Lord standing amid the clouds.

"How do you know all that?" Suhonen asked.

Juha disregarded Suhonen's question. His eyes remained on the painting. "This heavenly vision is oil on canvas and the theme was taken from the New Testament, Acts of the Apostles. The guy who's on his ass, blocking the light with his hand, is Saul. Old Saul here persecuted Jesus' apostles and wanted to imprison them." Saarnikangas's tone turned biblical. "And suddenly there shined round about him a light from heaven: And he fell to the earth, and heard a voice saying unto him, Saul, Saul, why persecutest thou me? And he said, Who art thou, Lord? And the Lord said, I am Jesus whom thou persecutest. But arise, and go into the city, and it shall be told thee what thou must do."

Juha turned his gaze to Suhonen. "Saul became the Apostle Paul."

Suhonen didn't reply.

"Art history, at the university. My short-term memory is shot, but stuff like this I remember." Saarnikangas attempted a grin, but the expression was sad. "Well, in any case, even though it's a Järnefelt, for practical purposes it's a copy of a painting by Vincenzo Camuccini from a church in Rome."

Saarnikangas fell silent. Suhonen didn't have anything to say, either. The few others in the church were still sitting quietly, and no one else had entered.

"Well," Juha said, running his hand through his filthy hair. "I'm not here to waste your time. We had a deal."

Saarnikangas held out his hand, and Suhonen slipped him two packs of Subutex with a hundred-euro bill rubber-banded around them.

"Da Vinci's *The Last Supper*," Saarnikangas said quietly. "Lord, who is it? Lord, is it I?"

Suhonen looked at the altarpiece.

"Hietalahti Shore Drive 17, the A entrance," Saarnikangas whispered. "Third floor. The door says Mäkinen. It's an old servant's apartment, a little studio. You might want to check it out. He might be armed."

Suhonen stood, but Saarnikangas stayed sitting in the pew.

Saarnikangas kept his gaze down until he was certain that the undercover cop in the leather jacket had exited the church.

Juha rose, stepped into the aisle, and moved closer to the altar. There was a man in a gray coat sitting in the seventh row, and Saarnikangas sat down next to him. There was a large shoulder bag at the man's feet.

"Thank you," Repo said quietly. "Is this going to cause problems for you?"

"No worries."

"What if the cop comes back?"

"I can handle him," Saarnikangas said. "He's not too bright. I made a reference to that Leonardo da Vinci painting *The Last Supper* and said, 'Lord, who is it? Lord, is it I?'"

Repo gave a slightly perplexed look at the long-haired junkie, who was smiling smugly. "And?"

"Well, who am I referring to with that quote?"

"Judas Iscariot?" Repo guessed.

Saarnikangas pursed his lips. "Agh, you don't get it either. It was Simon Peter, the most faithful disciple."

"What the hell are you talking about?" Repo said coldly.

"Look, I gave the cop a clue, but because he's so dumb he didn't understand that I'm not betraying you. So he deserves to be betrayed," Saarnikangas said with a smile.

"If you say so," Repo replied coolly. "It is what it is. Thanks for the pad. I needed the sleep. I won't forget you."

"Whatever it is you've decided to do, do it soon," Saarnikangas said, eyeing Repo's shoulder bag. "Those cops aren't kidding around."

Repo didn't get it, but began humming a hymn: "Now is the moment of truth, guide us as we seek the path to purity."

Saarnikangas put a hand to Repo's lips before any of the others could turn around.

* * *

Hietalahti Shore Drive 17 wasn't the easiest place to stake out. Suhonen had parked his Peugeot so that he could see the A entrance, which was located next to a bookstore. The main door of the yellow-stucco, seven-story structure was decorated with three large ornamental circles. The building's southern windows had a direct view of the shipyards and the terminal for the Tallinn ferries.

Suhonen had no idea as to whether the building had a basement. It probably did, because the uppermost floor looked like it had been added on to the original 1930s structure. The problem with basements was that they usually provided easy access from stairwell to stairwell, meaning you could use any of the building's exits, and Suhonen had no idea if the building had doors leading to an interior courtyard.

Red marquees hung over the bookstore windows. Lights appeared to be on inside, even though it was coming up on 9 p.m. Evidently someone was working late.

Suhonen had called in the information on Repo's potential whereabouts to Takamäki, who had decided to call in SWAT assistance. It would take a little while for them to get ready, and Suhonen had been sent to the scene to keep an eye on things. There were several lit windows on the third floor, so he couldn't deduce anything that way.

Turunen, head of the SWAT team, called Suhonen's cell and asked what the status was.

"There have been a few dog-walkers, but that's about it. You want me to go in and check things out?"

"Yeah," Turunen said. "Check if the main door is locked, and how we can get past it. But no further, okay?"

"Yup," Suhonen replied, getting out of the car. He dug a couple pieces of gum from his jacket pocket and tossed them in his mouth.

It was getting colder, either that or it just seemed colder near the shore.

Suhonen got to the main door and glanced up and down the street. Empty. The stairwell lights were off, so no one was exiting the building, either. Suhonen tried the door and immediately noticed that it had some give.

He pulled out his ATM card and shoved it into the crack. The card pressed in the tongue of the lock, and a few seconds later the door was open.

Suhonen spat his gum out into his palm and pressed it into the hinge side of the doorjamb. He let the door close carefully. It didn't go far enough for the lock to click into place. The SWAT guys would be able to open it with a tug.

In the lobby, Suhonen paused to think. The streetlamps were shining in enough that he didn't need to turn the hallway lights on yet. The corridor to the elevator was maybe twenty feet long, and the stairs rose to the right of the old-fashioned wire-cage elevator. On the left there was a door leading to the courtyard or the basement.

Suhonen looked at the name board—there really was an apartment on the third floor occupied by a Mäkinen. At least Saarnikangas hadn't been totally lying. Numerous companies also appeared to be in the building.

The undercover detective decided to punch on the stairwell lights and headed toward the stairs. He opened his leather jacket and instinctively checked his Glock. No point waiting in the corridor.

He chose the stairs; they rounded the elevator in a semicircle up to the second floor. Halfway up was a window to the backyard with streetlight shining through it. Suhonen stopped on the second floor for a moment. All was quiet.

He climbed up to the third floor. Mäkinen's apartment was immediately to the left of the stairs. Suhonen continued past the elevator door, climbed a couple of steps higher, and paused to listen.

He decided to take a closer look at the apartment. He crept up to Mäkinen's door and carefully cracked the mail slot. He could hear muffled speech inside. Evidently there was an inner door that was almost shut. Nevertheless, Suhonen was able to make out that it was human voices, not a radio or TV. He tried to think who Repo might be with—if he was in the apartment at all, that is.

Suhonen silently closed the mail slot and retreated back to the stairwell.

His cell phone began to ring! Goddammit, Suhonen silently swore. The sound would definitely carry into the apartment. He pulled his phone out from his jacket pocket and quickly descended the stairs.

"Hello," Suhonen answered. He punched on the stairwell lights at the second-floor landing, because someone talking on the phone in the light was probably less suspicious than someone talking in the dark.

"What's the situation?" asked Turunen.

"Where are you?" Suhonen asked.

"A minute away."

"Main door's open. Come on in."

"What kind of lock's on the door?"

Suhonen was confused by the question. "I just said it was open."

"No, I mean the apartment door," Turunen said. "I know you didn't stay outside or in the lobby to wait."

Suhonen chuckled. "Normal residential. You'll have no trouble getting in the door with your gear. It's on the third floor, immediately to the left of the stairs. Door says Mäkinen. There are at least two people inside the apartment."

"Listened through the mail slot, huh?"

"No, I levitated myself inside."

"All right, we're pulling up outside now."

"I see you guys," replied Suhonen, who by now had made it down to the main door.

The SWAT team was traveling in two vans. Three men in masks and helmets jumped out of the first one, and four from the second. One grabbed a big shield, and another a metal pipe meant for smashing locks. The others raised what looked like ski goggles from their necks to their eyes.

"Flashbangs?" Turunen asked one of the men, who nodded in response. A flashbang was a light-and-noise grenade intended to stun the target for a few seconds. Turunen put on a mask, too.

"You want one?" he asked Suhonen.

Suhonen shook his head.

"Well, here's a radio for you at least," Turunen said, handing him a headset.

Only about thirty seconds had passed since the cars had parked, and the police were already filing in the main door.

"How certain are we that Repo is in there?"

"Uncertain, but possible."

"So it might be some civilian's apartment."

Suhonen nodded. The SWAT leader's comment was a clear reference to the earlier pointless raid near the Kallio fire station. "I didn't call you in, Takamäki did."

Turunen clicked on his headset. "Change of plans: no flashbangs. Otherwise entry as planned."

The police climbed the stairs, treading lightly. None of their gear clinked or clanked. Suhonen and Turunen brought up the rear and had just reached the second floor when the point man, "Jack Bauer" Saarinen, whispered into the headset: "Ready."

"Okay, let's go in," Turunen ordered.

Suhonen heard a dull crash as the pipe crushed the lock. Then came the shouts: "Police! Don't move! Keep your hands visible!"

Suhonen had made it almost up to the third floor when an announcement arrived in his ear, "Apartment has been cleared. Three men in custody inside."

Three of the SWAT officers withdrew from the apartment as Suhonen entered. The entryway was small, it contained nothing but a coat rack. The room itself was furnished with a bed and a dining table. The apartment was clearly the sort that was rented out for a day or two.

Three men were lying on the floor in handcuffs, guarded by three members of the SWAT squad. Suhonen nodded at the lead SWAT man. Then he looked at the men on the floor, one at a time. The first had a greaser-style haircut, sideburns, and '50s clothes. It was Jorma Raitio, the guy from Järvenpää that Nykänen had mentioned during the meeting and whose phone the NBI had been tapping.

The second man was wearing a black sweater and army pants. His face was so lean that he could well be in the military. Suhonen didn't recognize him, but somehow he got the feeling the guy wasn't Finnish.

The third one he knew, however. All too well. Lying there on the floor was Salmela. The men's gazes met, but neither said anything.

Turunen tapped Suhonen on the shoulder and gestured him over to the dining table. There were some maps and other papers on it. Jewelry shop addresses were written on one of them. Neither of the police officers touched the papers. Let Forensics study them first.

"Take them all to Pasila," Suhonen announced, and the SWAT team roughly hauled the detainees up from the floor. As Salmela was led out, their gazes met again.

Turunen was the only one who stayed behind in the room with Suhonen.

"What is this place?"

Suhonen shook his head.

"Were they planning some robbery?" Turunen asked, gesturing at the papers.

"That's what it looks like. This is a job for the NBI," Suhonen replied, bending down to look under the bed. There was an ice hockey bag there, and Suhonen carefully pulled it out. It held three pistols and two sawed-off shotguns. Suhonen would rather have found Repo crouching in fear.

The undercover detective thought about Saarnikangas, and whether he had known who really was in the apartment.

"Goddammit." Suhonen exhaled heavily, whipping out his cell phone. He pulled up Nykänen's number.

# CHAPTER 17
## WEDNESDAY, 10:10 P.M.
## HELSINKI POLICE HEADQUARTERS, PASILA

"Well, well," Nykänen grunted. He was in the Homicide conference room, along with Takamäki and Suhonen. Joutsamo entered and said that a call had been made to Emergency Response from Karppi's landline that morning. The call had been logged as a wrong number, but Emergency Response had promised to pull up the recording. She didn't have any information on Karppi's cell phone yet.

Nykänen returned to the raid that Suhonen and the SWAT team had made. It was clear that the case would be transferred over to the NBI for investigation.

"I should've guessed this. We've been tapping their phones for a couple of months, but as soon as we tell you, it doesn't take even 24 hours and our suspects are sitting in jail."

His tone of voice was such that Suhonen couldn't tell if it was a reprimand or praise.

"I had no idea they would be in there," Suhonen explained. It was possible that they had moved too early on the potential perpetrators.

"Suhonen said something about some papers," Joutsamo said.

"Forensics is going through the fingerprints, but the places where getaway cars would be swapped were marked on the map, and the other list was of the targets themselves."

"So attempted grand larceny," Joutsamo said.

"Actually several attempts," Nykänen corrected.

Takamäki looked thoughtful. "The Supreme Court has decided that when planning of a crime has begun, it can be considered an attempt. Finding the plans indicates, of course, that something was in the works. Especially if we can connect it to the Manner recording."

"There's a felony weapons charge in there, in any case," Joutsamo said. "Those shotguns were sawed off."

"There's just one problem here," Nykänen reflected. "If those guys don't talk or if we don't find a connection from the call data or anywhere else to Manner, then he won't get his toes wet."

"I'm pretty sure these guys won't talk," Suhonen said. He made a mental note to swap out the SIM card of his off-the-record phone in the very near future, because if the number were found in Salmela's mobile phone, the NBI might decide to tap it.

"Well, at least we achieved our number-one goal. We prevented the crime from taking place," Nykänen grunted.

"For Manner we still have that hit-and-run, plus Espoo could also investigate the vehicular arson. We could also revoke his security company license," Takamäki stated, and then held a brief pause. He shifted his gaze to Suhonen. "You or me?"

Suhonen shrugged.

Takamäki elected to continue. "There's one more thing here that you need to know about, but it can't be discussed outside of this room, or used in any way in the investigation. Do I have your word?"

"How can I give you my word, if I *need* to know about it?" Nykänen asked.

"Let's just say it would be good for you to know," Suhonen corrected. "And we're only telling you this because you used to work in this unit."

"Okay," Nykänen rumbled, stroking his moustache. He wasn't sure what was going on.

Takamäki took back the floor. "One of the men apprehended in the apartment is Eero Salmela, whose son was killed a year ago. It was a witness protection case, if you remember."

"Hard to forget."

"Okay, but the thing is that this Salmela is a close friend of Suhonen's."

"A close friend..." Nykänen repeated.

Suhonen eyed Nykänen. "I'm sure you get the drift."

"Okay, I get it," Nykänen nodded. "Would he be interested in talking to us?"

"I can ask, but if it doesn't work out, then Salmela can't receive any special treatment during the investigation that would tip outside parties to... anything."

\* \* \*

Salmela was sitting in his green overalls in the interrogation room, with its light-brown table and gray walls. The guard let Suhonen in and closed the door behind him. Suhonen stroked his beard.

"How're you feeling?" he asked.

"How do you think?" Salmela answered.

Suhonen sat down on the wooden stool across from Salmela and tossed a pack of cigarettes onto the table. Salmela took one, and Suhonen scratched him a light.

Salmela sucked in a long drag and slowly blew the smoke out. "Fuckin' a," he said.

"Why?"

Salmela laughed.

"Is this some interrogation?"

"No."

"Is there a recording device in this room?"

"No," Suhonen repeated.

Salmela hung his head. The cigarette was in his right hand, and the smoke writhed up lazily toward the ventilation system.

"How did you guys know to hit the apartment?" Salmela asked. "Who gave us out?"

"Shitty luck. We were looking for Repo."

"Repo?" Salmela wondered, raising his head. "The escaped murderer?"

Suhonen nodded. "We heard he might be there. We found that apartment in the customs office register. Some cigarette smuggler used it last winter."

"Fuckin' a!" Salmela blurted out. "We rented it with cold hard cash from this old lady to make sure it wouldn't be in some police database. You can't trust anyone, goddammit."

"Got dealt a shitty hand."

"And it had to be a nobody like Repo. Fuck, if you would have told me he was such a big deal to you guys, I would have scraped him out of some dumpster till my fingernails bled."

"As I recall, I did tell you," Suhonen retorted. "Let's get back to the situation at hand. What do you want me to do for you?"

Salmela thought for a moment. "I don't know. How much do you guys know?"

"We know about your plan to jack those jewelry shops and that Manner is running the whole show."

"Fuckin' a!" Salmela blurted out again. "How? How the hell?"

"I'm not even sure," Suhonen said. "It's NBI's case. We've just been helping them out. But you do know where this will lead?"

"Time in the pen," Salmela said. "That's obvious..."

"So is there anything I can do for you?"

Salmela shook his head. "Yeah well, maybe a cup of decent coffee, because this is starting to look a hell of a lot like I'll be drinking freeze-dried from here on out."

Suhonen rose and returned a couple minutes later. He was carrying two cups of coffee.

"Black, if I remember right," Suhonen said, setting the cup down in front of Salmela.

"Yeah."

Suhonen sat at the table and let Salmela drink his coffee. He had some himself.

"Your son's thing, is that it?" Suhonen asked. A year earlier, Salmela's son had been shot during a drug deal gone bad. Salmela didn't take his eyes off his coffee.

"I guess. Everything felt pretty empty after that. Junkies sell me phones and computers and I front them. It seemed so stupid and empty. I thought, one big gig and that'd be it. Enough dough that I could take it easy, at least for a while. Okay, it's stupid to even think that way, but it was a chance."

"What, that you guys would hit several targets at the same time?"

"That, plus a few other jobs," Salmela said. "You're the only one I'm going tell this to. In the interrogations, it's going to be no comment down the line."

"What other gigs do you mean?"

"Do you remember that armored truck robbery in Mariehamn a few years back? First they set up a diversion by burning a car and then executed the robbery. Something like that. On a normal day there's max thirty to forty patrols in the greater Helsinki area. It wouldn't take much for half of them to be tied up in bullshit cases. Certain areas could be emptied of cops pretty easily. The idea was specifically in the massive scale."

"Whose idea was this? Yours or Manner's?" Suhonen asked.

Salmela winked. "Hey, we were all just execution. They told us we had to keep our eye on a couple of spots. My job was to chop down this big birch, because it was blocking the view from this one house. And if it fell on a couple of cars and tied up the police and fire & rescue departments, then that wouldn't have been such a bad thing."

"Right," Suhonen said, not believing a word of what Salmela said about the part he played. Someone who chopped down trees didn't need to know about any other robberies. Suhonen knew that there were many more perpetrators involved than the three they had behind bars, but figuring that out was the NBI's job. "I guess there's not much I can do."

"A man has to take what he has coming. Goddammit, I should have known after that car thing that this is going to get screwed up."

"What car thing?"

"It was no big deal. Just this one little thing, but I should have seen it coming."

"What happened?" Suhonen asked.

"You know Skoda Sakke?"

Suhonen nodded.

"Well, he was supposed to be the driver for the Espoo vehicle, and he had headed over to scout out the area around Sello early this week. In Manner's car. Well, he didn't dare to say anything at first, but later he told Manner that he knocked over some cyclist out there. Sakke hadn't hung around, of course. When Manner heard, he had a conniption. Kicked Sakke's ass and then made him burn the car. Sakke's debt grew by twenty grand, even though Manner's going to claim the insurance money too, of course. So then the Espoo police got in touch with him."

"Sounds like a clusterfuck."

"That it was."

Suhonen snagged the cigarette pack from the table.

"One more," Salmela said, pulling a smoke from the pack in Suhonen's hand. Suhonen lit it for him.

Joutsamo rushed in. "Suhonen, I need to talk to you. It's urgent."

"Take your time, enjoy your smoke," Suhonen said to Salmela, before following Joutsamo out of the room.

Joutsamo withdrew thirty feet down the corridor from the interrogation room door and kept her voice to a whisper, even though she was well aware that the interrogation rooms had solid soundproofing. "Saarnikangas called the phone that was in the jacket on your desk. I didn't answer, but I listened to the message. Said he had something urgent. His voice sounded agitated, maybe even alarmed."

Suhonen didn't particularly care for other people listening to his messages, but he accepted Joutsamo's decision. "What was he alarmed about?"

"He didn't say, but he asked you to come to the Chaplin Bar on Mannerheim Street right away. Has some information on Repo, apparently."

Suhonen considered whether Saarnikangas was trying to finagle more pills, or if he really had something new. Either way, he'd have to check it out.

"I'll probably head over, then," Suhonen said. He'd have plenty of time during the drive to call Takamäki to let him know what Salmela had said about the hit-and-run. The problem was, of course, that the information could never be used, because then the crew would find out that someone was talking to the cops.

"How's Salmela?" Joutsamo asked.

"Pretty bummed," Suhonen said, returning to the interrogation room.

Salmela's elbows were on the table, and his head was resting in his crossed hands. The cigarette was burning between the index and middle fingers of his right hand. A quarter-inch stub of ash curled down from the tip. Salmela raised his head, and the ash shivered onto the table.

Suhonen sat.

Salmela broke the silence. "You gonna send a Christmas card to me in the pen, or you think you'll have time to drop by?"

"I'll be by. Outside normal visiting hours, of course," Suhonen said, looking his childhood friend in the eye. He didn't really know what else to say, and nothing else was needed.

# EARLY THURSDAY MORNING

# CHAPTER 18
# THURSDAY, 12:40 A.M.
# LAUTTASAARI, HELSINKI

Repo pulled a suction cup and the glass-cutter he had bought from the sale bin at the Anttila department store from his coat pocket. He pressed the suction cup to the window and used the pencil-like tool to incise a circular hole around it. The glass didn't come loose on the first try, and Repo was forced to make a second incision.

The window was triple-paned, so Repo had to cut through the internal windows as well before he was able to push his hand through the hole and open the back door.

He stopped to listen. The house was quiet. Repo noticed his pulse quickening, and yet he felt calm. He had planned this for a long time.

The house was a large one by Finnish standards; Repo estimated at least 2000 square feet. It was a single-story brick home with a flat roof. The location was secluded, too—on the northern shore of Lauttasaari Island, right next to the Lauttasaari soccer fields. The marina was a hundred yards away. A long line of townhouses stood on the marina side of the house; on the other, a couple of ramshackle wooden homes.

Inside was dim, but the living room looked to be completely decorated in black and white. The couch and the table in front of it were white, the armchair was black. Black-and-white paintings hung from the walls. The flat-screen TV had been picked to match the decor.

There seemed to be an aquarium over to the side, but it was dark.

Everything looked tidy and well-kept but stark. Repo eyed the furnishings and shut the back door behind him. He walked across the carpet without taking off his shoes. He removed his gray coat and tossed it across the sofa, but kept the shoulder bag with him.

The living room was set lower than the rest of the house, and Repo had to climb a couple of steps to get to the main level. The black-and-white decor continued in the dining room. The largish dining table was black, and the ten chairs white. The dining room was separated from the living room by a low railing. Behind the dining space was the kitchen.

Repo silently continued into the front entryway. Several coats and a woman's black fur hung from the coat rack. A door to a room led off from the entryway. Repo opened it quietly and peeked inside. The streetlamp illuminated it enough for him to make out an office. It looked more normal than the black and white of the other rooms. In front of the window, there was an oak desk and a computer. The walls were lined in bookshelves. The room also accommodated a big, brown leather armchair with a small table at its side. Repo caught a faint whiff of cigar.

Repo turned back toward the living room. On the left was a door bearing a small plaque—"Toilet." Next to it was another door, which Repo guessed was a combined shower and sauna space.

One final door stood before him.

He carefully placed the shoulder bag on the floor and quietly opened the zipper. He found everything he needed except the Luger and Karppi's cell phone. Goddamn Saarnikangas must have snagged them, which meant he now knew what else was in the bag. Repo pulled a red-handled, all-purpose Mora knife from the bag. He had found it in one of the Anttila sale bins, too, for four euros.

Repo slowly thrust the door inwards and hoped it wouldn't creak. It didn't. The house was well tended. The owner probably paid someone good money for that.

It was the bedroom, as Repo had guessed. First he saw the red numbers on the digital alarm clock—00:45 a.m.—and heard the breathing of two people. The man was wearing black pajamas and sleeping on the far side of the bed, near the window. The woman slept closer to the door.

The knife was in Repo's hand, and he moved closer. His advance was cut short—the man turned over under the blue blanket and cleared his throat, but didn't wake up.

Repo held the knife in his right hand. The woman's mouth was slightly open. She was a blonde, about fifty years old. I could do it this way, too, Repo thought, twirling the hollow-handled blade in his hand: slit her throat just like that. The thought horrified him.

He bent down next to the woman's head just as her eyes flashed open. Surprise and disbelief morphed into fear when she saw a man in a black suit standing over her. "What...?"

"Death comes to call," Repo said in a low voice, clicking on the nightstand lamp. The woman shrieked, and the man sat up in bed.

"What the hell?"

"Judge Fredberg," Repo said with feigned politeness, yanking the woman over in front of him so the knife was at her throat. "Nice to see you again."

"What is this? Who are you?" Fredberg managed to spit out. "Put that knife away immediately."

Repo simply smiled. "The Lord is my shepherd; I shall not want."

The insanity of the situation began to dawn on Aarno Fredberg, chief justice of the Supreme Court. "What do you want?"

"What do I want?" Repo said, pressing the blade more tightly against the woman's throat. "What do you think? If I slit your wife's throat..."

Fredberg tried to pacify him. "Don't hurt my wife. Leena, stay calm. Everything's going to be fine."

"...who would you send to prison, Judge Fredberg?"

Fredberg didn't answer. He tried to think of who this man was, but couldn't come up with the answer.

"Answer me," Repo shouted. "If I slit your wife's throat, who would you send to prison?"

Fredberg hesitated. "You, because you'd be guilty, but I wouldn't be able to judge the case, because it would be a conflict of interest. What is it you want? I have money."

"If I wanted money, I would have robbed you," Repo said. "Do you know who I am?"

Fredberg shook his head. "No. Should I?"

"Yes. You sentenced me to life in prison for the murder of my wife eight years ago in the Kouvola Court of Appeals. Timo Repo, nice to see you again."

For a long moment, Fredberg wondered if he should lie and say he remembered the man. Maybe it would be best to keep up the conversation.

"I've seen thousands and thousands of cases over my career. Unfortunately I can't remember all of them."

"Have you ever made a mistake?"

"As a judge? I don't think so. Everyone is innocent until proven otherwise."

"But you did make a mistake!"

"Did I?" Fredberg said. He thought about how he could surprise the knifed man, but under the circumstances it would be impossible. Fredberg was in decent shape and believed he could beat the intruder in a struggle. But the knife at his wife's throat dampened his enthusiasm.

"You sentenced me to life in prison for murder."

Fredberg was still unable to connect the man to any of his cases. He was a little ashamed and afraid, because admitting this could lead to catastrophe.

"What mistake did I make?"

\* \* \*

Suhonen left the silver-gray Peugeot on Mannerheim Street across from the Swedish Theater. It was parked illegally, but Suhonen didn't care. He stepped out of the car, locked it with the remote, and headed into the Chaplin Bar.

Four black men were scrapping on the sidewalk in front of the bar. Suhonen didn't get involved in the Somalis' argument, but was pleased to note that the refugees had evidently successfully integrated into society, because the men were screaming at each other in Finnish.

Suhonen stepped into Chaplin. There was a bar at street level and a billiards room in the basement. Suhonen wove between tables toward the basement stairs. A blond guy with a long-haired woman tattooed on the back of his hand was sitting at one of them, alone. Suhonen tried to place the guy but couldn't. He definitely looked shady, though.

The basement billiards room was divided into two areas: smoking and non-smoking. On the smoking side, there were about ten billiard tables; on the non-smoking, five. Saarnikangas had said he'd be in non-smoking. There was also a big screen TV and a bar on the smoking side.

The link between tobacco and the game invented in France five hundred years earlier was apparent. The tables on the smoking side were full, while on the non-smoking side there was no one but Saarnikangas. He had racked the balls and was just about to break when Suhonen stepped into the doorway. Behind the billiard table stood a lonely-looking pinball machine.

Saarnikangas noticed Suhonen and didn't strike. Suhonen stepped up to the table. "You had something to tell me," he said in a serious voice.

"Chill," Juha said. "That last tip was a good one, wasn't it? I'd guess Repo wasn't there, but some other bad boys were."

Suhonen wondered whether he had a disagreement with someone from the criminal crew, maybe Salmela.

"You had something to tell me," Suhonen repeated.

"Should we play a round?" Saarnikangas suggested. "You can't be in that big of a hurry."

"Actually, I am," Suhonen said. "I gotta go to bed."

"Then I don't think I'll tell you anything."

"I've got chalk in my pocket."

Saarnikangas didn't get it. "Huh?"

"I'm going to draw your outline on the floor in a second," Suhonen said. He felt like smacking the druggie in the head with one of the billiard cues and putting an end to his games. Instead, he took off his leather jacket and hung it on the back of a chair. "What are the stakes?

"If you win, I talk. If I win, I get one more pack of Subu..."

Suhonen snorted. The guy was incorrigible. On the other hand, he seemed to know things, for instance about the apartment they just raided, so it was a relationship worth cultivating.

"You're on."

The tattooed guy from upstairs walked up to the pinball machine. "You guys probably don't mind if I punch the machine a bit, do you?"

Suhonen shrugged and prepared to break.

Tattoo Guy dropped a two-euro coin in the South Park pinball machine, which, as was only befitting, came to life with a fart. He hit the flippers and the machine squawked, "They killed Kenny. You bastards!"

Suhonen's break dropped a stripe into the corner pocket and he continued. His next hit sank a second ball.

"I am not gay," announced the pinball machine. Mr. Hankey the turd howled softly in the background, and the machine farted at a steady pace. Evidently Tattoo Man knew how to play, since Mr. Hankey yelped in delight and announced "Multi-ball!" But the noise from the machine didn't distract Suhonen.

He sank the balls one by one, without Saarnikangas ever getting a chance to hit. At the same instant as the winning shot, the eight ball, dropped into the left center hole, the pinball machine popped out a free ball and yelled, "Kick ass!"

"All right, let's talk," Suhonen said, glancing at the blond guy, who was concentrating on his game. "But over here to the side."

"You coulda let me hit a couple too," Saarnikangas complained, as Suhonen dragged him away.

"You had something to tell me," Suhonen said.

Saarnikangas was still carrying his stick. "Yeah, well about Repo. I saw him later that evening after you had left the church. We had some coffee, and he seemed a little confused. I decided to call you just so you don't think I'm mixed up in his crazy scheme in any way."

"What scheme?"

"Well, he was talking about some sort of revenge he was going to take on the chief justice of the Supreme Court. He had apparently unjustly sentenced him to life in prison in appeals court."

"What do you mean, revenge?" Suhonen asked. His eyes were on Pinball Guy, who was concentrating on his game. The machine made so much noise that he wouldn't be able to hear their conversation.

"Well, I was a little surprised too, but I'm pretty sure he's serious."

"How so?"

"When he went to take a leak at the café, I took a look in his bag," Saarnikangas said.

"What was inside?"

"A knife, rope, cable ties, electric wires, and sticks of dynamite," Saarnikangas listed, leaving out the pistol and phone he had stolen.

Suhonen looked dead-seriously at Saarnikangas. "Are you positive?"

Saarnikangas nodded. "Sure. And you know his background?"

"What background?"

"Before his wife's murder he was in the military. Some sort of explosives expert in field ops. Probably knows how to use dynamite."

\* \* \*

Suhonen turned off the Western Expressway at the Lauttasaari interchange, where the road rose up to an overpass and circled southward across the expressway. The car's tires hadn't been changed for winter yet;

Suhonen drove slowly down the snow-covered street. The sleet continued to fall.

Once he passed the apartment buildings, Suhonen turned the car westwards onto Lauttasaari Road. He recalled that this was the spot, where Soviet army captain Ivan Belov had been shot in November 1944. Finland had by then exited World War II, and was being supervised by the Allied Control Commission. Belov was shot by a sniper, who was never caught, and the Soviets threatened military action. The Finnish government responded by setting up one of the largest manhunts in its history. That incident had been explosive at the time, and so, apparently, was the present one.

It had taken one phone call for Suhonen to get the address of the chief justice of the Supreme Court, and he had headed straight from the bar the couple miles west to Lauttasaari. He thought it was better to go check things out first rather than send over a patrol. Suhonen hoped he'd make it to the house before Repo.

An elementary school stood on the left, with a park behind it, where a monument, a 76mm anti-aircraft cannon from WW II era, rose up from the bedrock. Suhonen had staked out this place from the nearby woods in the '90s, when one drug gang had used the cannon's base as a cache.

Suhonen had wondered whether he should call Joutsamo and tell her about the visit to Lauttasaari. The tip was worth checking out, of course, but Suhonen felt that at this point it was enough that he'd go have a look. Joutsamo might easily overreact, and if Saarnikangas's tip was nothing more than a lure for Subu, a quieter approach was better, since they were looking at the chief justice of the Supreme Court. In any case, he'd have to call in a patrol to watch the place for the night—and probably for the next days, too. But it was still better to check things out first.

Suhonen turned the Peugeot right and drove under the expressway into a graffiti-scrawled tunnel. The marina brought back good memories. On one summer night in the mid-eighties, Suhonen and Salmela had been on the shore hucking rocks at an empty buoy thirty yards out. The bet had been that the one who didn't hit the buoy had to swim around it. Fifty throws later, both found themselves in the water. The shore was so full of boulders that they had scraped their legs and sides raw.

Suhonen passed a complex of low-slung townhouses. Fredberg's house was twenty or so yards away. In between there were woods and some sort of hedge. Suhonen drove past the house and turned into the soccer field parking lot.

After pulling on a black ski cap, he walked back down past the house and to its far end. The streetlamp illuminated the relatively small front yard. No footprints could be seen in the snow. The place looked silent and peaceful. For a second Suhonen wondered whether he should ring the doorbell. Maybe it would be best to circle the house first.

There was no point trying to peek in any of the windows, because there were curtains drawn across all of them, and he found the same on the left side of the brick house. He found no footprints, but the snow was coming down pretty hard.

Suhonen made it to the edge of the back yard. Part of the yard was covered in stone pavers; the centerpiece was a large brick grill and a wooden table set. The other side of the yard looked like it was filled with berry bushes.

Suhonen tried the back door, but it was locked. Shivers ran up and down his spine when he noticed the hole that had been cut into the window.

The curtain on this side of the house was drawn too, so Suhonen couldn't see inside. For a second he wondered what to do, but then decided to stick his hand through the hole and open the back door. But first he opened his leather jacket so his Glock would be easily accessible. The gun stayed in its holster for now.

Suhonen was careful not to cut his hand on the sharp edge of the glass. He got a grip on the door handle and twisted down. The door opened outwards. Suhonen slowly drew the curtain to the side. The living room was dark, but it looked enormous. Suhonen immediately noticed the woman lying on the sofa. The position she was in was somehow unnatural: her hands and legs were together. It only took Suhonen a second to realize she was bound, but was she alive? What had happened in the house?

Even though the soft carpet muffled Suhonen's footfalls, he crept over to the sofa. The woman watched him approach, and Suhonen hoped she wouldn't scream. Her eyes were full of terror. Suhonen raised a finger to his lips.

She didn't make a sound.

Suhonen made it over to her and whispered, "Police. Shhh."

Despite his instructions, the woman immediately spoke, luckily at a whisper, "That crazy man has my husband. He's going to kill us."

"Stay calm," Suhonen said, pulling his switchblade out of his pocket. He cut the ropes from the woman's hands and legs.

"Out," Suhonen ordered. "And quietly."

He slipped his knife back into his pocket and took his pistol. The woman had made it to door when the living room lights blazed on. The sudden brightness momentarily dazed Suhonen. He noticed the woman pause.

"Go!" he ordered.

"Stop!" a man yelled inside the house, but the woman ran out the back door.

Suhonen saw two men of approximately the same build, both dressed in black. One was wearing a suit, the other pajamas. Suhonen recognized the one in front as Fredberg, chief justice of the Supreme Court, and the one in back as the escaped convict Repo.

"Police," Suhonen announced loudly, aiming his weapon at Repo. "Stay calm."

"Kiss my ass!" Repo shouted.

Only now did Suhonen notice the harness wrapped around Fredberg; it had been strung with light-brown tubes bearing red triangles. Explosives, probably dynamite. Electric wires led from the sticks to a detonator in Repo's hand.

"Stay calm!" Suhonen shouted back. At least he had played for enough time to get the woman out of the house. "Everything's all right."

"I'm going to blow him up!"

"If you do, I'll shoot you."

Repo was surprised by the police officer's aggressive stance. He began to laugh. "You're tough for a cop!"

"Timo Repo, this game ends now. Put the detonator on the floor and let him go."

Repo glanced at the pale Fredberg. "Look, judge, some folks even recognize me!"

Suhonen's gun remained trained on Repo. He could see Repo's forehead through his sights; the escaped convict was less than thirty feet away. He would definitely die if Suhonen pulled the trigger. The problem was that Suhonen wasn't sure about the detonation mechanism—often hostage-takers used devices where the bomb was set off not by pressing a switch, but by releasing it.

"Repo, listen! This is your final chance. Let's end this now."

Repo's eyes drilled into Suhonen. "I don't have any reason to die, but I don't have any reason to live, either. If you want, I'm happy to end this now. You really want to?"

Suhonen's finger gripped tighter around the trigger. There was not an iota of give left. One tiny tug and the bullet would leave the barrel and pierce Repo's forehead. But what about the detonation mechanism? The chances were about fifty-fifty. If Suhonen shot and releasing the button triggered the explosives, Suhonen would die too. The odds were on Repo's side.

Repo closed his eyes. "The Lord is my shepherd; I shall not want."

Suhonen had an impulse to rush for the door. That way maybe his legs would get lacerated, but he might save his head. He didn't follow through on the impulse, though.

"Repo, stop." Suhonen lowered his weapon. Repo muttered something Suhonen couldn't make out.

"No one needs to die. Let's just calm down here," Suhonen said.

Repo opened his eyes, his gaze was intense. He didn't say a word.

"Peace and love and all that," Suhonen said. "If it's okay with you, I'm going to head out that door, and we can talk more soon by phone."

"You can't leave," Fredberg wailed.

Repo smiled. "Listen to the judge, officer. He'll slap you with a police misconduct conviction if you leave him here with me alone."

Suhonen tried to lighten the mood. "Sure, I can stay. I don't have anything against it. There's probably some expensive cognac around here somewhere. Let's light a fire, pop open a bottle, and watch a late-night talk show. But I'm going to keep this Glock in my pocket. Is that okay? Huh?"

"Out," Repo ordered coldly. He was unsure about what to do, but he needed to get the police officer out of there no matter what. It felt like the simplest solution, since the woman had already slipped away.

Suhonen obeyed and walked out the back door. He could have tried to stay inside, but he needed backup. As soon as he was on the patio, he broke into a run. He wondered where the chief justice's wife had gone. He found Leena Fredberg out on the street in her nightgown, sobbing and shivering by the mailbox. Suhonen gave her his coat and started walking her down the snowy street to his car.

The undercover officer pulled out his phone and called the Emergency Ops Center before he did anything else. The gist was that there was a hostage situation on Marina Road. An ambulance and lots of backup were needed on the scene.

The second call was to Takamäki, whom he woke up. Suhonen informed his lieutenant that he had good news and bad news. The good news was that Repo had been found. The bad news was that he was holding the chief justice of the Supreme Court hostage.

Takamäki said he'd be there in fifteen minutes.

Suhonen told him to dress warmly.

# CHAPTER 19
## THURSDAY, 2:05 A.M.
## LAUTTASAARI, HELSINKI

"Briefing!" Takamäki growled. The lead van had room for four: Joutsamo, SWAT chief Turunen, and on-duty lieutenant Helmikoski were inside with Takamäki. Joutsamo was sitting in the rear left at the computer, next to her boss. Turunen was across from her, and Helmikoski had spun the swiveling front seat backwards. The van's sliding side door was open with Suhonen and a couple of uniformed sergeants standing outside; wet snow was falling on them.

The van was parked at the edge of the soccer field, where Takamäki had set up the command center. Four police vans were parked nearby. The target was less than a hundred yards away, behind a small grove of trees. About twenty officers from the cities of Helsinki, Espoo, and Vantaa were on the scene, and more were streaming in.

"Suhonen, you start," Takamäki said. "Tell us what happened."

"Sure," Suhonen said from outside the van, wiping the snow from his beanie. "This evening I got a tip from the field that Repo might be inside this house. I came to check it out and entered through the back door, which had already been broken into. Fredberg's wife was tied up in the living room, and I freed her before Repo and Fredberg came in. The wife escaped, and then Repo and I had a pretty intense conversation."

"How intense?" Turunen asked.

"I was looking at him through the sights of my Glock, and he had a detonator in his hand. The dynamite was strapped around the judge's body, and I came to the conclusion that, under the circumstances, I wouldn't be able to bring the situation to a peaceful resolution."

"Good call," Turunen said.

"Yeah, maybe. In any case, I got the woman out of the house. She was pretty hysterical, but I got the basics out of her. Repo had broken into the house and woken both of them in the bedroom. She didn't have any idea who the intruder was, but it had turned out that he had something to do with her husband's work. He repeatedly claimed to be innocent of some murder."

"What about the dynamite?" Turunen asked.

"Slim, light-brown sticks that had been strung around Fredberg in some sort of harness. There were wires leading to the detonator in Repo's hand."

"What sort of detonator?" Turunen continued, as an ambulance curved onto the field.

"Guess how hard I was trying to figure that out while I had a bead on Repo's forehead."

"You didn't see whether Repo was pressing a button or switch down or whether his finger was on top of it?"

Suhonen looked seriously at Turunen. "If I would've been sure it wouldn't go off when his finger was released from the switch, I would've taken the shot. Definitely. I didn't dare take the chance, because that could've meant three bodies."

Turunen nodded. "Okay. Another good call. Did he have a firearm?"

"Didn't see one. The woman mentioned a knife, but he didn't have it in his hand when I saw him."

Turunen continued his quizzing. "Was Repo drunk or high?"

"Not noticeably, at least."

Joutsamo asked from the back seat, "Where's the wife now?"

"Ambulance took her to the hospital. I don't know which one."

"Okay," Takamäki said. "And assess Repo's state of mind for us."

"Hmm, what could I say about that," Suhonen said. "There were probably several pounds of dynamite on those harnesses, so I'd consider him really damn dangerous. He didn't present any demands, so I'd assume this is some sort of vendetta. Did this Fredberg preside over Repo's case?"

Joutsamo nodded in the back seat. "Yeah. Fredberg was chair of the Kouvola appeals court when Repo was resentenced to life in prison."

"So a vendetta," Turunen huffed. "Suicidal?"

Suhonen shrugged. "The woman remembered him having said, 'I don't have any reason to die, but I don't have any reason to live, either.' And, he said the same thing to me, but he didn't blow us up once I got the woman out of there, so in that sense we still might have a chance."

"Okay," Takamäki said. "Suhonen, you can get out of here. We don't need you anymore, and you can't be involved, given your confrontation with Repo."

Suhonen smiled. "Hey, I'm not going to argue with you. So I can go take a hot shower now?"

Takamäki nodded, and Suhonen left. After a couple of steps, he stopped. "Oh yeah, I think I'm going to head straight home and return the car tomorrow."

"Get out of here," Takamäki said, turning to Joutsamo. "What's your analysis of the situation?"

"That was basically it. Repo sees Fredberg as having unjustly convicted him of murder. Repo's father's death triggered something, and whether he planned it or it was a momentary impulse, Repo decided to escape. Evidently Repo has been staying at his father's neighbor's Karppi's place, who was found dead this morning. At the moment, we don't know whether Repo was involved in Karppi's death. We might want to remember that, at least based on my investigation, the guy could actually be innocent in this old case."

Turunen looked at Joutsamo. "You're saying he might've been innocent and still was sentenced to life?"

"Quite possibly. Even likely," Joutsamo said.

"And he sat for eight years? Shit, he might be pretty goddamn bitter. If he's actually sober in there, then the situation's pretty bad."

"The thing that makes it even worse is that thirty pounds of dynamite was stolen from a construction site after Repo's escape and hasn't been recovered. The explosives could well be from there. Thirty pounds makes a pretty big bang."

Takamäki's gaze circled his colleagues inside and outside the van. "Okay. The chief justice is still alive, and Repo didn't kill Suhonen either, so we might have some negotiating room. Does anyone have any other questions about the background?"

Everyone shook their heads. Outside, a few officers in uniform were hooking up a generator to the lead van and the other vehicles containing all the hi-tech equipment. The team's computers, radios, and other equipment devoured so much current that the vans weren't able to generate it themselves, even with their engines running.

"Good. Like Turunen said, we're up shit creek, but we're going to make it through this. Helmikoski," Takamäki said, turning toward the stout man. "What's the situation now?"

The on-duty lieutenant pulled out a notebook from his breast pocket and flipped through it. "The area has been almost fully cleared. Marina Road has been cordoned off at both ends, and the houses in the vicinity have been evacuated. A police boat has been called in to patrol the water, but it might take an hour or two to get here. So the area is relatively secure, although our command center might be a little too close. As I recall, at construction sites, the safety distance for two pounds of dynamite is about 200 yards, and now we're less than a hundred yards from that house. And we have men a lot closer. Of course the building would block some of a blast, too."

"Well, we can't pull our men out of there until things get really acute," Takamäki reflected. "Helmets on, everyone."

"And anti-radiation blankets," Helmikoski added. "Protects you from the sleet, too."

"Looks like we'll have to cut off the expressway and expand the evacuation zone around those nearby homes as well, but let's call in some expert from the Army or the Safety and Chemicals Agency," Takamäki said. He didn't have a precise understanding of the damage a thirty-pound dynamite charge would cause if it detonated inside the house, but he remembered the car bomb that had exploded a few years back in downtown Helsinki. Eight pounds of dynamite had obliterated the car and caused relatively heavy damage to nearby buildings. "Helmikoski, look into these safety zone issues and cut off the expressway."

"Okay, we'll set up detours at the Lemissaari and Katajaharju exits."

Turunen jumped in. "That Lemissaari exit might be too close. It might be better to cut off the expressway back in town and route traffic across the old bridge and along Lauttasaari Road. We've also called in TeBo. Their bomb squad will be here as soon as they get their equipment together." TeBo was an abbreviation for the national Terrorist Bomb unit.

"If this goes on till morning, we're going to have huge traffic jams," Helmikoski said.

"Not our problem," Takamäki replied. "Turunen, what's the situation in the immediate vicinity of the house?"

"I have eight men stationed around the house. No one will get out without being noticed, but we don't have the men for a raid. We can bring in another group in a few hours, and then we'll have the men to go in, too. Since the guy's a former army explosives expert, that dynamite is ready to blow. Suhonen didn't see a firearm, but the risk of course lies in the detonator. If it's the kind that detonates when the finger is lifted off it, we've got one hell of a situation on our hands. Usually those switches have some sort of safety, because no one has the concentration to press a button for hours and hours, but the detonator's still easy to activate, of course. If the standoff continues and he falls asleep, that obviously means the safety is on, but how are we going to know for sure when he's sleeping in there?"

"Do we have a listening device in the house?"

"Not yet," Turunen said. "We're bringing them in as we speak, and once they get here we'll plant a few on windows. We'll be able to hear what's being said inside, and if we hear any snoring, then that's when we should strike. We're also bringing a mobile base station, so we can listen in on all cell-phone communication in the area. We're getting the blueprints for the house, too."

"Okay," Takamäki said. "If we had to go inside now, what would be our chance of success?"

Turunen's expression was grave. "Elimination of the target would be inevitable, and because we don't know what kind of detonator it is, my best guess is the hostage would have a 50 percent chance of survival. Since we're dealing with a bomb, the survival probability is that same 50 percent for the policemen entering the building."

"So it's not a suitable alternative at the moment, but have a plan ready to go just in case we need it, and have the men entering wearing bomb suits, just in case."

"Right," Turunen said. "They're not comfortable for hours on end, so if things heat up, let me know."

"Sure."

Joutsamo felt like mentioning Fredberg's criminal-coddling interviews. You'd think he'd know how to handle this Repo himself: all he'd have to do is promise him money and a place to live. What did he need the police for?

"So our plan is to let things cool off," Takamäki clarified. "Let's allow Repo to settle down, and I'll contact him by phone. Time is on our side."

"Should we cut off electricity to the house?" Turunen asked.

Takamäki shook his head. "No. We might need some media assistance here," he said, glancing at Joutsamo. "Give Römpötti a call."

Turunen gave Takamäki a perplexed look. "The reporter?"

"Yup. Let's see if we can defuse his bitterness that way. Helmikoski, when the press starts arriving, set up a lemonade stand over on the far side of the expressway where the reporters can get their information. I'll try to drop by at some point. The photographers will grouse for a chance to get closer. Let's promise them a tour at some point, because I don't want them to start fooling around on that old ski jump," Takamäki said, gesturing at the hill rising behind him.

"Just so you know, it was torn down thirty-four years ago, back in 1973," Helmikoski noted.

"What?" Takamäki asked.

"The ski jump," Helmikoski said in a snarky tone. "But guess what the record was?"

Takamäki, Joutsamo, and Suhonen shot looks of disbelief at the on-duty lieutenant.

"Um, tell us," Takamäki said.

"96 feet, 9 inches," Helmikoski said, proud of his knowledge.

Takamäki looked out the van window toward the hill. "Really?"

Helmikoski nodded.

"In Herttoniemi we did 160-footers."

"Wasn't the Olympics," Turunen noted. "I'll get us keys to the locker room at the soccer field. We'll make it our break room. We probably won't even have to wait too long to get a coffeemaker in there."

* * *

Repo cautiously glanced out into the front yard through the kitchen curtains. The streetlamp on Marina Road was off. He could see the cars down at the soccer field, but couldn't make out anything closer up. Repo knew that the police were out there, though.

The house was dark, because Repo didn't want to give the police any unnecessary advantage. Light shone from the aquarium in the living room, as he hadn't been able to figure out how to turn off the timer. On the other hand, it was good that the house wasn't totally dark. The police had night-vision equipment. He didn't.

Repo carefully closed the curtain. The arrival of the police officer with long hair had thrown off his plans. Had Saarnikangas squealed on him after all? Originally he was going to leave Fredberg and his wife in the house and set up the dynamite on a timer to go off in an hour. That was no longer possible. Plenty had gone awry: Karppi's death and now this hostage situation. He needed to come up with a new plan, but thinking gave him a headache.

Fredberg sat in a chair less than ten feet away. Repo had tied him to it with double zip ties, tightly pulled around both wrists and ankles, and then looped around the chair. There was no way Fredberg could wriggle free.

The judge sat still in the chair, and a ten-foot wire led from the strapped explosives to Repo's detonator. The device, which was about the size of a TV remote, lay on the table. Repo had left the safety on.

Fredberg's gaze followed Repo incessantly. Repo sat down at the table and picked up the detonator. "Are you afraid of dying?"

"I don't know," the judge said. His forehead itched, but he couldn't scratch it. "I've never thought about it in terms of being afraid, because it's inevitable, a given fact."

"Do you believe in God?"

"Yes, although I consider myself a Christian by convention rather than conviction."

Repo stared Fredberg in the eye. The judge was trying to look somehow dignified, even though his hair was a mess and he was wearing nothing more than pajamas.

"I lost my faith in God eight years ago."

"What hap...?" Fredberg started, quickly swallowing the rest of the sentence.

"Were you going to ask what happened?"

"I was, but I already figured out the answer."

Repo didn't immediately respond.

"Who was it who said, 'That which is not just and fair may not be law'?"

"What do you mean?"

"Answer!" Repo roared, causing Fredberg to flinch.

"Olaus Petri, of course. In the 1530s. All judges know that."

"I read those principles in the prison library. They compared judges to God."

"Yes, well." Fredberg chose his words with care. "I'd say that's reading a little too much into it."

Repo's eyes remained locked on Fredberg's. "Because the judge is charged by God to judge rightly, he must strive with all his might to know what justice is," Repo cited from memory. "The judge acts at God's command."

Fredberg didn't dare to contradict him. "I believe that's correct."

"God urges us to mercy, and according to Olaus Petri, justice must include mercy as well."

"I fully agree with you."

"So why wasn't any shown in my case?"

Fredberg tried to remember the case, but he couldn't recall the details.

"If the court acted wrongly, that can be corrected. I can personally look into the case and act as your advocate."

"You should have advocated for me eight years ago," Repo said. "Now it's my turn to be the judge."

\* \* \*

252

Sitting alone in the lead vehicle, Joutsamo dug her cell phone from her pocket. Takamäki, Turunen, and Helmikoski had gone for a round to get a better picture of the situation. The snow had turned to rain, but slush still covered the ground.

The number rang six times before a sleepy voice answered. "Römpötti."

"Good morning!" Joutsamo said, feigning perkiness.

"Anna, what the hell?" the reporter growled. "It's three in the morning."

"That's right, We've still got an hour to play before the bars close. Come party."

"Give me a break," Römpötti moaned. "I haven't gotten a good night's sleep all week. And now I probably won't be able to fall back asleep."

Joutsamo was amused by how slowly the human brain worked when it was roused from slumber. "Come on! Let's go!"

"No!" Römpötti shouted. "No way!"

Joutsamo decided to end her teasing. The risk was that Römpötti would hang up and turn off her phone. "Listen. It's about work. Are you sure you're awake?"

"Work? At this hour?"

"Yup. Cops never sleep."

"Neither do reporters, at least not this one. Tell me," Römpötti said, her voice more alert.

"We found the escaped convict in Lauttasaari. He's holed up in a house on Marina Road. There's a pretty big police operation going on here."

A slapping sound filled the air. Joutsamo glanced up and saw a red helicopter landing further down the soccer field. The air current from the rotors whipped the water-drops harder into the van's windshield.

"The air ambulance just arrived."

"Holy shit! I'll call a cameraman and be right over."

"There's one more thing. He has a hostage."

"Wow. That's not good. You know who it is?"

"Yes. Fredberg, chief justice of the Supreme Court."

Römpötti was silent for a second. "You gotta be kidding me. That's a huge story."

"And a serious situation."

"Are you going to get him out of there alive?"

"We're doing our best."

"How close can I get? We're going to broadcast straight from the scene."

"Takamäki said your team can come onto the soccer field. I don't know exactly what he has in mind."

Römpötti's voice was thoughtful, "Is that so? Are we going to be part of some police operation?"

"He'll probably tell you more himself, but I can always call some other network and see if they want to bring a van up on the field."

"We're on our way."

Joutsamo looked at the helicopter, which had cut its engine. The blades of the rotor still spun, drooping lazily. All of the ingredients for a massive catastrophe were in place.

# CHAPTER 20
## THURSDAY, 4:10 A.M.
## LAUTTASAARI, HELSINKI

Turunen brought a thermos into the lead van and produced three paper cups from his pocket. "Sorry, all I got was coffee. Black, no sugar."

"No worries," Joutsamo said. She was sitting at the computer. Takamäki was next to her.

"None at all," he agreed.

Turunen pulled the side door shut and sat down in the passenger seat. He set the cups down next to the laptop and poured out steaming java.

Joutsamo got hers first. "What's the situation?"

"Same as an hour ago. Both are in the dining room. Haven't moved," the SWAT leader informed them. Takamäki knew that the SWAT team had a device they used to see people's movement through walls. The system worked like radar, except the waves transmitted by the equipment penetrated walls and bounced off people. They hadn't managed to set up cameras to produce any helpful images.

Earlier, Turunen had also laid out the plan for entering the home. Since Repo was apparently not in possession of a firearm, they only had to deal with one threat: the detonator. If it was the release-type, they would have to successfully cut the wire between the explosives and the detonator, which would require a major diversion. In practice their best chance was if a police officer was allowed to bring food or something else to the house. The problem of course was that there was presumably plenty of food inside the house.

Their other opportunities would arise if Repo fell asleep or if somehow they could catch him off guard when the detonator's safety was on.

"No contact has been established?" Turunen asked.

"No. We've been calling at regular intervals, both the landline and Fredberg's cell phone. No answer," Takamäki reported.

"Is this technically a hostage situation?" Turunen pondered. "We don't know what Repo's demands are. Some sort of demand is necessary for a hostage situation to arise."

"Save it for the court room," Takamäki said, taking a sip of coffee. "If and when some lawyer finds fault with our decisions here."

"What have they been talking about in there lately?" Joutsamo asked. One of the tech vans was continuously recording any conversation transmitted by the window mics.

"Not getting much of anything. Repo's got the same record on repeat: mercy, the verdict, and a judge's responsibility. He's really bitter about that conviction," Turunen reported.

"So the same as before," said Joutsamo.

"It's a vendetta," Turunen said. "Not much to add. We hear a lot of threats like these, but almost no one carries them out."

"Yeah, thinking more about Repo's mindset...I guess our society has become so individualistic nowadays that advancing your own interests is now the most important thing, or the only thing, in some instances," Joutsamo reflected. "That means the justice system and state bureaucracy are constantly working more and more like the business world, where money and productivity are the priority."

"You mean the state doesn't act in the best interests of individuals," Turunen clarified.

"In the business world, it's the company's job to protect its own interests. Bureaucrats will start doing the same as this business-type thinking is shoved down their throats. The purpose of the system will change from looking after the interests of the people to ensuring the functioning of the system itself. When that happens, any person lodging a complaint about civil servants becomes a burden, and those who do it repeatedly become branded as nuisances who won't be taken seriously, like Repo. At the same time, the government grows more secretive, and any missteps within the system get covered up. All this feeds into the thinking that things can only be resolved by taking the law into your own hands. Repo is probably a pretty good example of this."

Turunen nodded. "If Fredberg manages to get out of this alive, the first thing he'll probably do is demand a bodyguard. And when one judge has a bodyguard, all the others will think they need one, too."

"And they're not necessarily unjustified. I think we're going to be seeing more and more situations like this."

No one had anything to add. Turunen's phone rang, and he summarized his brief conversation for Takamäki and Joutsamo: "We've also got the landline tapped now."

"No other phones have turned up?" Takamäki asked. The police had set up a base station that pulled in all cell phone calls in the area and allowed them to listen in. The caller didn't notice anything. Cell phones were programmed so that they sought out the nearest base station, and the police's base station offered the best alternative. But the police would have to comb through all the calls in order to be able to pinpoint Repo's phone.

"No," Turunen said. "Not even any calls from reporters yet."

Takamäki grunted. He remembered a situation where a reporter at the scene of a siege had called his source at the police department without knowing that the call was being intercepted. The incident had led to an official reprimand for the source.

"Who's going to get the warrants for all this?" Joutsamo asked.

"Karila or Kafka can take care of that," Takamäki answered. "And Helmikoski is handling the expressway closure. He already wrote up a press release."

Two armored Pasi personnel carriers from the military turned onto the soccer field from the marina end. The streamlined tanks had six wheels, and the military identifiers were already covered by police stickers. The intent, aside from providing safety for the police officers, was to present a show of strength to the hostage-taker.

"Should we try again?" Takamäki wondered out loud. Joutsamo nodded and gave the computer the command to start recording. The phone Takamäki was using was connected to both the computer and a speaker.

Takamäki pulled up Fredberg's landline from the phone's memory. The phone rang.

Turunen's radio beeped and a voice announced: "The target is moving inside the house."

Takamäki looked at Turunen, who turned down his radio. His expression was hopeful.

"Hello," answered a male voice.

"Hello," Takamäki said in a firm, neutral tone. "This is Lieutenant Kari Takamäki from the Helsinki Police Department. Is this Timo Repo?"

A moment of hesitation. "Yes."

Takamäki thought Repo's voice sounded relatively sober, despite the fact that he had only spoken two words.

"How are things in there?"

"Calm," Repo answered.

"Good. It's pretty calm out here too, even though this sleet doesn't look like it's going to let up anytime soon," Takamäki said. He had a single objective for the conversation: bring the standoff to a conclusion in such a way that no lives were lost. "Do you have any suggestions as to how we could resolve this situation?"

Repo grunted. "Pack your bags and get out of here. Then there won't be a situation."

"As I'm sure you're aware, that's not possible."

"Well, do you have any suggestions?"

"Timo," Takamäki said, intentionally using his first name. "I think we could resolve this by you and Fredberg coming out nice and slow and leaving the explosives inside."

"I'm not going back to prison," Repo announced, his voice determined.

Takamäki's and Joutsamo's eyes met. A lack of willingness to compromise on a key negotiating point was a bad sign.

"You don't want to go back to prison because you were wrongly convicted, as an innocent man," Takamäki said. He wanted to communicate empathy and avoid conflict. That being the case, he wouldn't be mentioning Karppi's death.

Repo was silent.

"We've looked into that old case during your escape. It seems to be full of irregularities."

"Irregularities!" Repo burst out.

"Major errors that can be fixed."

"And how would you fix them, lieutenant?"

"The case can be reopened, and retried, and if you are found not guilty, you'll receive significant compensation for the past eight years," Takamäki said. He was trying to feed Repo the idea that he did have an alternative to the detonator.

"I don't believe you! I tried for a couple of years to get it overturned, but no one lifted a finger. I was branded a habitual complainer. None of my appeals were taken seriously."

"The situation has changed. I'm on your side," Takamäki said, wondering for a second if he was going too far.

"You're just saying that because you want me to come out with the judge."

Takamäki had anticipated this response. That's why he had asked Joutsamo to call Römpötti.

"I'm willing to state it publicly, too. Do you want me to say it on live TV on the 6 a.m. news?"

Repo was silent for a minute, and Takamäki didn't pressure him.

"Judges should be the system that ensures justice is served, not be an extension of the state bureaucracy," he finally said. "No. I was convicted as an innocent man, so I own the right to kill as compensation for my lost life. I don't want anything from you." Repo cut off the call.

Joutsamo stopped recording, and neither she nor Takamäki said anything for a minute.

"The last part was pretty bad, but maybe you got him thinking," she said. Joutsamo knew that during hostage negotiations, the main objective was to bring the target out of their emotional turmoil and get them to think rationally.

Turunen nodded approvingly. "Owning the right to kill for doing time as an innocent man. That's pretty heavy."

"It's just a reflection of his bitterness," Takamäki said. "We can influence that feeling. At least we can try. But what he said about not wanting to go back to prison sounds serious."

Joutsamo nodded. "He might've ended up in prison anyway because of Karppi, but now he definitely will for this siege."

"True. After we defuse this situation, we can think about what comes next," Takamäki said. What happened at Karppi's house should not be brought up here, unless Repo wanted to address it himself. Now they needed to concentrate on defusing Repo's bitterness.

"Anna, tell Römpötti I'll give her an interview at six regardless. Let's try to establish contact with Repo before that."

"Is there any food out in that changing cabin?" Joutsamo asked.

"Sandwiches," Turunen answered.

Raindrops struck Joutsamo in the face as she stepped out of the car. Luckily she was wearing boots, so her toes would stay warm.

\* \* \*

Veteran SWAT officer Jarmo Eronen was sitting in the back of the tank, right next to the rear doors. The army vehicle was as bare-bones inside as it was out. Eronen's partner, "Jack Bauer" Saarinen, was sitting further in, eyes shut. They switched places every twenty minutes to maintain their alertness.

Eronen, who was almost thirty, had been on the SWAT team for about five years. His older brother had died about ten years earlier in a police operation on an island off of Helsinki. The incident had inspired him to apply for the police and the SWAT team.

The back door of the Pasi had a small hatch where Eronen could look out down the barrel of his MP5 submachine gun. It had a laser sight under the barrel, but it wasn't on. The house was about 20 yards away. Eronen could see the front yard and the right facade of the house. He had night vision gear, but neither he nor Saarinen wanted to use it. In spite of the rain, the city lights gave off enough light.

They had seen no movement. Nor was there any reason to have. The team had managed to get a radar sensor close to the house, and an announcement would come over the radio if any movement was detected inside.

Eronen was a trained sharpshooter. Nonetheless, his Heckler & Koch MSG90 rifle was on the bench of the Pasi in its black canvas holster. The distance to the house was short enough that the MP5 would suffice.

Eronen was happy that the tanks had shown up, because just half an hour ago he had been lying on the ground under a poncho. The Pasi wasn't comfortable, but it was noticeably better than the wet ground. When you were lying outside, you had to piss by rolling up on one side. At least in the Pasi there was a canister.

No movement. In a couple of minutes it would be Bauer's turn to take over.

The SWAT officer was used to waiting. It didn't bother him in the least. It was better to get situations resolved without violence. Some time ago, Turunen had informed them that contact had been established with the target. That was a good thing.

No hint of movement.

\* \* \*

Takamäki was sitting in the lead van alone, looking toward the house. The house itself was not visible; other vans were in the way. The scene reminded Takamäki of some old Western where the pioneers formed their wagons into a ring. Takamäki was at the computer, reviewing the log of all that night's developments.

Deputy chief of police Skoog had called to tell Takamäki that he'd remain in charge of the operation. Command could be reevaluated in the morning if the unpleasant incident, as Skoog had termed the siege, still continued. That suited Takamäki just fine, because they would have to change shifts in the morning anyway. He and all the others who had been at the scene overnight would be sent home to get some sleep.

Skoog had also pressed for Takamäki's prognosis about the eventual outcome, but Takamäki hadn't been able to give him an answer.

Takamäki tried to think where things had gone wrong—why had a normal manhunt for an escaped convict ended up in a high-profile siege? The search for Repo had been taken seriously, with several officers dedicated to tracking him down. Agh, he thought. He could process all that later.

The numbers on the van clock read 5:32.

Takamäki decided to try calling Repo. As per Joutsamo's request, a speaker had been pulled from the tech vehicle to the lead van, but things had been quiet inside the house for the past half hour.

He reached over to the computer to turn on recording and picked up the phone. The number was still in the phone's memory, and it rang three times before Repo answered. This time the radar man didn't announce anything about the target moving, so Repo probably had a cordless phone.

Once again, Repo answered with a simple "Hello."

"Hi, this is Lieutenant Kari Takamäki. How are we doing?"

"You tell me."

"Pretty well, I'd say."

"Is that so?" Repo's scornful tone sounded ominous to Takamäki. But he didn't give up.

"Yes. The sooner we resolve this situation, the sooner we can start clearing up that old case. Rectifying the wrongs that happened."

"How are you going to rectify those wrongs? By throwing cash at them? That seems to be the way the government works. When civil servants make mistakes, they can escape justice just by paying for it out with the taxpayers' money. But nothing happens to them. I think that's wrong."

"No one has come up with a better system yet."

"You civil servants all just protect each other, because you don't know whose actions will be the subject of the next investigation. The atmosphere of fear keeps everyone quiet."

Takamäki felt like disagreeing, but he didn't want to escalate the argument. On the other hand, he couldn't let his opponent humiliate him, either.

Repo continued. "If you can guarantee that Fredberg and that shit-head Leinonen, the lead investigator from Riihimäki, are charged with misconduct, I'll come out right now."

Takamäki thought for a moment. Repo wasn't stupid. But there was no point stepping into the trap.

"I'm a police officer. I can investigate it, but the prosecutors decide who gets charged," Takamäki said. "I can, however, guarantee you that I'll investigate it."

Repo chuckled sarcastically. "Maybe you're a straight-shooter after all, at least you're not lying to my face. Unfortunately, investigating it isn't going to cut it. But you were saying something earlier about a TV interview. I could consider coming out if you present an apology to me on behalf of all Finnish police officers, and especially on behalf of that dunce in Riihimäki."

Takamäki was getting pissed off, but he had to keep his feelings out of it. He reminded himself of his goal: bringing the situation to a peaceful resolution. "You want me to order you a pizza while I'm at it? Empire Special? Salami, shrimp, and garlic?"

"Garlic's hard on my stomach," Repo replied. "It got used to cabbage in the pen."

"Seriously, though," Takamäki shifted into a more sober tone. "I think we've been making progress. I've promised that we'll investigate the old case. We've established that the actions of all civil servants involved in your case will be thoroughly scrutinized. That we agree on, right?"

"Sure. You did promise that," Repo said.

"Good. Your old case will also be re-opened. By the way, we sent the clothes from the old murder scene in for DNA analysis. So you can be sure that if anything new turns up, we'll do everything we can. We probably agree on that, too, right?"

"Yeah," Repo said.

"Well, so help me out a little, too. What's still standing in the way of us ending this whole stupid siege? What's eating at you here?"

"The fact that the authorities destroyed my life with their sloppiness. I could've still..."

"Could've what?"

"Even though Arja was killed, I could've continued my life with Joel," Repo said. Takamäki could sense the emotion in his voice.

"You said your wife was killed," Takamäki interjected. "Who killed her?"

"I know who did it. He told me himself."

"Your father?"

Repo was silent for a second before continuing. "A couple of years after the incident, he came to visit me in prison. We hadn't ever talked about it before, but he wanted to come tell me. I had passed out, and he and Arja had had some massive fight that had ended in a single knife-slash. They had been standing across from each other and Arja had challenged him, told him he wouldn't dare. Well, he dared to do the slashing, but he didn't dare to take responsibility. Afterwards he panicked, put the knife in my hand, and left. He called the police from some phone booth," Repo chuckled. "That's back when there still used to be phone booths."

"Did you tell this to anyone?"

"No. And after that, I stopped all my appeals, too."

"Why?"

"I couldn't. Okay, so he was a shitty dad and played a shitty trick on me, but I couldn't do it to him. Besides, I had already been labeled a habitual complainer, so it wouldn't have mattered. Who would've believed me? You?"

Takamäki didn't answer. If Repo wanted to talk, let him talk.

"Somehow it all bubbled up that weekend when Dad's funeral was coming up, and I read in the paper that Fredberg had become the chief justice. I had really trusted the appeals court and overall system. I thought, OK, district court sentences can be sort of be based on whim, but I thought the appeals courts actually had better judges. But there was just this goddamn asshole who doesn't even know how to do his job," Repo said. "See, the only thing you learn in prison is how to hate."

266

"Why did your dad kill your wife?"

"I don't know. He never told me the exact reason. Some argument," Repo said.

"And your father didn't want to take responsibility later either, even though he knew he was dying?"

"He didn't want to die. According to the hospital papers, he demanded the best care. He was probably afraid he'd be left in a prison cell to rot. Like what happened to me. After Arja died, I had two paths ahead of me: life with my son or prison. The authorities chose prison for me. Thanks a fucking lot."

Takamäki was mildly horrified. It was good that Repo told him his story, because it brought them closer together. Takamäki had a better chance of influencing Repo's choices. There was also something troubling about the way things were headed, though. Repo was telling him things he hadn't ever told anyone before, and was up in the red zone of his emotional barometer again.

"You said in your last phone call that judges were supposed to ensure that justice is served, not be an extension of the state bureaucracy. I agree with you."

Repo laughed drily. "You're telling me. My case is a perfect example, and hopefully it will be remembered. But listen, Takamäki, I'll be watching you on TV at six. After that, I'll decide what I'm going to do."

"Follow your head, not your feelings," Takamäki said. "And call me first. Do you have my number?"

"Yeah, I can see it here on the phone."

"You're a unique case who can do some good for the system."

"Bullshit, I'm not unique in any way. Open your eyes and ears, man."

Takamäki feinted once again. "You promise to call?"

"Ha! I promise to look into whether I can call," Repo retorted. "Oh yeah, one more thing. I didn't kill Karppi. I

267

was there, but he fell and hit his head by himself," Repo said and hung up.

Takamäki reflected on the call. Good or bad?

# CHAPTER 21
## THURSDAY, 6:00 A.M.
## LAUTTASAARI, HELSINKI

The morning TV broadcast began with the show's soothing theme music. Takamäki couldn't hear the sound, but he could see the show's intro graphics on the monitor that had been set up next to the satellite van.

Wearing a black leather jacket, the reporter Sanna Römpötti was holding a large umbrella at Takamäki's side. In front of them stood cameraman Ike Karhunen, his large camera wrapped in plastic and trained on them. Karhunen had also set up lights, which initially made Takamäki squint. The lights would of course be visible from the besieged house, but Takamäki had allowed their use.

Römpötti had explained beforehand how the beginning of the broadcast would go. The anchor would kick things off at the studio, but the broadcast would quickly shift to Lauttasaari, with Römpötti answering a few of the anchor's questions. Takamäki's turn would come a few minutes later.

Takamäki gazed silently at the monitor—the host was talking. The text "Supreme Court Chief Justice Held Hostage" appeared on the screen. That made the incident major news. If Repo had kidnapped, say, his former lawyer, that also would have been news, but nothing on this scale.

Römpötti appeared on the screen and answered the first question that she'd heard through her ear mic.

"The situation here at Lauttasaari is very serious. Timo Repo, a convicted murderer who escaped from prison a few days ago, has barricaded himself in that house there behind me," Römpötti reported, gesturing toward the stand of trees. "He is holding the chief justice of the Supreme Court hostage. Let's take a look at some footage of how the situation developed here over the early-morning hours."

Material that had been shot earlier that night was shown on the monitors. Römpötti had presumably edited the clip in the satellite van.

Römpötti turned toward Takamäki. "This will take a good sixty seconds. Then you're on."

"So you'll ask and I'll answer."

"That's usually the way it goes," Römpötti smiled. "Shitty weather, huh?"

"At least we have an umbrella. Those guys on the front line don't."

Takamäki watched the footage of the siege. Pictures of the armored cars arriving and the medic copter waiting on the field were being shown when the cameraman announced that they would be continuing the live broadcast in ten seconds.

Takamäki thought once more about Repo in the house. He was definitely watching the broadcast, because five minutes ago the radar man had announced that there was movement in the living room. After that, the sounds of the TV had been heard coming from the room. What would the hook be that would convince Repo to give in?

"We're back broadcasting live from Lauttasaari," Römpötti announced into the mic, "where convicted murderer Timo Repo, who escaped last week, is holding Aarno Fredberg, the chief justice of the Supreme Court, hostage. The police operation here is being led by

Detective Lieutenant Kari Takamäki of the Helsinki Police Department's Violent Crimes Unit. Lieutenant Takamäki, what's the latest status?"

Takamäki kept his gaze on Römpötti. "Things are very calm at the moment, and have been for several hours now. In order to ensure the safety of the public, we have had to take precautionary measures of cordoning off a large area and rerouting Western Expressway traffic. Of course that's going to cause a lot of headaches for commuters traveling from Espoo to downtown Helsinki."

"Have you established contact with Timo Repo?"

"Yes," Takamäki said, but did not elaborate.

Römpötti was caught a little off guard by the one-word response, but recovered quickly. "What are his demands?"

"Repo was sentenced to life in prison in 1999 for the murder of his wife. The Helsinki Police Department has, in conjunction with the escape investigation, conducted a preliminary review of that case, and there appear to be some anomalies in it."

Römpötti bit. "Anomalies? What do you mean?"

Takamäki turned his gaze directly to the camera, so the words would be targeted personally to Repo.

"The Kouvola Court of Appeals upheld Repo's life sentence, but the case definitely demands a more detailed investigation."

"So Repo has, perhaps, been wrongly convicted?"

Takamäki's gaze stayed on the camera. "It's very possible. The matter must be investigated in detail as soon as this situation here has been resolved."

"So an unprecedented situation?"

"You could say that," Takamäki said, turning back toward Römpötti.

"Supreme Court chief justice Aarno Fredberg used to sit on the bench at the Kouvola Court of Appeals, and he was one of the judges that sentenced Repo to life in prison. Can we assume that there's a connection here?"

Takamäki nodded. "That is the case."

"What kinds of demands has Repo presented? How can this situation be resolved?"

"The police are approaching the situation as calmly as possible. As I said earlier, we have been in contact with Timo Repo and negotiations are ongoing. The old case will be reinvestigated at a later time, and for right now the police are, of course, working toward a peaceful resolution." Römpötti understood Takamäki's tone of voice: it was time to end the interview, but she wanted to ask one more thing.

"The police statement earlier read that Timo Repo was not considered particularly dangerous. Presumably that's no longer the case?"

Takamäki didn't care for the question. "The police are seeking to resolve this in a peaceful manner and are continuing negotiations."

Römpötti turned toward the camera. "And so the siege that began last night here in Lauttasaari continues. Now back to the studio."

The morning host came back on screen. Photos of the judge appeared, quickly followed by clips from Römpötti's recent interview with Fredberg.

"Thanks," Römpötti said to Takamäki. "Nice interview."

The cameraman turned off the lights.

"Good," answered Takamäki. "You might want to keep those cameras rolling and aimed at the house. Something might happen soon."

"What?"

"If I only knew," Takamäki said, as he strode off toward the lead van, twenty yards away. He heard Römpötti order Karhunen to keep the camera filming the house.

He ran into Joutsamo outside the van. "Good interview, maybe," she said. "Repo's on the line. He called as soon as you went off the air. Said he'd hold until you made it to the phone."

Takamäki's face was grave. "Okay, tell Turunen to get his men ready. We might be going in soon."

"The moment of truth?" Joutsamo asked.

"The moment of doom."

"Helmikoski also got a pretty serious barrage of calls from the other media outlets. They want to move in closer from their cordon on Lauttasaari Road. In the name of equal treatment."

"That interview wasn't journalism, it was a police operation. The message was intended solely for Repo."

"I know that," Joutsamo said, as they reached the door of the lead car. "But explain it to them."

Takamäki's phone rang. Blocked number. "Hello?" he answered.

"Hi there, Mary J. Juvonen from *Iltalehti*..."

Takamäki pressed the button marked with a red receiver.

"Explain it to her if she calls back," Takamäki said, handing the phone to Joutsamo. Takamäki stepped into the van, where Kirsi Kohonen was sitting. Joutsamo followed.

"Hi," his red-headed subordinate said. "Call for you."

Takamäki sat down on the seat of the van, took a deep breath, and picked up the receiver. "Hello."

"Hello, it's Repo."

"Hi," said Takamäki. At least the fugitive's voice didn't sound overly tense.

"You did well on TV."

"Ha," Takamäki grunted. "Good, if that's what you thought. I hope you understand that I'm serious about this now."

"Yeah, I understand that, and I'd sincerely like to thank you for your empathy."

"After that publicity, your case and the two bureaucrats will definitely be investigated with a fine-toothed comb."

"That's wonderful," Repo said laconically. "Do you remember who Jorma Takala was?"

Shivers went up Takamäki's spine. "Of course."

"The explosion at the market square in Mikkeli twenty-one years ago changed a lot of things about the way police conduct their operations."

Takamäki knew what Repo was referring to. Takala had robbed a bank with a shotgun and dynamite in Helsinki, then taken hostages that he drove 130 miles north to Mikkeli. In the middle of the night, the police stormed the car, freeing two of the hostages. The officer shot Takala, but he still managed to detonate explosives killing himself and one hostage and injuring ten officers. This led to the police becoming much more cautious in hostage crises. Nowadays, the police always had time to wait, and the focus was on a peaceful resolution.

"There always has to be a crisis before things change," Repo continued. "Now that you told the country on TV how this situation came about, hopefully it will have a similar impact on the justice system that Takala had on the police. Judges should be the part of the system ensuring that justice is served, not an extension of the state bureaucracy. Maybe they'll think a little harder about that after this."

Takamäki gave Joutsamo and Kohonen a concerned look. "Come on, don't say that."

"Hey, Takamäki," Repo said. "Listen to Johnny Cash's song 'Hurt' once this is over. He's an ex-con. After that, you'll know how I feel."

"I..." Takamäki tried to interrupt.

"I said, listen to the song when you get a chance. Johnny Cash, 'Hurt.' My English isn't great, but the song starts off with lyrics saying that he has to hurt himself so he'll know he's alive. That's the way it is in this case, too. Society needs to be hurt in order for it to function properly."

"Timo," Takamäki raised his voice. "Don't do anything foolish..."

"I'm not going to do anything foolish. You have one minute to pull back all your officers. I don't want to do them any harm. But the outcome is inevitable now."

"Give us two minutes so we can get everyone out from around the house," Takamäki replied.

"Okay," Repo agreed. "And thanks."

Takamäki sighed and ended the call. Two minutes wasn't much time.

Turunen sprinted the fifteen-foot trip to the lead car. "Not looking good?"

"No. Pull everyone back. Immediately."

The radio reported, "Movement in the house."

"And we're not even going to try to go in there?"

"No. Let's minimize the damage. Not a single officer is going to die today. At least at Lauttasaari this morning. We have no choice."

Turunen took the radio and announced the order to pull back at least a hundred yards from the house.

\* \* \*

Eronen had been manning the gun for twelve minutes when the radio announced that everyone was to retreat to at least a hundred yards. Saarinen was startled awake. The driver of the Pasi heard the command and revved up the vehicle's diesel engines.

The army sergeant at the wheel confirmed the order with the police officers: "Pull back?"

Eronen looked at the house. There was no movement.

"Yeah, follow the order," Eronen replied, but at that very moment he saw the back door of the house opened. A man in black pajamas stepped out, or at least that's what it looked like. He wasn't wearing shoes. He took a few tentative steps and looked around.

"Stop!" Eronen shouted, and the Pasi, which had just been rolling backwards, shuddered to a halt. Eronen opened the back door and hurled himself out. He was moving fast and slipped on the wet asphalt—his legs were stiff from crouching in the Pasi. He smacked his knee but leapt back up. Saarinen had already made it to his side. Eronen waved at the man who had emerged from the house, who darted toward the policeman.

Eronen glanced at the house. It appeared peaceful. The man in the pajamas came running toward the police officers barefoot. He didn't have any explosives strapped to him.

Eronen was anxious about the imminent explosion and wondered if they'd make it back to the tank, or whether they should just hit the ground. If he climbed on top of the guy in the pajamas, the protective clothing would shield the other man too. Eronen now recognized him as the chief justice of the Supreme Court. Even though he had said all kinds of crap on TV, he still needed to be protected.

Saarinen was the first one to make it to Fredberg and drag him along, forcing him to move faster. Eronen aimed his weapon at the house just in case Repo decided to come after them. No one did.

"Faster!" Eronen yelled, turning to follow the other two. He caught up to them five yards from the tank, he was running right behind Fredberg. At least Eronen's gear would protect the judge from any shrapnel.

Eronen and Saarinen tossed Fredberg into the Pasi. The judge yelped as he banged his leg against the edge of the back hatch. Saarinen jumped in, and Eronen followed. The policemen slammed the hatches shut and ordered the sergeant to drive.

Eronen was winded from the exertion, but he switched his ear mic to Talk. The man in the pajamas lay quietly on the floor of the armored vehicle. Saarinen was pointing his automatic weapon at him just in case.

"A man exited the house. Looks like the judge. We'll bring him to the lead van."

"Please repeat," Turunen said.

"A man exited house just as we received the order to retreat. We took him into custody and have him in the vehicle," Eronen said, taking a closer look at the man's face. "This is Supreme Court chief justice Fredberg. Identification is positive," Eronen continued, before turning off his mic.

"Good," Turunen said. "Everyone pull back. The target informed us that he will detonate soon. You have about 20 seconds."

\* \* \*

Römpötti was antsy. The morning show was interviewing some local politician about the westward extension of the subway, and it had taken a second call to the producer to get him to interrupt the interview. On screen, the morning host was rapidly repeating the news on the siege.

"Our reporter Sanna Römpötti is at the scene. Sanna, what's happening there now?"

Römpötti was in the shot for the first two seconds, after which Karhunen shifted the camera to what interested people more.

"The situation has developed dramatically here over the past few minutes. The police have retreated, and the tanks are on the move. According to eye witness accounts, someone exited the house, but those reports are still unconfirmed..."

Römpötti's sentence was interrupted by an enormous explosion. Flames burst out of the house's windows, and the roof appeared to jump up a few feet before collapsing. Roof tiles showered down on the soccer field, with the nearest ones coming down fifty feet away. Heavy smoke rose from the corner of the house.

The first one to say anything on the TV broadcast was the Green party politician whose microphone had remained on in the chaos. "Oh my god! How horrible!"

The anchor rapidly took control of the situation, since she didn't know if Römpötti was okay.

"Viewers, you are watching a live broadcast of the dramatic end to a siege. A convict who escaped prison earlier this week took the chief justice of the Supreme Court hostage, an incident that evidently came to a conclusion in this explosion. We do not know if there are any casualties. Our reporter Sanna Römpötti is on the scene. Sanna, are you all right...? Sanna!"

The explosion had popped Römpötti's ear drums, and it took a minute before she could hear anything. Karhunen, the cameraman, waved his hand behind the camera, and the stunned Römpötti understood that she should talk now.

"There has been an explosion here. We don't have any details yet," Römpötti said in an unnaturally loud voice. "Heavy smoke is rising from the building. Just a moment ago, escaped convict Timo Repo and Supreme Court chief justice Aarno Fredberg were in that house together. We do not have any information on the fate of either. The motivation for the siege was Repo's potentially wrongful conviction for his wife's murder. Fredberg was..."

Takamäki was typing up his notes from that morning. He was tired, but it was best to record the chain of events while it was still fresh in his mind. Joutsamo, Kohonen, or the department secretary could transcribe the calls with Repo for the appendix, and Takamäki would still have a chance to edit his text. In any event, multiple parties would be demanding a report.

Skoog burst into Takamäki's office and started praising him as soon as he walked through the door. "Congratulations!"

Takamäki raised his gaze. "What for?"

"For a goddamned well-handled situation. You had about a zero percent chance of resolving it, but you got the hostage out of there."

"There are a lot of ways of looking at it. Repo let him go. Fredberg said Repo had spoken about mercy at the door as he let him go. Mercy he wasn't shown himself."

"Well, he wouldn't have let him go if you hadn't succeeded in influencing his judgment."

"Hard to say," Takamäki said, noticing a rare smile on the lips of the stern deputy chief. It didn't suit his stony face in the least. Maybe that was because even though the mouth was smiling, the eyes were still hard.

"I spoke with Fredberg, and he is truly grateful to the police that the standoff was resolved this way. Even apologized for giving an interview to the press in which he had disparaged the police."

Takamäki nodded. "I still don't consider the incident a success. The aim was to resolve it without a single victim."

"Of course that would have been preferable," Skoog admitted. "But there's nothing to complain about either. The hostage survived. That's the most important thing. At least four officers are going to get a cross of merit for this. Suhonen for saving the wife, Saarinen and Eronen for their last-minute actions, and you for leading the operation."

Skoog's praise felt good in a way—and yet it didn't.

"The press conference is a little over an hour away. You're going?" Takamäki asked.

"I was thinking I'd attend."

"Do I have to?"

"Yes," Skoog said. "Several networks are broadcasting it live. You deserve the recognition."

Takamäki looked thoughtful. "That old Riihimäki case is definitely going to surface. What are we going to say about it?"

"I had a brief word with the attorney general about it," Skoog said. "It clearly falls under the area of due process, and they promised to reopen Repo's old case for review."

"So it'll be transferred there?"

"I agreed that you'll drop by within the next few weeks to brief them as to what you feel the problem is."

"Fine," Takamäki said. "Maybe it's better that the AG's office looks into it, because it's a difficult spot for the police to be in. The wrongly convicted and the potential perpetrator are both dead, so from that perspective we have no interest in the case, since there is no one to prosecute."

Takamäki doubted they would find strong enough evidence to overturn Repo's conviction. The clothes that Joutsamo had sent in for DNA analysis might reveal that Erik Repo had been in the apartment, but that didn't make him a killer. In all likelihood the case would remain open. Without the Repos' testimony, finding out the truth was nearly impossible. In any case not a single police officer or judge would be charged with misconduct, even if there were cause.

"Repo told me his father's account of events over the phone. It's on tape. Should we turn it over to the attorney general's office?" Takamäki asked.

Skoog thought for a second. "Yes, if they think to ask for it, but we're not going to actively mention it. It is, of course, nothing more than his version of events, and it's not of great importance. But back to the matter at hand: the plan now is to stress Repo's mental health problems. And that'll be our theme at the press conference, too."

"Did he have any?"

"Of course he did, if the guy was capable of resorting to a solution like that. We don't want the media making him into some sort of martyr, victim of the system, or innocent murderer. We're not going to speculate about his innocence, we're just going to say that the attorney general is going to investigate. In the end, what we're talking about are the unlawful actions of a mentally unstable man. We'll also raise the fact that we're investigating the Karppi incident as murder, and that Repo is—or, I mean, was—the prime suspect. In other words, before taking a hostage, Repo is suspected of murdering his father's closest friend. We'll knock him off that pedestal he wanted raise himself up on. Repo's nothing more than a common criminal."

So this is how the system works, Takamäki thought.

* * *

Takamäki turned his Toyota station wagon into his townhouse lot. He drove into his parking space under the garage, stepped out, and locked the doors.

The day was extremely gray, and the rain continued to drizzle down. Takamäki strode to his front door and stepped in. The lights were on, and Jonas was downstairs, sitting at the computer with one arm in a cast. Some black girl was shaking her booty on the music channel on TV.

"Hey," Takamäki said, and Jonas turned the TV down.

"Pretty intense day, huh?"

"Yeah."

"I watched you on TV this morning and during that press conference just now."

"Well, what did you think?"

Jonas gave a little smile. "That was a really cool explosion, even the reporter went totally speechless."

Takamäki sat down on the sofa. "A person died there."

Jonas looked at his father. "He was one weird dude, killing his dad's friend and all. Must have been pretty messed up. Was he innocent in that old case, by the way?"

"That's what he told me on the phone."

"Do you believe him?"

Takamäki thought for a second. "In a way I almost want to, but I don't know for sure."

"No, seriously. Tell me," Jonas insisted.

"I really don't know. Seriously. Someone's going to look into it, I guess, but it's pretty hard to get new evidence in an old case like that. The clothes are being analyzed for DNA. Maybe something will come out of it. Maybe not."

"There you go with the cop talk again," Jonas laughed. "You should have just said 'No comment' like that Skoog dude did on TV."

Takamäki changed the subject. "How's the arm?"

"Still attached to my shoulder. A little hard to surf the web with one hand. With the mouse it's fine, but typing's tough. How do one-handed people turn on their computers? For me at least that Control+Alt+Del you have to do at the start was pretty tricky."

Takamäki lay down on the sofa. "I need to sleep for a couple of hours, but feel free to hang out on the computer. It doesn't bother me."

"Okay," Jonas said, looking at his dad. Takamäki fluffed up the pillow and put his hands behind his neck.

"Hey, Dad?"

"Yeah?"

"That accident I was in. Did you guys find out who the driver was?"

Takamäki answered without opening his eyes. "Yes. This one criminal."

"Is it going to go to court?"

"I don't think so."

"Why not?"

Takamäki thought for a second and rose up on his side. How could he explain this? Suhonen had found out from Salmela that a guy called Skoda Sakke had hit Jonas. They couldn't use the information, though, because it would have immediately let the criminal league know that someone from the gang had talked to the cops. They couldn't investigate the hit-and-run unless someone confessed to it, and that was extremely unlikely. Takamäki regretted having told his son that that they knew who the driver was.

"Why not?" Jonas repeated.

Takamäki sat up on the sofa to explain. "Is it enough if I tell you 'No comment'?"

"I guess, but I don't get it. If you guys know who the driver is, why doesn't he have to go to court? It was his fault. And who's going to pay for my bike?"

"The bike's easy. Insurance will take care of that," Takamäki said, trying to formulate his answer. Salmela had told him that Skoda Sakke had gotten his ass kicked and been forced to pay him back for the burnt car. "Let's just say that the guy knows he did wrong and was made to pay."

"Did someone ice him?" Jonas asked gravely.

Takamäki laughed. "No, it wasn't that bad. But I can't tell you the details."

Father and son looked at each other. Jonas was the first to talk. "So do you think that's a good thing?"

"Good question," Takamäki answered diplomatically, buying time to frame his thoughts. As a police officer the answer was easy; of course it was. But as a father and parent, this wasn't the way things should go. He should be able to tell his son that justice is carried out in society. Lying wasn't Takamäki's style, though. "Your hit-and-run not ending up in court will let us protect one of Suhonen's sources."

"Oh, Suhonen's informant?" Jonas said. During his visits, Suhonen had taught Takamäki's boys that snitch was a forbidden word, informant was better.

"Is that okay?"

Jonas shrugged his healthy shoulder. "Fine by me. Is Suhonen coming over for Christmas again?"

"I don't know yet," Takamäki said, lying back down on the couch. "Of course we'll invite him."

"That would be cool."

Takamäki closed his eyes again. "Wake me up at one o'clock at the latest. I don't want to sleep too long, because then I won't be able to fall asleep tonight," he said. "Oh yeah, one more thing: find Johnny Cash's song 'Hurt' and play it for me."

# SIX WEEKS LATER

## CHAPTER 23
## TUESDAY, 2:20 P.M.
## HELSINKI POLICE HEADQUARTERS, PASILA

Joutsamo stepped into the room, and Takamäki raised his eyes from the computer.

"Got a sec?" Joutsamo asked. Without waiting for an answer, she entered and closed the door behind her. She was wearing a gray sweater. November was coming to an end, and it was already growing dark outside. The temperature was teetering above and below freezing.

"Well?" Takamäki asked, as Joutsamo sat down in the chair across from him. Takamäki was still wearing a white shirt and tie, because that morning they had had to attend some pointless meeting at the Ministry of the Interior. His sport coat was hanging from the back of his chair.

"I have a theory."

"About what?"

"Everything, of course," Joutsamo smiled. "But especially about this Repo case."

Takamäki nodded. It had been six weeks since the explosion. The incident had been in the media for a few days, but had then been overshadowed by other news. The Office of the Attorney General had started investigating the matter, but nothing much had been heard from there. This came as no surprise to Takamäki—the office was known for its glacial pace.

"Lay it on me," Takamäki said.

"I got the final DNA reports this morning, and I've been thinking about them. Of course they found Timo Repo's and his wife Arja's DNA on the belongings. But in addition, they were also able to pick up DNA from Arja's shirt that belonged to Erik Repo."

"That's interesting, but it doesn't prove..."

"Listen, I know it only indicates that Erik Repo was at the scene. It doesn't put the knife in his hand. All I said was that I had a theory."

"Continue," Takamäki said.

"The items also included a stuffed animal that had been found on the kitchen floor, because it had blood on it, too. It turns out that it was—as I expected—Arja's blood. But they found something else on that stuffed animal, too. In other words, the child's DNA, of course, which was determined by that blood sample we acquired. Which leads us to my theory."

Takamäki was listening.

"The child's DNA looked strange, and my friend at the NBI lab took a closer look at it. Arja was the boy's, Joel's, mother, but Timo Repo was not the father."

"Theoretically speaking, that would give Timo more of a motive."

Joutsamo shook her head. "I checked the calls from the night of the explosion. Repo mentioned his son twice. He didn't know."

"But Grandpa Erik did?"

"Or found out," Joutsamo said. "It's pure speculation, but it fits the picture. Timo Repo passes out. Erik and his daughter-in-law start to bicker about something. That's what Erik had told Timo, and according to the old interrogation reports, it wasn't the first time. The situation escalates. They're drunk."

Takamäki interrupted, "As far as I can recall, in the preliminary investigative reports no one mentioned anything about shouting."

"Maybe they didn't shout. Maybe they just argued. Maybe they didn't want to wake up Timo, who was passed out. Anyway, Arja insults her father-in-law and he dishes it right back. At some point, she pulls out the big guns and insults the family by telling him that the child was the result of an extramarital affair. Grandpa Erik can't stomach it and slashes her throat. Then, in a panic, he frames his son."

"Why?"

"This is just a theory, but maybe he considered his son just as worthless as the woman he killed," Joutsamo said.

"Cruel father," Takamäki said.

"Wouldn't be the first. But like I said, this is just a theory. And we won't be able to take it any further."

Takamäki nodded. "I also have a theory. A drunk married couple gets into a fight. The woman insults the man by telling him the kid is someone else's. The man panics, kills the woman, and doesn't remember anything. They don't always. The man's father is on the scene or happens to come in a little later and sees what happened. He flees the apartment in horror and doesn't call the police until he's outside the building."

"Cruel husband," Joutsamo said.

"But the dad isn't so bad after all. He sees his son languishing in uncertainty in prison and decides to ease his pain. He lies to his son that he committed the crime. He knows he'll lose his son, but he'll save him from going insane," Takamäki said. "But this is just a theory, too. And we won't be able to take it any further."

"But the courts did, once upon a time," Joutsamo mused. "All the way to a murder conviction."

# Also by Ice Cold Crime

### Jarkko Sipila *Helsinki Homicide: Against the Wall*
#### Winner of 2009 Best Finnish Crime Novel

Detective Lieutenant Kari Takamäki's trusted man Suhonen goes undercover as Suikkanen, a gangster full of action. In pursuit of a murderer, he must operate within the grey area of the law. But, will the end justify the means?

### Jarkko Sipila *Helsinki Homicide: Vengeance*

Tapani Larsson, a Finnish crime boss, walks out of prison with one thought on his mind: Vengeance. Larsson targets Suhonen, the undercover detective who put him in prison. With every string Suhonen pulls, he flirts with death itself.

### Jarkko Sipila *Helsinki Homicide: Nothing But the Truth*

A mother of a 12-year old girl is a witness in a murder case. After testifying in the trial, she finds herself the target of an escalating spiral of threats. As the threats mount, the witness is torn between her principles and her desire to keep her family safe. How much should an ordinary citizen sacrifice for the benefit of society as a whole?

### Harri Nykanen *Raid and the Blackest Sheep*
#### Winner of 2001 Best Finnish Crime Novel

Hard-nosed hit man Raid travels around Finland with Nygren, a career criminal in the twilight of his life, wreaking vengeance him and paying penance. Soon, both cops and crooks are on the trail of the mysterious pair.

### Harri Nykanen *Raid and the Kid*

Hard-nosed hit man Raid is reluctantly mixed up into the world of drug trafficking in this twisting tale of cops, criminals, and those who blur the lines

### Seppo Jokinen *Wolves and Angels*
#### Winner of 2002 Best Finnish Crime Novel

With attacks on the disabled and ailing, Detective Sakari Koskinen and his eccentric team spring into action in a gripping story about the struggles of the disabled coping with their new lives and the strains on those who care for them. Nuanced depictions of interpersonal relationships and personal challenges make Jokinen's characters come to life on the page